LOSING SPRING

V.C. Andrews® Books

LOSING SPRING

V.C. ANDREWS®

GALLERY BOOKS

New York   London   Toronto   Sydney   New Delhi

G

Gallery Books
An Imprint of Simon & Schuster, Inc.
1230 Avenue of the Americas
New York, NY 10020

Following the death of Virginia Andrews, the Andrews family worked with a carefully selected writer to organize and complete Virginia Andrews's stories and to create additional novels, of which this is one, inspired by her storytelling genius.

First Gallery Books trade paperback edition October 2023

For information about special discounts for bulk purchases, please contact Simon & Schuster Special Sales at 1-866-506-1949 or business@simonandschuster.com.

Interior design by Erika R. Genova

Manufactured in the United States of America

10 9 8 7 6 5 4 3 2 1

Library of Congress Cataloging-in-Publication Data
Names: Andrews, V. C. (Virginia C.), author.
Title: Losing spring / V.C. Andrews.
Description: New York : Gallery Books, [2023]
Identifiers: LCCN 2022059249 (print) | LCCN 2022059250 (ebook) |
   ISBN 9781668015933 (hardcover) | ISBN 9781668015902 (paperback) |
   ISBN 9781668015926 (ebook)
Subjects: LCGFT: Novels.
Classification: LCC PS3551.N454 L67 2023 (print) | LCC PS3551.N454 (ebook) |
   DDC 813/.54—dc23/eng/20221220
LC record available at https://lccn.loc.gov/2022059249
LC ebook record available at https://lccn.loc.gov/2022059250

ISBN 978-1-6680-1593-3
ISBN 978-1-6680-1590-2 (pbk)
ISBN 978-1-6680-1592-6 (ebook)

LOSING SPRING

To every thing there is a season, and a time to every purpose under the heaven:

A time to be born, and a time to die; a time to plant, and a time to pluck up that which is planted;

A time to kill, and a time to heal; a time to break down, and a time to build up;

A time to weep, and a time to laugh; a time to mourn, and a time to dance;

A time to cast away stones, and a time to gather stones together; a time to embrace, and a time to refrain from embracing;

A time to get, and a time to lose; a time to keep, and a time to cast away;

A time to rend, and a time to sew; a time to keep silence, and a time to speak;

A time to love, and a time to hate; a time of war, and a time of peace.

Ecclesiastes 3, King James Bible

PROLOGUE

My mother told me that who you are is already determined when you are born. However, you can still determine much about who you will be.

She set down the rule.

If you have faith in yourself, you won't be afraid of the choices you make.

If you don't have self-confidence, other people will decide who you will be.

1

I have come to believe that I was almost wrong to be a child, to be a prisoner of hope and good dreams and see brightness and color in a world that could quickly rain down darkness and rage.

Daddy used to say, "At the moment you are born, you get your first hint that bad things can happen. That's why babies cry.

"It might be the last time they're right."

Fortunately, until I was nearly thirteen, I really had never known deep unhappiness or dreary silence. My days were filled with music. There were balloons on birthdays along with funny talking cards, toys, books, and pretty clothes and shoes. I overheard my early grade-school teachers, in whispers, praise my mother on how nicely dressed she kept me. At times I felt more like a precious doll than just another little girl. But most of all, there was music, lively and fun. It was almost like a soundtrack in a movie accompanying whatever we did or wherever we went. Our house was rarely silent and shadows were never foreboding. They were simply pauses in the stream of sunshine, like commas in a sentence, and certainly nothing to fear.

Like most children whose view of the world was formed in comfort, having all the love and attention needed, living in a safe community as well as attending a good school with caring teachers, I thought my joy and contentment would last forever. I had only glimpses of poverty, social injustice, and crime. My mother especially shielded me from all that when I was very young. "There will be plenty of time later for this horror," she might say when turning off something on television.

Daddy didn't agree, but he didn't argue vociferously about it. The most he would do was issue a warning. He would almost sing it: "You'll be sorry if you turn her into a turtle."

Sometimes, when I was five, I tried to imagine what that would be like. I would crawl under my blanket and poke my head out at the foot of the bed and then quickly pull it back under as if I had seen something ugly there or something to hurt me. It wasn't terrible, but it was boring under a blanket. In that special place in my heart where I kept secrets, I put this one: I agreed with Daddy. I didn't want to be a turtle. I wanted to be more like him and be strong enough to face down anything ugly, anything mean.

But for all my early childhood years, there was really nothing terribly unpleasant in my personal world from which I should hide anyway.

Consequently, for me there was only one season back then: spring, when everything brightened and everyone wore a bright, warm smile like the smile of the sparrow in the preschool picture book I had, *The Laughing Sparrow*, a wide grin with eyes that gleamed with happiness and hope. Remembering those early years, even for a few moments, washes away the dreary fog that settles every morning at the bay windows of my bedroom in my grandfather's mansion, a bedroom that is at least three times as large as my bedroom was at home, but with ten times the emptiness.

Whatever, remembering my happier spring days doesn't keep the haze from returning here almost daily. It is almost like a bad memory that challenges me to forget it and dares me to even try.

The seasons are so different now, never bursting out like some wonderful surprise in the morning, but instead tiptoeing into my life almost as if they were asking for my permission to emerge. "Should we move the year ahead? Does it matter?"

Birds don't ever seem happy like the ones I saw in my children's books or around our home when I was younger. Now they look as confused as I am, fluttering about this magnificent, regal estate that has become my whole world, a prison with all the necessities of life save one: normal childhood and adolescence. Here I have no friends; I play no games. I don't dance. I don't go to birthday parties, not even my own.

"It's time to put aside all that nonsense," Grandfather Sutherland often said, even before I was brought here. True to his word, he doesn't celebrate his own birthday with parties and gifts, and if anyone should forget and give him something or wish him a happy birthday, he roars his displeasure. "I don't need you to remind me," he might say. I recall hearing that when I was younger, and I remember my mother brought him a birthday gift, more to annoy him than to please him. She gave it to him with that wry smile on her face. He reluctantly celebrated Grandmother Judith's birthday and celebrated their anniversaries with parties and dinners because she insisted on that.

Now other happy events that would please and excite someone as young as I am only happen out there beyond the walls and gates, but I don't see them. I don't even hear about them. It occurred to me that if your birthday was treated like just another day, you might eventually forget how old you were. Maybe my grandfather is simply afraid of his birthday. Perhaps he wants to make a fist around the hands of a clock and stop them from moving one second more. I have no doubt that he believes he can hold back time for himself and can mold my world, even diminishing my peepholes, eventually turning me into a turtle.

I have a computer but with all sorts of censorship devices inserted, squeezing it into a narrow road out with *NO* at any possible turn that could lead to even an imaginary escape, let alone an internet friend. And I haven't got a television set because my grandfather believes it's "mostly garbage dumped into the innocent minds of children. And look how they're turning out!"

There is no point to my having a phone, as there would be no friend to call, and anyway, I'd be ashamed to tell a friend anything about myself now. I never had the chance to say goodbye to anyone I knew. Maybe they know I live here or wonder where I have gone, but by now most of them, if not all of them, likely have lost interest in caring about or finding out exactly what happened to me.

And even in here, inside the grand house with its high ceilings, its elaborate gilded chandeliers, its tiled floors with expensive area rugs, and its luxurious drapes, I know I will never be happy. Even if I please my grandfather, *no* for me is written in many places. I will never enjoy any of it. There will always be so many doors locked to me in my grandfather's mansion. Right now, windows are shut almost mechanically at certain times of the day, and opinions and orders are filtered to prevent certain words and ideas from reaching my ears. My grandfather's employees look like their mouths are zipped shut when they see me. Some even seem surprised that I am still here and are even afraid to ask me how I am. The chains on secrets are so heavy that they can't be lifted.

The walls and the door to my room are thick enough so that I don't overhear anyone talking in hallways, especially the dark corridor where my room is located. No wonder, then, that I think of my grandfather's estate as someone would think of a turtle shell. How right Daddy was. I did end up in there.

It's almost as if beyond the gates there is only emptiness resembling outer space. We're set so far from a main highway that I can barely catch the sounds of passing cars and trucks, their horns baaing like frightened sheep. When I was finally permitted to go out for fresh air, I could only get a glimpse of them through a small space in the surrounding seven- or eight-foot large evergreens, objects jutting by, colors and shapes barely identifiable. Grandfather's small army of uniformed gardeners, who wear dark brown uniforms and white gloves with his company insignia on the backs above their knuckles, keep them nourished and healthy: the thick green wall.

But how I see everything has changed anyway. Although I don't wear glasses, it feels like I do; it feels like I'm looking through lenses that paint shade over sunshine and make flowers that bloom look more like memories stuck between pages of a diary, faded, threatening to crumble. When I gaze back at everything that has happened, I am looking through a prism that promises to feed confusion and nourish lies. Every sound I do hear is louder here; every command is harsher. I wake to the image of snapping whips in the long, wide hallways. Threats seep through the walls and echo in corners. How different it all is from my earlier childhood.

Neither my mother nor my father really yelled at me because of something wrong I had done back then. My mother always chose to show me why I shouldn't do it and then made sure I understood. "Are you clear, Caroline?" she would say. "Do you see?" she would ask, always with a smile.

During my early years, my father could sound firmer and curt, but I never felt great anger from him or saw in his eyes the distrust I saw in my grandfather's and even my grandmother's eyes afterward. Despite what he might say now, I know I'll never see anything else in my grandfather's look.

My father's favorite words were *correct* and *incorrect*. He never said I had done something bad. And he'd rarely raise his voice above a loud whisper when he said, "That's a mistake. Don't do that, Caroline." At worst, he might repeat it three times. He told me most people didn't listen the first time, even the second.

Pleasing my mother and father was so important to me anyway that I was upset more with myself than I was at them when they reacted to something wrong I had done. I'd punish myself. *You can't have that cookie now*, I'd think, or *Don't touch those toys or that doll for at least an hour*. But those moments were truly rare during my early childhood. Most of the time it was as if we had bells ringing with laughter and joy in our house. I thought I was growing up in a world where every day was Christmas, so I had to be careful not to do anything that would change it, whether I was inside my house or outside it. In fact, I thought we were so special that we lived within a bubble. What I didn't consider was, like any bubble or balloon, something could poke a hole in it and that buoyant, Christmas-like feeling would leak out, which it did.

Before that, every day was a sort of Christmas. When it was cold and we went outside, I was amused and fascinated by the sight of my breath. I'd watch the way ice crystals on tree branches changed colors as the day waned. Sometimes, when Daddy was home and I was much younger, not even in kindergarten, he'd play with both Mommy and me in the snow. If it was snowing, he'd say, "Let's see how many flakes you can catch." But they always melted before I could even start to count. I loved mittens, and although it was a struggle sometimes to put on my shoe boots, they were worth the effort because they were pretty, with pink shoelaces and furry tops. I even regretted my mother putting them away when spring had sprung almost like the clown in my jack-in-the-box.

Early spring for us back then was filled with fun things to do around the house, or at least they seemed like fun to me. I remember preferring to help with work over playing with my toys. There was always some touch-up painting to do, and cleaning up the front lawn and the backyard. I even had my own small paintbrush and rake. Somehow the snow, rain, and winds had brought debris from other homes in the neighborhood to us— debris like pieces of old newspapers, mail advertisements, and food boxes washing onto our property. Once there was even a postcard of Niagara Falls with all the writing faded. You couldn't even guess the words. Daddy studied it when I showed it to him. He put his finger on the postage stamp and then said, "It was sent three years ago." He laughed the hardest I could remember when I said, "It took a long time to get here."

At the start of spring, my mother loved reorganizing clothes and shoes, polishing furniture, and especially washing windows that had gone through months of rain and snow streaks. There was always music playing when she worked. Sometimes she'd pick me up and dance when one of her favorite songs was being played. And if Neil Diamond's "Sweet Caroline" came on, she'd scream and dance as if she was on a stage. When I was old enough, I'd mimic her and she'd laugh and hug me. Later, when Daddy came home, she'd play the song and show him how we danced. Mommy tried to get him to join us, but he always backed away, palms out to pump the air between us, saying he'd make her look bad.

"Didn't Daddy ever dance?" I asked my mother once.

She paused as if it was the first time she had ever thought about it.

"At our wedding," she said. "Because my father told him he should."

Every spring my mother redid our garage, storing what we didn't need in cabinets, sometimes so efficiently and quickly that Daddy complained he couldn't find something. In those days there was no "Where the hell is it?" There was only "Hey, I can't find . . ." followed with a laugh or a little apology and a quick retrieval.

"I'd swear you'd put *me* away for the season," Daddy might joke. "And they call the people who do my work such perfectionists that they practically have OCD."

When I found out what that meant, I wasn't as surprised as I was curious. Could he be someone like that?

They'd banter and end even small tension with a kiss or my mother tapping him with her small fist gently on the shoulder. He'd pretend it hurt and threaten to report her to the police for domestic abuse, which sounded scary. "Oh, you poor, sensitive thing," she'd say, and make believe she was on the verge of tears.

Even at four and five, I would stop whatever I was doing and watch them with some wonder. In my early years especially, my parents could be my most cherished entertainment, but more important, they could cause me to feel happy or sad, frightened or safe. If they were smiling, their smiles floated like soap bubbles to land on my face. If they were sad, the day darkened even when there were no clouds.

The low, rolling thunder that came approached subtly at first, seeping in like smoke. The silences that began to form between them eventually became places with no bottoms, deep holes into which I could fall and tumble forever and ever, only, unlike Alice, I would find no Wonderland at the bottom, at least not one any girl would want.

I can say with certainty that I was nearly thirteen when the thunder began, because what finally happened had happened right before my thirteenth birthday, the first birthday my father didn't attend. Sometimes we had to celebrate in the morning because of his work, but the important thing was he was there; he cared. I knew that Daddy had a very difficult job as an FAA air traffic controller. Often he was in the airport tower late at night and slept until early afternoon, and that made life different for us from what it was for other families in our neighborhood.

I saw other fathers at home with their wives and children more often, and there was always something more casual about them, about how they dressed and how they moved about their lawns, that made them seem like they were ice-skating or floating. I don't think the other little girls my age, though they were a bit younger or older, liked being in our house because it was kept so neat and organized, mainly because of how my father wanted it. They were afraid to touch anything and hated having to sit so still. With forbidding eyes, their mothers, visiting with my mother, kept them on invisible leashes. They fidgeted and leaped off their seats like frogs when it was time to go.

I didn't know it when I was little, but back then neighbors called us the "Robot Family," maybe because of the way we moved about, how everything was correctly placed, and how perfectly we were always dressed. They'd pause to look at us the way people paused to look in a store's showcase window, stepping to the right or left to get a better view. My mother coordinated her clothes with a fashion model's adherence to colors and styles. She never stepped out of the house without her hair and her makeup being perfect. She even looked that way when she worked in the garage or the yard—looked like someone who seemed too fancy to ruin her hair, her nails, or her lovely clothes doing household chores.

"You could be on the cover of *Vogue*," Daddy once said, and held up the magazine she had received in the mail. She did look prettier than the woman on the cover. And then mysteriously, he added, "Too perfect to be touched."

That didn't sound right, and sure enough, Mommy snapped back at him.

"What about you, Morgan? You are the dapper man. You might be on the cover of *Esquire*."

I understood why she would say that. Daddy always wore a starched, clean long- or short-sleeved white shirt, a black tie, and black slacks, with comfortable black leather loafers, polished and shiny, to work. His cuffed pants had to have perfect, sharp creases. He had at least two dozen white shirts and pairs of black slacks and five pairs of the same loafers, all neatly organized in his closet. Mommy said he was always ready for inspection.

His dark brown hair was military trim, or at least that was what Mommy called it. At six foot two, he had the lean build of a professional tennis player or a swimmer, both of which my mother claimed he did well: "He won't do anything if he can't do it well."

Like dancing, I thought.

But Daddy had perfect posture because he was conscious of it. If he forgot for a moment, he would snap to attention as if he had a spring in his spine. He was afraid he would become stoop-shouldered, sitting and leaning toward a radar screen for hours. He was always after me to take care of my posture.

"You're never too young to worry about it. Stand straight, Caroline. Pull your shoulders back. Hup, hup!"

My mother nicknamed him Captain Bryer, even though there was no such rank for him at his work. She'd say, "Yes, Cap'n, sir," to tease him and even saluted whenever he told her to do something in that commanding and authoritative tone of voice he brought home from work. She had me saluting him, too. In the beginning he laughed, but there came the time when he snapped, "Stop that," at both of us and walked off after saying, "It isn't funny anymore."

She stopped calling him Captain Bryer, and I never saluted him again.

But as far back as I could remember, my mother called him an "exact" man because of how he had been brought up and how detailed and accurate his work had to be. There was little room for mistakes and no room for careless errors at his job. People's lives depended on him being perfect.

So I thought he was perfect and that, because of him, we would be.

He was similarly exacting in his personal life. We lived in a remodeled dark green two-story Queen Anne house with white shutters in Colonie, New York, which was only five miles from the Albany International Airport, where Daddy worked. I think I was born under the sound of a passing jet plane. Nevertheless, I never got used to it; when I was playing outside, I always stopped what I was doing to watch an airplane take off or approach the airport for landing. If my mother was nearby and saw me look, she would proudly say, "Your father is ensuring the safety of all those people so they can go home to their families. He's probably talking to the pilots now."

Because she was so impressed, I was impressed, even though it took me a while to really appreciate why that was justified. When I fully understood that a mistake, even a small one—a little to the right or to the left, something done just a short while too soon or something not clearly understood—could mean a terrible, often fatal accident, I had more respect and understanding for how my father behaved and kept his personal things.

My parents' bathroom had been completely redone before we had moved into our house. There was a sink and cabinets for my mother and a sink and cabinets for my father across from hers. The white marble counters were immaculate "because your father wants the house to look like an operating room," Mommy said, and sighed. "But I'm not hiring an army of maids like your grandfather had and his father had. This is a home, not an institution."

Daddy's side always did look cleaner and more organized than my mother's. Nothing was ever moved from the spot in which he had placed it. His toothbrush and shaving things were set the same distance apart, almost as if they were done with a ruler, and if Mommy happened to shift something, Daddy always corrected it. I knew because I was often with her while she was cleaning the bathroom. She'd turn to me and say with a smile, "You'd think I stopped the world from spinning. The soap dish was slightly too far on the right."

Her side was messy compared to his mainly because my mother seemed to be in more of a rush or in a frenzy when she had to wash, dress, and do her makeup and hair to be sure it was always flawless. She often had to soak in a bubble bath first, the floral scents rising with the steam. She told me that relaxing was key to looking pretty. She'd almost fall asleep in the tub. Before I was five, I'd sit on the floor while she was bathing and pretend to read to her from one of my favorite books. I had actually memorized all the words. She'd lie back with a soft smile as if I was singing to her.

Afterward, she would sit at her vanity table to do her makeup so carefully that it was like watching someone rise out of herself to become extra beautiful. As if I was observing an artist painting a masterpiece, I was mesmerized, even before I understood any of it: why mascara was important, why foundation was so necessary, and why the technique for putting on lipstick had to be done correctly. She had learned it all at the all-girls prep school she'd had to attend when she was sixteen, but she didn't regret it.

"Don't you just hate to see women with a little smear on the side of their mouths?" she asked. I didn't remember noticing that, but I thought she was talking more to herself and didn't expect me to answer.

When she started on her hair, she seemed to take extra care with every strand, telling me that your hair was really the frame of your face: "I know the plainest-looking women who can suddenly become attractive because they've done their hair so well, a mediocre painting in a gilded frame."

Daddy would poke his head in and say, half jokingly, "Why didn't you start yesterday?" He'd point at his watch.

"We don't have to be the first ones there," Mommy would reply. "Your father is really a watch repairman, or should be," she'd tell me.

Daddy hated even being almost late for anything. He was well prepared ahead of time. My mother said he spent most of his day riding on the second hand on a clock the way cowboys rode a horse, crying, "Giddy-up." She told me that when a doctor listened to his heart, he heard "tick-tock." Daddy didn't think that was funny. He lost his smile, anger pooling around his eyes. But I still believe to this day that he looked at clocks more than he looked at me.

I remember that it wasn't that he moved to the ticktock of a clock as much as he moved cautiously, firmly, and deliberately, almost as if he had counted the number of steps from here to there, whether it was going from one room to another or out to get the mail. He never took a step less or a step more when he retrieved our mail, if and when he was home to get it. I knew because when I watched him, I counted.

I think I was more fascinated with how he went up the stairway, never taking two steps at a time and always stepping in the middle. Mommy was frustrated when he wouldn't fill both his arms or his hands with things to take up. He would have a free hand for the banister and make a second trip.

"One would think you were in your eighties," she once said to him with a tone of frustration and a little ridicule. That tone of voice never seemed to bother him back then.

"One would think I want to *reach* my eighties," he would reply. Sometimes he smiled when she said things like that to him; sometimes he sounded more like her teacher, because he repeated his answers word for word. Sometimes she smiled; sometimes she turned and walked away with a comment like "Suit yourself. We'll add another hour to the day."

I remember one of Mommy's friends saying to her, "Is he as careful and precise when he makes love?"

I had no idea what it meant at the time, but it sounded funny. *How do you make love?* I wondered. Was there a recipe, or written directions in a book? Mommy did laugh.

"Surgical," she replied, and they both laughed even harder. "He always calls it a perfect set-down or a great takeoff."

She tilted her head and thought before she added to her answer.

"But I wouldn't go so far as to say it was passionate. Perhaps men aren't as much as women. What's the quote: 'Don't make the perfect the enemy of the good'? I wonder if that applies to love."

I would learn from my classmates in grade school that, unlike their fathers, my father's precision even applied to me, to how my mother dressed me before we went out, even simply going shopping. "Her hair needs to be brushed or pinned," he would say. "There are loose strands all over her forehead." Or "Why do her socks look so sloppy, Linsey? They look like they've lost their shape, washed out. Her shoes could be cleaner. Their sides and the fronts look like she's been kicking the walls. Don't tell me it's a tween thing or something like that, either. Everyone makes excuses for their children, blaming poor appearance on peer pressure. You take such care with yourself. Why not her?"

Usually, my mother would fix me because she didn't disagree, but closer to my thirteenth birthday, she would grimace when he complained about how I looked and say, "Why don't you buy her clothes and shoes and, while you're at it, lay out her clothes each day yourself, Morgan? Besides, she's not a baby anymore."

Whatever lightness and joy had surrounded us had begun to evaporate by then. Of course, until it happened, until that shocking morning, I truly didn't anticipate the end of forever spring. At first, I really didn't know how I should react. Truly, it was as if the world had tilted beneath me so that nothing looked as centered or as correct as it once had.

My parents' marriage and their love had seemed to be made of unbreakable glass. Was I blind? Was I wrong to believe it, accept it? During those earlier years, they kissed when Daddy returned from work as if he had been gone weeks. "Landed!" he would cry from the entryway. We'd both hurry to greet him, me tossing aside whatever I was holding or doing. There was no "Hi" without a kiss for Mommy until things had begun to change, at first in subtle ways like the way he would simply come home from work, hang up his jacket, and go upstairs to change out of the clothes he had worn to work. If I was there, sitting in the living room reading, he'd glance at me strangely, suspiciously, and before I could jump up to greet him, he was gone.

It wasn't only kisses and hugs that made everything about them seem all right before that. Later Mommy would tell me Daddy didn't actually kiss her; he stamped her: "I almost heard him say, 'Delivered.'" I had no idea what that meant then. During the springtime days, they looked after each other all the time: my mother anticipating something he needed or wanted and rushing to get it; Daddy moving quickly to fix something that she needed fixed. If he couldn't, he would immediately replace it and so fast that my mother told me, "Your father has everything in his back pocket." I really had no reason to think, even imagine, that my parents would change. We all lived in my fairy tale, and characters in fairy tales don't become someone else every time you read them.

Maybe it was childish, but I did believe our lives were magical. When

I was about six and according to my first-grade teacher reading on the level of someone about eight, my mother talked about herself and my father as if they were characters in one of my children's books. Even later, when things were breaking between them, perhaps to make excuses for herself, for how it had all begun and how quickly she had agreed to marriage, she always referred to him the way people refer to movie stars: "He was so handsome, stunning, with those gray-blue eyes and his dark brown hair, rich, thick, and trimmed as if he was going to be filmed or photographed. The features of his face were sculptured like the face of a god on a Roman statue. I never saw a man, including my father, who was so sure of himself. Maybe you can't understand this yet, Caroline, but I immediately felt so safe with him.

"I think," she muttered, almost under her breath like someone really talking to herself, "it was that rather than love that drew me to him. I was always too fragile, vulnerable to changes around me . . . like one of those planes he oversees affected by the weather. He always steered me away from trouble and danger the way he would warn a pilot about a storm or a downdraft. I never flew below the radar when it came to your father. And boy, did I need to be on that radar back then."

She'd throw her head back a little and have a rippling laugh when she talked honestly about herself. Her laughter circled her eyes and brightened them. "I was brought up to be a little princess, you see," she said. "There was always someone to wash my hands and clean my clothes. I can barely recall when I began to cut my own meat. Even when I was your age!"

She would pause, go into deep thought for a moment, and then firmly, angrily add, "I'm not going to bring you up that way, the way my parents raised me. I will protect you always, Caroline, and try to keep what's ugly away from you as long as I can, but you're going to be harder, more independent, and so much less vulnerable than I was when you get to be my age and especially than I was when I was a teenager, my sweet Caroline."

She'd rock me and sing the Neil Diamond song. I never stop hearing it, even here, in the shell built over and around me. Perhaps I hear it even more because I am trapped in it and my mind is full of echoing memories.

My grandfather, my mother's father, J. Willard Sutherland, was a very wealthy man at an early age—"before most young men graduated from college," my mother told me after I had entered school and she was helping me with homework. "His father, your great-grandfather, Raymond Sutherland, was a genius when it came to choosing what would become valuable commercial property," she said. "He was rich, but my father is wealthy. Believe me, there is a big difference. Rich people live well, but wealthy people have power, real power, over other people. And they enjoy it. Especially your grandfather.

"By the time I graduated from Skidmore, my father, who had inherited the business, was worth more than a billion dollars. He was and still is a workaholic. He'll never have enough or too much money. It's too simple to say that he's greedy. His work, basically making money, is his life. Profit and loss is like breathing in and out. His picture could be next to the word *businessman* in the dictionary. He really only respects people who make money.

"When I graduated from Skidmore with my degree in liberal arts, he told me that my official document and five dollars would get me a city bus ticket. 'Knowledge for the sake of it might improve your dinner conversation,' he said in his arrogant style, making it sound like an obvious, universal truth, 'but not your bank account.' My older brother, your uncle Martin, went right into working with our father when he graduated with a Harvard business degree two years before me, and a year later married Aunt Holly, his high school girlfriend. They had been going together since seventh grade."

She paused. I anticipated what she might say next.

"They started their marriage with a tragedy when their baby girl, Annabelle, died at three months from sudden infant death syndrome. Of course, I felt terribly sorry for them, especially for Holly, who fell into months of depression. I think her getting pregnant with Simon was a lifesaver.

"Anyway, Martin was a perfect son for my father because he never liked having choices. Your grandfather made all his decisions for him. I used to call him 'one-flavor ice cream.' When we were younger, I could kid him, but I stopped after Annabelle.

"Nevertheless, I didn't want to become his secretary, so my father decided I should work in the bank of which he was president."

"And then you married Daddy almost three years later," I said. She had told me the story enough times for me to remember it almost word for word. "He was the man for you."

"Yes, yes, but I never had a real boyfriend until your father came in to start an account," she said. "I mean, I had boyfriends here and there, but none of them really mattered to me. I didn't even go to my high school prom. So many of my classmates were in cliques. I hated the chatter and the gossip. Maybe that was your grandfather's influence. And too many thought I was some sort of princess. As far as boys went, your grandfather thought anyone who showed the slightest interest in me was too immature. 'Young men and women are more like seven-year-olds these days,' he'd say. When I was in college, he told me, 'To find a man in his twenties who is an adult is like finding gold.'

"So you see, your father was not only special to me; he had my father's stamp of approval. I often wonder how much difference that made," she added, tilting her head and thinking like she always did when something had just occurred to her. "I can still see my father mouthing 'I do' when I said it during the marriage ceremony, like he was willing it to be said, like it was all under his control, even love. Yes, even that . . ." she muttered, her voice trailing off like the sound of a bird's song being carried off in the wind.

Maybe she was doing it for me more than she was doing it for herself, but she always tried to make her early days with Daddy seem more like something magical and enchanting. She even began with "Once upon a time, there was this young girl working in a bank . . ."

"And you wouldn't have been there to meet Daddy if it wasn't for Grandfather," I always interjected, as if we were telling the story together, performing it for some unseen guests.

"He'll tell you that more times than I will—tell you how I was so lucky to find a man who could support me and a family decently. For my father, it has to be that way. A woman has to have a man to provide for her and her children. She can never really do it herself. He thinks it's funny to call those who do provide for their families 'woe men' instead of 'women.' Your grandfather is definitely a reincarnation of Attila the Hun."

"Who?"

"No one you want to know," she said, and then laughed. "Sometimes I thought he imagined I was born with a hairy mole on the tip of my nose and couldn't find a man myself. He was worried about it more than my mother was. My mother was always more romantic, trusting in faith. That's for sure. My father thinks being romantic diminishes your control. He thinks he moved my brother and me like pieces on a chessboard. Everything I have and that has happened to me and your uncle was part of his grand design. Checkmate."

"Checkmate?"

"Yes. You're about to lose. Your opponent warns you, not that either of us put up that much opposition to our father when we were younger. Like all young girls, I was confused about myself, certainly more confused about myself than Martin was about himself. He fell into place quickly, a marching soldier, whereas I'd question every feeling, everything I did. It's why I tell you self-confidence is so important, maybe more important these days for women than it is for men.

"However, when your grandfather sits in that ruby-red, thick-cushioned chair with his hand-carved mahogany walking stick at his side—a stick that he doesn't need; it's just an affectation—you'd think you were meeting some king who raised his hand and lowered your life over you," she said, not so much bitterly as matter-of-factly.

I did hear my grandfather say that my mother met my father because of his foresight to have her there in that bank. It was at one of the rare formal dinners at Sutherland.

"Things don't just happen," he said. It was practically his mantra, a quote from his own bible. He always stroked his trim, silvery-gold, thick mustache with his right thumb and forefinger when he made his pronouncements. That's how you knew they were coming. "People who have bank accounts have money or good reason and validity to borrow. They are stable with purpose. A vulnerable young woman doesn't have to wonder if the man she met in my bank, especially my bank, is substantial. We don't coddle ne'er-do-wells."

"What vision you have, Daddy. Like some Old Testament prophet," my mother would say. "Maybe you can part the Red Sea." She'd smile after saying something like that, but the mood of the dinner would sink like a rock in a murky pond. I wasn't too young to feel it. When Grandfather Sutherland raised his voice at the dinner table, I'd reflexively cower. Was I like my mother when she was my age?

Grandmother Judith would come to his defense and say something like "Your father is always looking out for his children. He needs to be appreciated. We all have wonderful lives because of him."

My uncle and his wife, Holly, would be silent, and their son, Simon, two years older than me, would barely move or blink his eyes. He was probably thinking about his math homework. Everyone was calling him a genius already and predicted he would surely be the one to discover the cure for cancer or something equally spectacular. My mother once told me that Simon had a heavier burden to carry. He had to be as successful as two children, "assuming the possibilities for the lost Annabelle as well as his own."

When Mommy would challenge Grandfather Sutherland or, as she had done, ridicule his arrogance, Daddy would stare ahead as if he was watching a radar screen, patiently waiting for a storm to pass, and later tell my mother, "That mockery of your father wasn't necessary."

"It was for me," she'd say.

Daddy wouldn't argue, but he had a way of clenching his teeth and pulling back his lips that told me he was upset. Consequently, we only went to my grandfather's estate home for my grandmother's birthdays, my grandparents' anniversaries, or the celebration of some major business accomplishment my grandfather had achieved, mostly because my father insisted we attend.

I didn't mind going to dinners and parties at Grandfather's home back then. His home was so impressive, with all the gates and rolling hills, trees, and the greenest grass, even late into the fall. The original structure was historic. My great-grandfather kept adding to it, buying all the land around it. I knew very few people lived like that. I imagined at least twenty homes in our neighborhood could fit comfortably on Grandfather's property.

The house itself is a true mansion, and with its gray-silver stone exterior and grand, oval-shaped copper and mahogany front doors, it does look like a medieval castle from one of my adventure stories. Those doors open to a large atrium with fountains and a slate walkway, bushes, and flowers in the spring and summer. Behind the house, there are two tennis courts, a large oval pool, and even a nine-hole golf course. My grandfather had the gardeners create a brook, water gurgling over rocks and then pumped back to run over them again and again. My mother said nothing pleased my grandfather more than improving what his father had done. "He's trying to be the better man, you see. Everyone fights with his own ghosts."

I had no idea what that meant then. Who were the ghosts? How could you fight with one? But because of my grandfather's home, I believed in any fantasy my mother created. Look where she and my uncle had grown up. The estate was so grand that my grandfather had given it a name: his name, Sutherland, as if that was a famous place on a map. It hung in what looked like gold-plated scrolled letters above the main gate, looming over anyone who drove up to it.

When I asked my mother if it was a famous place, like those on maps, she said, "That's what your grandfather thinks everyone thinks.

"And you know what?" she added, obviously reluctantly. "That's what they do think."

I wondered why she didn't sound prouder of that, despite the father-daughter conflicts.

I don't wonder now.

2

I don't remember exactly when my mother's friendship with Natalie Gleeson became very special to her, but the first time they met at Mr. Gleeson's funeral, I saw that there was something different about them when they were together. Daddy did, too, although he didn't say so that day. Natalie's father had been our real estate agent for the house we were in. Her mother, Marlene, was often my babysitter when I was much younger, and we had been to the Gleesons' house for dinner a number of times, but never when Natalie was there. We saw her picture, of course, and my mother inquired about her. Her parents were very proud of her and did show us pictures of her with very important people, even the president.

When she was speaking to Natalie, Mommy's smile was warmer. They looked like they had known each other since they were little girls. They hovered about each other and almost totally ignored anyone else, even me. Daddy was off in a corner most of the time, looking annoyed at being ignored, too. After a while, he interrupted them to say he had to get home to prepare some work for his next shift. He said goodbye to Mrs. Gleeson and left.

Since they had been seeing each other so often, I asked my mother if Natalie was now her very best friend. She thought a moment, smiled, and nodded.

"How do you know she's your best friend?"

"You know. Here," she said, holding her hand over her heart. "It doesn't happen overnight. A real friendship is something that just flows into you gradually but steadily, Caroline. You can almost feel it beginning. There's a happiness that comes over you, maybe overwhelms you, when you see each other, when you talk. You don't talk at each other like you see most people talking to each other. Half the time they look uninterested, just being polite. No, being together with someone special to you suddenly becomes a wonderful thing, a burst of sunshine on a gray, rainy day."

I didn't have a friend like that, someone who brought me and to whom I brought such joy. When would I? I wondered. My mother made it sound so wonderful. Was I too young? And yet some of my classmates seemed to have special friends, friends from whom they were practically inseparable. Was something wrong with me? Of course, later that would become the biggest question, my grandfather's biggest concern, and the justification for Dr. Kirkwell. Despite my resistance, deep down I couldn't help wondering: Was Grandfather right to be so concerned?

"Don't look so worried, sweetheart," Mommy said after she had described what a best friend was. She put her arm around me and cradled my head on her shoulder as she brushed her fingers through my hair. "You'll always be my very best, best friend. And you do like Natalie very much, too, right?"

"Uh-huh," I said. I almost said, *But I don't think Daddy does or ever will.* I swallowed that back, sensing how angry that might make her. For now, maybe it wasn't that important, I thought. Daddy could change his mind or keep his opinion to himself. Sometimes Mommy had to ask him about something a number of times before he would reveal his opinion, but when he did, there was never a doubt that he wouldn't change his mind.

I remember that when her deep friendship with Natalie began, I sensed the magic leaking out of our house. She never seemed as interested in the other women she met when she and Daddy went to dinner with them and their husbands, and although she occasionally went shopping with someone, I didn't see that friend often, not as often as I would Natalie. She didn't talk to anyone as much on the phone, either, and many who called my mother from time to time stopped calling altogether, maybe because my mother rarely called them. It became even rarer when my mother and Natalie began to see each other almost daily.

I couldn't imagine any other reason. My mother never had bad arguments with any of those women or was unpleasant to someone, so I didn't think anyone was especially mad at her. With her soft, bright smile, Mommy would make anyone feel comfortable, especially some of the women whom Daddy's friends and coworkers were dating or had married. I knew that deep down she didn't like many of them, but they couldn't tell. Maybe Daddy could. I know I could.

I knew how to read every blink of her eyes or the way she tightened her lips when someone she wasn't fond of spoke to her, gave her an opinion she didn't like, or just ignored what she had said. I could even see it in the way she clasped her hands like someone anticipating a disaster. Sometimes her face was so still that she resembled a person who had forgotten how to smile or even grimace. I knew my mother better than I knew myself. At least, I thought so until we met Natalie Gleeson.

Natalie lived with her mother in a ranch-style house with pretty cut fieldstone walls at the end of our street, the cul-de-sac, but she had been mostly away from home during the years we were the Gleesons' neighbors. She had been working in Washington, D.C., and then was working for the U.S. ambassador to France. She rushed back from Paris when her father died unexpectedly from a heart attack. My father said, "Most people who die that way die unexpectedly."

It was the first time I had gone to a funeral. In fact, Mr. Gleeson was the only person I knew personally who had died, and I was already in the eighth grade. Death wasn't something my classmates and I talked about at school, excluding tragic deaths or ones that made headlines. Of course, I heard about airplane accidents. Daddy always analyzed them aloud, and when he did, Mommy often reached for my hand, because Daddy always spoke so angrily that he frightened us both. It didn't have to happen. "Someone was careless or ill-trained," he would declare in a booming voice.

I believed Daddy was right to be angry, because in my mind, especially when I was much younger, death seemed like something you could prevent or at least delay until you were very, very old. "Just follow the rules and be alert," he would say whenever I expressed how nervous or afraid I was of something. "Most people convince themselves nothing bad will happen to them. Ignoring something, Caroline, doesn't make it go away. Don't believe that junk about turtles living longest. They've got to come out sometime, and when they do, they're not properly prepared. The odds of being hit by lightning are one in five thousand, so unless it's a bolt of lightning, you could prevent it."

But Mr. Gleeson didn't die in a plane accident or get killed crossing a street because he didn't look both ways. Even though he had followed the rules, at least as far as I could see, he had simply just died. One day he waved to me from his driveway, and now he would never wave and smile at me again. Was that a bolt of lightning?

My mother saw how upset I was the moment we heard. She took my hand, sat me down at the table, and held on to my hand as she explained it this way: "Mr. Gleeson has left to live with his mother, father, and older brother in heaven, and so you won't see him anymore. Everyone is sad, especially Mrs. Gleeson, because she can't see him again until she goes to heaven, and that could be a long while. So we have to try to help her and her daughter Natalie feel better, okay?"

I nodded, thinking she was talking to me like I was a younger child because she didn't want me to cry. Neither my father nor my mother spoke very much about heaven or God. "The only thing my father worships is the Almighty Dollar, and whenever my mother mentions church or prayer, my father goes into a rant about religion destroying most people's ambition. He calls it a 'refuge for failures,'" my mother said. "He donates to the church, but mainly because my mother insists. Of course, being so rich, he always likes to appear benevolent." Nevertheless, it was all still quite a mystery to me: God, heaven, hell, prayer. I wasn't sure what I should believe.

The only thing Daddy ever said about religion, heaven, or God was that he believed only in what he saw or heard and God hadn't called him lately: "God's not on the radar." He didn't even like the word *believe*. He said he'd rather *conclude*, which was why my mother compared him to her father.

"Radar screen or adding machine. What's the difference, Morgan?" she said. "You both hypnotize yourselves with facts and figures. Maybe you're both hiding behind them."

Daddy didn't seem pleased about that. I had never seen him glare at her so angrily, but like most of the time when she had upset him, he simply snapped his paper and started reading again or turned on the television.

What should I believe in? I wondered. What was worth the faith you had in it?

I did believe that my mother was the most beautiful woman in the world. Even though our neighbors called us the Robot Family, they admired my mother's beauty. Other fathers stopped what they were doing to look at her, and when their husbands weren't there, women gave my mother more compliments, admiring her strawberry-blond hair and her eyes. She had my grandfather's velvety blue eyes and my grandmother's perfect nose, what Natalie called a "button nose." She really did have the face and the figure to be a *Vogue* cover girl or a cover girl for any magazine, for that matter. Until I met Natalie Gleeson at her father's funeral, I didn't think any woman could compare or hold my interest as well as my mother held mine.

It wasn't that Natalie was more beautiful; it was more the intensity I felt when she looked at me or anyone else. She seized your attention and held it while she spoke to you. It was hard to look away or even think of something else at the moment, not that I wanted to. She focused her kelly green eyes on you as if she could tell everything about you in a few moments and decide if she wanted to continue talking to you. I watched her closely, as closely as I watched my mother when she was around other people. If Natalie didn't like someone or was bored with him or her, she'd blink like pulling down a window shade, smile, nod her head, and, with one big step as if she was stepping over a puddle, politely move to someone else or to do something else.

Natalie was a little taller than my mother, but her figure was not as perfect. She was smaller-bosomed and a little wider in the hips. I wouldn't say her posture was as flawless as Daddy's, but there was something just as authoritative about it. She moved with Daddy's firmness and sense of purpose, moved as if she wanted to be sure that everything she had done or would do and everything she had said or would say wasn't a waste of time. She shook hands as firmly as Daddy did. Some of the women Mommy knew or who were friends and wives of Daddy's coworkers had handshakes that felt and looked more like feathers trembling in someone else's palm.

Natalie spoke with a different sort of accent, which I later realized was only because she was so precise with her pronunciation. When I first heard her speak French, however, it sounded melodious. It was difficult not to fixate on her, which was one of the reasons I understood Mommy's welcoming her to be her best friend. There were many reasons, but I thought the most important was that Mommy envied her from the very beginning. Daddy didn't understand it as much as I did, maybe because Mommy told me, "Natalie has done things I always dreamed of doing. She has courage."

"Like a soldier?"

"In a way, yes. When she graduated from high school, she went right on to study at the Sorbonne in Paris. The only time I've been to Paris was with my parents because my father had a business meeting there. He put my brother Martin, my mother, and me with a group of tourists. We really didn't see Paris. We saw a travel brochure." She sighed with envy. "Natalie lived in Paris, went to the groceries and drugstores Parisians went to, and ate in restaurants off the tourist maps. She took trips to the countryside and went to small villages and towns few visitors to France saw. She really learned what France is. And all by herself, too!"

Days after Mr. Gleeson's funeral, my mother rambled on about Natalie while Daddy and I sat and listened to the stories and details Natalie had told her at the Gleesons' house, almost fed her like a starving child. I think that was the first time I realized my mother had lived in such a closed, controlled world, even when she attended college and started to work in the bank. What she had accepted as her fate was suddenly not enough, not nearly enough. And she never missed an opportunity to tell me there was no reason why it should be for me, either.

Maybe Daddy always had the same suspicions about what drove Mommy to become so close to Natalie, only he didn't see Natalie's stories as being as amusing and exciting as I did when Mommy retold Natalie's tales of Paris, of grand ballrooms and banquets and official visits to world-famous cities. Instead, he saw a threat in her admiration of Natalie and her life, and then, in his own way, he became a turtle.

I liked Natalie a lot. Another daughter, especially if she was an only child, might have resented her, right from the beginning. She was taking my mother's attention away, not only from Daddy but from me. What early on was just annoying to Daddy obviously became infuriating to him. I would see something I had never seen in his face or even imagined. He would become wounded, and deeply, in ways it would take me some time to understand. Perhaps I could just as easily say I never knew my father and my mother. What a horrible realization for a young girl to have. Could there be a greater loneliness?

Eventually, then, whatever I had once thought was perfect and wonderful about my life would be swept away. Playing in the yard, basking in the spring sun, and dancing to "Sweet Caroline" would become the lost pieces of my heaven. A dark pall would fall over our home, and what replaced it wasn't enough, at least for me, even though it seemed to be enough for Mommy, maybe more than enough.

After we had gone to the Gleesons' home for the funeral reception, I heard Daddy tell Mommy that Natalie was too stuck on herself. "She's inhaled too much Paris perfume."

"What? What does that even mean, Morgan?"

"For starters, isn't she, like, thirty-two and still single? There's no man she thinks is good enough for her?"

"What's the point of bringing up her age, Morgan? Women don't rush into marriage as a safe haven as quickly anymore."

"Safe haven, huh?"

"You know what I mean. More women are willing to wait for the right person and focus on their careers rather than rush into marriage just for the sake of it. Why fault her for it? I should think you of all people would admire her ambition and accomplishment. You're always telling me how little there is of it these days."

"Yeah, well. I still think she's too into herself. Diplomatic corps. American aristocracy. Some career. In a few years, she'll wish she had never gotten involved. It's all politics. A wasted life."

"Oh. Please. What isn't political? Hasn't my father convinced you of that? He's convinced you of so much else. If he declares it, it's gospel."

Daddy turned on the television to watch news. Their arguments were what my grandfather would call "one-punch fights." I wasn't sure back then whether that was good or bad, but now I realize that if you're upset with someone you love or who loves you, it's important to settle it before you go to sleep. Otherwise, it will be like a small cavity that will grow bigger until it hurts you when you least expect it. And it doesn't matter who is right, who wins. It's almost worse to win an argument with a friend or a member of your family. There will always be some pain when you see his or her embarrassed look of defeat. It hurts more when it's a friend or a family member. But according to my grandfather, it was especially dangerous when you fought and won arguments with strangers in business.

"Never turn your back on someone you've defeated, family or not," he preached. He pulled me closer to him until I could smell his licorice lozenges. "In the garden of victory, there are weeds called revenge. Never forget it."

Even though we didn't see Grandfather Sutherland that much, whatever he had said when we did see him seemed to settle in me forever. Daddy said Mommy wasn't so wrong about her father. He told her that her father did speak with the authority of someone who recited the Bible. "You may mock it, Linsey, but he's a man with a sense of conviction. That's different from someone simply egotistical."

"Conviction? 'Closed-minded' is a better description. You don't know what it was like for me growing up in his shadow, Morgan," Mommy told him. "And Natalie Gleeson doesn't come close to that. She's willing to listen. Yes. It's true. My father has great conversations, open-minded ones, but only with himself."

"Well, he hasn't suffered for it," Daddy said, looking to end the one-punch fight.

But I wanted to ask Mommy what Daddy meant. How could Grandfather suffer for great conversations anyway? What did that mean? However, I could see the glow of anger in her eyes and knew it was better to leave things alone. Even at my age, I already knew that some questions were better left floating, even floating away.

I certainly knew what Daddy had meant when he said Grandfather Sutherland spoke with such authority. I couldn't help but pay attention to him whenever he revealed his thoughts to us at dinners and events. Daddy was right about that, but Mommy was also right about Natalie. People listened to what she said, too. But it was different, at least for me. Even though, like Grandfather, she commanded my interest, when she spoke to me, she mixed so many French words in with English that it made whatever she had said wonderful and important, but somehow softer. I didn't want to resist or challenge anything deep inside me. I really wanted to believe what she believed, as opposed to feeling I had better believe what Grandfather did or he'd be angry or I'd be punished. When he wanted me to believe something, he usually added, "Or you'll be sorry." On the other hand, Natalie simply smiled with confidence. The most she would say was "You'll see. It's true."

Shortly after Mr. Gleeson's funeral, Mommy was chatting with Natalie in the driveway of our house, and she spontaneously invited Natalie and her mother to our house for dinner. I heard Natalie tell my mother that her mother wasn't ready to socialize. She really wasn't up to doing much. She was sleeping a lot. Her husband's death and the aftermath had exhausted her. Natalie surprised me when she said that she practically had to spoon-feed her mother to get her to eat. "Like a child."

"What comes around goes around, doesn't it, Linsey?" she asked, her eyes glazed with tears.

"'They say an old man is twice a child.' *Hamlet*," my mother replied.

"Ah, *oui*."

"Somehow my father will skip it," Mommy said, and they both laughed and then hugged.

Later, Mommy told Daddy how concerned both she and Natalie were about Mrs. Gleeson. His eyes widened and he looked up from the newspaper he was reading. Sometimes he would do that, pretend he was reading and wasn't really listening.

"So what you're going in a circle to tell me is that it's just her coming to dinner?" Daddy asked. Mommy looked so disappointed. Even I knew he had missed her point. Daddy was too smart for that not to be deliberate, but Mommy said nothing more than yes.

"Thanks for the warning," he said. "I'll do one of the guys a favor and take over his hours," he said, then snapped his paper and started reading again, which clearly upset her even more. For a moment she stared at him so hard I thought the back of his neck would burst into flames.

"You might read a radar screen well, Morgan, but you miss a lot on the people screen."

"People screen?"

He laughed, but when she walked out, he glanced at me, and I could see that he didn't look happy. I followed her out quickly. I never wanted to be with my father when he was that angry. It felt like his rage would spread over me like hot sauce. She stood in the kitchen staring out the window toward Natalie's house. Her velvet eyes gleamed. Ironically, when Mommy was terribly upset, every color on her body brightened and made her look more beautiful. Her strawberry-blond hair looked combed with sunlight. Some candle inside her was lit. After a few moments, she realized I was standing there and smiled.

"Let's think about what we're going to prepare," she said.

And just like that, as if the light in her body had traveled into mine, despite what Daddy had said, I was excited about Natalie coming and eagerly helped Mommy fix dinner. I set our dining room table, funnily enough taking extra care placing silverware and dishes so it looked precisely how Daddy liked it. Afterward, Mommy had me wear my pretty green dress.

"For the Irish," she said, smoothing it down. She explained the meaning, telling me all about Saint Patrick's Day even though it was months away. We were in mid-September, but it was one of those cooler falls when the fall leaves were starting to creep into the forests and the yellow and brown could be seen flowing through the mountains. Mommy called it nature's work of art, every gold and rust brown color done in brush-strokes. The breeze had a slight chill in it. People seemed to walk faster.

Birds were fleeing already, too.

"I think this is going to be a colder winter," Mommy predicted. I didn't understand at the time that she was talking about more than the weather. Something mysterious and secret was happening between Mommy and Daddy. I could almost see the shadows in our house growing thicker, wider, and longer.

"Silence speaks the loudest," Grandfather Sutherland once told me when I started to speak while he was still finishing a long and, as Mommy would say, "winded thought." But silence did speak louder than words in our house. I think I noticed it as soon as it had started. Mommy and Daddy spoke less and less to each other after Mommy had begun to spend more and more time with Natalie Gleeson. Toward the end, when our bubble burst, my parents did move like the shadows, unheard, darkly, almost sliding toward wherever they were going in the house and taking care not to brush against each other.

I don't know when that started to frighten me, but it did long before either of them said anything to me about it. I suppose I could say that from that first dinner with Natalie, I saw a difference in Mommy's feelings about Daddy. She was so upset with his comments about Natalie and his decision to work that I thought she would stop working and cancel the dinner, or maybe plan it for another day and not tell him so he couldn't get out of it. She would leave the table dressed and set so it would shine like a bright light in his eyes. She would do it just to spite him. But as the time grew closer, she was buoyant, adjusting my dress, fixing my hair, and putting on music. Her excitement filled me with even more excitement. I hurried with her to the front door when the buzzer sounded.

Natalie looked very pretty in a dark blue pantsuit. Her amber hair was up, which changed her face, made it softer. She wore much less makeup than Mommy, but there was what looked like strokes of pink at the crests of her cheeks, maybe to cover the small freckles. The only jewelry she wore was a very expensive-looking watch, which Daddy had noted at the funeral, a Cartier that I thought was similar to Grandmother Judith's. Natalie wore no rings. Mommy wore four, two on each hand, and a ruby bracelet that matched two of her rings. Natalie handed her a bag.

"It's a Château Pontet-Canet," she said. "The ambassador's favorite for Italian. You did say Italian."

"Oh, yes, veal piccata with a side of angel hair."

"Sounds wonderful."

"Thanks for the wine."

"*Un avant-goût de la beauté pour le beau,*" Natalie said.

Mommy blushed. What did it mean? How did Mommy know? I rarely heard her say anything that even resembled French. Daddy knew more, I thought. Although all the pilots he helped spoke English, Mommy said he liked to welcome them in their native languages. He knew how to say it in five or six different languages, even Turkish.

"*Merci,*" Mommy said. "I'm afraid Morgan had to go to work to cover for someone tonight."

"Oh. I was so looking forward to talking to him about his work. Fascinating, I'm sure."

Mommy rolled her eyes. There was a good second or two before Natalie took her eyes off Mommy and looked to Mommy's side and saw me standing there.

"What a pretty green dress," she said.

"For the Irish," I said, and Natalie's face burst into a smile the way the rose in full bloom looked in my book of flowers. She laughed, her eyes sparkling. She reached for my hand.

"Can you escort me in to show me your house, *s'il vous plaît?*"

I looked at Mommy.

"Natalie's escorted our ambassador to France many times, I'm sure," she said, and then, realizing I didn't exactly know what it meant, she added, "It's a real honor, Caroline. You show your respect for whomever by walking him or her into a party or a place."

"There was also security escorting us," Natalie said, smiling. "But I don't need security here, right, Caroline?" She was still waiting for me to take her hand, which I did quickly. *What a funny question to ask me,* I thought. *Security? Here? Like at the airport?* Neither of us spoke for a moment, and then Natalie realized I was holding her hand.

"Shall we start the tour?" she asked.

"I can show you my room first," I said. I don't know why, but it seemed very important to me for her to see it before she saw anything else.

"Of course. *Mais bien sûr,*" she said.

"That's what it means in French," Mommy explained. "Of course. Right?" she asked Natalie.

"*Oui, oui.*"

Mommy laughed.

"With Natalie around, you'll learn French fast, Caroline. I'll learn, too. Public schools don't require a language. English is spoken everywhere by necessity, Morgan says."

"Don't tell the French," Natalie said, and they laughed. I loved how they laughed together. "Anyway, school-learned French isn't exactly how the French speak. I was lucky."

"How so?" Mommy asked.

"There was a French family in this neighborhood back then, and I became good friends with the girl my age, Edith," Natalie said. She smiled. "She sang also."

"Piaf."

"*Je ne regrette rien.*"

They both laughed again. I could almost feel the warmth between them. It was as if they already had secrets.

What Natalie had said in French wasn't what interested me, however. *Whatever happened to that little girl?* I wondered. *How long were they friends? Were they best friends? Does she still live here?* I didn't want her to think of that little girl now. I didn't want her to be friendlier to any other girl even though Edith would be as old as Natalie or Mommy. I didn't even want to hear about another little girl she had admired. What if I wasn't as smart? And that girl sang? I sang by myself, but not around anyone but Mommy.

Vaguely I wondered if my father would be upset with my caring about that so much. He often said, "Your mother is rubbing off on you too much," as if she was covered in wet paint.

Mommy stepped back, and I walked Natalie to the stairway.

"It's upstairs."

She made a gesture with her hand for me to continue. I looked at Mommy. I suddenly felt very important. She could see it in my face and laughed.

"Would you like a cocktail first, Natalie? A French 75?"

"Oh, *oui, oui*," she said. I had no idea what a 75 meant, but as we walked up the stairs, she recited: "That's gin, champagne, lemon juice, and sugar."

"I know. I practiced," Mommy revealed from the foot of the stairs. I had seen her mixing and sipping a drink at the bar earlier, testing it. Because it was so important for her to do things that pleased Natalie, I decided I would, too.

Natalie laughed, and we turned at the top of the stairway toward my room. I suddenly realized no adult besides Mommy and Daddy had ever come in to see it. My Sutherland grandparents had never visited us, and Daddy's parents lived in Maui. I had seen them only on a Zoom call. They were both too sick to do a long trip and had actually been in assisted living for the past four years. His mother was nearly forty-three and his father was forty-seven when he was born. He called himself "a true afterthought between overseas missions," whatever that meant.

The walls of my room were a warm shade of pink. On the right, just over my desk, Mommy had hung a collection of my early baby pictures, two with her holding me and one with Daddy holding me on his shoulders, my arms out like the wings of an airplane. All the frames were a light shade of blue. Natalie turned right to them.

"I think you look more like your mother," she said, "but you have your father's brow." She pointed to it on her face. I looked at my pictures. It had never occurred to me to wonder who I looked more like. "You have your mother's beautiful eyes and that heartthrob nose. But people's looks change when they get older," she added. "You certainly look like you'll be even more beautiful than your mother."

My eyes widened. More beautiful than my mother? Would Daddy say I belonged on a magazine cover?

"I love your furniture. I bet your mother picked it all out."

I smiled and looked around as if I were just now first seeing the room. I never had thought about my mother doing it all, although I remembered my mother saying she was determined to make my room a real little girl's room. She told me that the room she had grown up in at Sutherland "could have been a boy's or a girl's. My father has always had a penchant for, an inclination to go with, dark or subdued colors," she said. "My mother's opinions were smothered to death an hour after she agreed to marry him. I always felt it was more of a contract than a marriage certificate. It was, after all, his family's house, his family's money, and his family's destiny. She was like someone who had stepped onto a train while it was still moving in one direction. It was in her marriage vows. Sit down or jump off."

My mother often went into similar rants about her life at Sutherland. Most of it went over my head, but I did remember those words, probably because she repeated them or something similar as she worked on our house, adding knickknacks, paintings, fake flowers, and pretty lamps, almost in a frenzy to forget Sutherland. I went with her to choose rugs for the living room and rugs for both our bedrooms and the guest bedroom. She said she was determined to bring the sunshine in, even on cloudy days. "Weather report at Sutherland: gloom seven days a week, slowly changing to rain," she muttered. "Weather report here: cloudless skies forever."

Did she really believe that? Forever?

My father was nothing like her father when it came to designing and furnishing most of our house. Mommy had told me that he had his interest centered on the things that would be his and left the designing of everything else up to her. My room was the first room she had planned after she and Daddy had decided to buy the house. It had an ornate, decorative rug with pink and green flowers and a darker pink border. It ran just under the front feet of my tufted bed frame. A crystal chandelier hung at the center of the ceiling. The two bureaus and my desk were in white. On the shelves were the dolls and stuffed animals my parents had bought me, and at the center of one shelf was a model of a 747 jet plane. It even had the faces of people looking out the windows.

"Oh," Natalie said, picking up a book my mother had read completely to me twice when I was younger. I had done a book report on it already this year. I kept it on the table at the side of my bed. "I love this. *The Secret Garden*. Do you love it?"

I nodded.

"I got an A-plus on my book report on it."

"Did you?"

"It was our first English assignment."

"That's right. School has started. You're in the eighth grade?"

"*Oui.*"

She laughed.

"My father bought this for me when I was a little girl. It was my first book. As a gift, that is."

She looked thoughtful again for a moment, with a soft smile on her lips as she might have during the moment her picture was being taken or while an artist was painting her, and then she put the book down and gazed at the rest of my room. I think I decided then and there to be like her, to smile like she smiled and move as pointedly as she did. Where Mommy was buoyant, Natalie was decisive, but in a more graceful way than Daddy. Perhaps the right word was *elegant*. That would be the way Mommy would describe her. Daddy called it snobbery.

"How beautiful. You keep it well, too. It looks like a *vitrine*."

"What's that?"

"Oh. French. I'm sorry. It comes to me first often. So, your room could be a room in a store window, but I see your father did contribute something," she said, walking over to the model plane. "He does have a very important job. I think I flew here in a plane like this. He might have guided my plane's pilot into the airport."

She picked it up and studied it.

"That even looks like me in the third window from the front," she said, laughing and showing it to me. "I'm always surprised with the end of a flight."

I had to look. Did it? It was just the face of any woman, I thought, more like a cartoon character with her big eyes. She put the plane down and gazed around again, nodding to her own thoughts as she did so.

"Your first room is something you'll never forget," she said, sounding so wise and sure, just like Daddy or Grandfather could. "You don't really miss it until you leave. There are so many little sacrifices we make to grow up. It's wonderful and painful at the same time."

I looked at her, completely puzzled. Painful? Growing up? Why? She saw the confusion in my face.

"Oh. Don't mind me. I get too philosophical sometimes." She put her hand on my shoulder. "Well, we'd better get down to see what your mother's up to. Shall we? *On y va?*"

"Does that mean 'Shall we?' in French?" I asked quickly.

"*Mais oui.*" She took my hand. "You're very bright. Do you want to learn French?"

"*Mais oui,*" I said, "but like you did."

She stopped, pulled her head back, and smiled widely.

"My long-lost youth." She leaned to whisper. "I warn you. Learning a language from someone makes you great friends."

Why should she warn me? She took my hand in hers again.

"Would you like us to be great friends, *bons amis?*"

"*Oui,*" I said with such enthusiasm that her rose bloom smile came again.

I walked to the stairway and descended with her as she began to describe what it was like for her to grow up an only child and then go off to college in France at the Sorbonne. She expressed how excited she was, as were all the other students who came from different countries. It obviously made her happy simply to remember it and have someone to tell it to.

"Good memories, happy memories, when recalled, are like polishing a valuable jewel," Mommy once told me. That was what Natalie looked like she was doing, polishing the jewels in her life.

"It was so much fun for all of us new students to share our backgrounds and learn about other places. Sometimes we'd spend hours and hours just talking. I think we were all a little scared and happy to meet someone else who was a little scared. After a while, we were too tired to be afraid."

"Why should you be afraid?" I asked, thinking of what Daddy had said about being afraid.

"Oh, you left home and you're in a different world with strangers. You'll understand when you go off to college, but never be afraid to be afraid."

That was almost exactly what Daddy had told me, but everything she said, everything she described about herself, seemed like it came out of a book or a movie, whereas what Daddy said sounded like it came out of a training manual.

We met Mommy in the living room, where she was sitting at the little bar, curved with a marble granite top. There were five high-backed black leather stools.

"Your cocktail awaits, *mademoiselle*."

"Breaking news," Natalie said. "In 2012, François Fillon, the prime minister, called for the official deletion of the word '*mademoiselle*' from all official documents."

"What should I call you?"

She looked at me.

"Nattie," she said. "What they called me when I was Caroline's age."

"Let's toast to it."

"Me too," I said, eager to be part of anything they did together.

"Your Shirley Temple is right here, honey." Mommy handed it to me.

"Oh, she's old enough for a sip of wine, *n'est-ce pas?*"

Mommy raised her eyebrows.

"If you don't tell your father," she said.

I looked at Nattie, who was smiling. Secrets from Daddy?

Mommy poured me a couple of inches of wine. We lifted our glasses.

"*À votre santé*," Nattie said. "To your health," she whispered to me.

I sipped whenever they sipped, the wine feeling so forbidden on my lips. Their eyes locked on each other. I hardly moved while I listened to them talk, my mother revealing much more about her early life than I had ever heard: how much she had hated the private school her parents had enrolled her in, especially the finishing school; how controlling her father was when it came to whom she could be friends with; and how Grandmother Judith was more interested in her canasta teas and her charity events than she was in spending more quality time with her. I was surprised to hear how her housekeeper, Mrs. Lawson, had much more to do with her everyday life, to the point of buying her clothes and shoes and even taking her to the doctor and the dentist! She was still working at Sutherland. Mommy called her "despicably immortal," whatever that meant.

"The privileged life is often antithetical to family," Nattie said. "Too many traditions, codes of behavior subduing feelings."

"What's 'antithetical to family' mean?" I asked, and they both looked at me as if they just realized I was with them. Both laughed. "And why to yours, Mommy?"

"We'll explain it later when you can best understand, Caroline," Mommy said.

"When you're about twenty," Nattie joked.

When they laughed together, they seemed like they could share anything, anytime. I remember that was the first time I felt a little jealous. Suddenly, Mommy had someone else to focus her attention on just as intensely as she did on me, if not maybe even more so. It was like they lived on a level above me. So much of what they said and meant to each other floated above my head. Explanations were pushed to "later," meaning I couldn't understand until I was older. I never hated still being considered a child as much as I did then.

However, after the cocktail hour and during the early part of our dinner, Mommy and Nattie talked to me a lot, maybe because I had interrupted them and made them realize they were ignoring me too much. Nattie explained things about Paris and France, all of it sounding so fantastic that it was as if I was hearing her describe a world as far away as a planet or star. As they spoke, Nattie was teaching Mommy words in French, too. They laughed about their college experiences, each having boyfriends they said were "too into themselves."

"I used to use that old joke, which some understood and others looked like it was smoke floating over their heads. You know, 'Enough about me. Let's talk about you. What do you think of me?'" Nattie said.

Mommy laughed.

"I must say, Morgan could get distracted, but never with himself, at least that way. However, when he fixes in on something, I could be doing somersaults or standing on my head and he wouldn't notice. Guys in his job have true tunnel vision."

"That could be very . . ."

"Exhausting," Mommy said, "and not just for him!" They both laughed. I had no idea what that meant. Why would it make her tired? She wasn't working at the airport. "Oh," she said, finally noticing me again. "Caroline's eaten everything on her plate!"

"It was a wonderful meal," Nattie said. "How did you become such a good cook?"

"That was one positive about my life at Sutherland: Mrs. Wilson, our cook—or chef, as my mother insisted she be called. It was practically an obscenity to call her a cook. She's still there. It's the only reason I like going to dinner at Sutherland. I spent lots of time with her learning about food. It was one of the warmest places in my father's mansion, and not just temperature-wise. Mrs. Lawson, who was practically my guardian, considered conversation with someone so young a waste of her time. I believe she was ordered to cry at birth and never changed. I think I was my own best friend back then."

They laughed. What did all that mean? How could you be your own best friend?

"I totally get it, and this dinner, too," Natalie said. She looked at me. "You liked your mother's meal just as much?"

"Uh-huh."

"Usually she leaves enough to have Morgan tell us how his father would make him eat his dinner leftovers for breakfast. My father always liked that story . . . the old 'Waste not, want not' chant. I think that's what he likes the most about Morgan: the belief about getting the most out of everything you own and everything you eat. My father imprints himself on people. He's like a tattoo."

Nattie stared at her for a long moment.

"What?" Mommy asked.

"Maybe I shouldn't say it."

"Now you'd better."

Nattie shrugged.

"Because of other things you've told me, it sounds a lot like a father fixation," Nattie said.

Now they were both very silent, deeply silent. For a moment, I thought Mommy might be angry at what Nattie said. Then she nodded.

"Can you love and hate someone at the same time?" Mommy asked her.

"*Le plus certain*. Especially if the love is not reciprocal. Calling up the amateur psychiatrist in me, and without having met your father, I'd say he suffers the same ambiguity."

"Don't tell him; it will break his heart. 'Doubt' is a curse word in his dictionary. But enough about me. What do you think of me?" Mommy said, and they laughed again as if they had been laughing together all their lives. Everything between them seemed so deep, philosophical, and mysterious.

Now I truly felt like I had disappeared suddenly and been forgotten.

"I was just hungry," I said, enthusiastically filling a rare moment of silence between them.

"What?" Mommy asked.

I pointed to my plate. They both laughed, but only when they looked at each other, as if they wanted to be sure it was proper.

"That's very good, honey," Mommy said. "Your father would be proud of you."

I smiled. I really didn't realize I had eaten everything until she looked at my plate. I guess I was too into their conversation to notice. I was like Daddy with his tunnel vision.

"We can have an after-dinner drink on the side patio," Mommy told Nattie. "It's not much of a patio, but it's still warm enough. There are some throw blankets if we need them. I have a Domaine de Canton French ginger liqueur."

"Oh, my, you really went *explosion coupable*."

"Well, it's not every day we have so important a guest for dinner, someone who works for the U.S. State Department. Right, Caroline?"

"*Mais oui*," I said.

Mommy smiled and brushed her hand through my hair. "My brilliant little girl, starting eighth grade—and so well, too."

"I'm giving that up," Nattie said. It sounded like something that just burst out of her, a secret she had been keeping. Mommy froze, her fingers still in my hair.

"What do you mean? Giving what up?"

"I've decided to stay with my mother and change my life. Government life has . . . *Qu'est-ce-qu'ils disent?* Run its course? At least for me. Besides, there'll be a new American president soon who will appoint a new ambassador to France, and the ambassador is talking about running for the Senate. I really like him, but I'm not into that campaigning gig."

"Really. What are you going to do?"

"I was thinking of getting my real estate license and assuming my father's business."

"You mean, live here again? That's amazing," Mommy said, putting her hand on my shoulder. "I mean . . . a real estate agent . . ."

"Not so amazing as you might think. It's all really selling, politics, diplomacy, real estate. *La même chose*."

"Morgan said something similar about diplomatic work, but he meant something different," Mommy said, but immediately looked like she regretted saying it.

"I don't blame him. It is what it is," Nattie said. "I've never romanticized my work."

"Yes, well, Morgan doesn't romanticize anything, even *Casablanca*." Nattie laughed.

"Maybe he'll change as time goes by."

Mommy laughed and then just stared at her, and suddenly, realizing she was, she moved more quickly to clear the table. I started to help and so did Nattie.

"You did say you were in the business world once," Nattie said.

"Oh, you mean working at my father's bank? Hardly the business world. I was nervous as hell that everything I did was being reported. What if my totals were under by a penny, or even over? My father would find out. I would have loved doing something on my own."

"Why didn't you?"

"Cowardice," my mother said instantly. "My father served it daily to me. I wouldn't be able to do this; I wouldn't be able to do that. I didn't know how hard this or that was. He smothered my ambitions. And he even admitted it was his fault, but always a 'good' fault. Truthfully, he wasn't wrong. I was too protected to survive in the man-eats-man world."

"I think your father will be surprised to learn it's become a many-women-devouring-their-male-competitors world," Nattie said.

Mommy laughed.

"I often imagine him faced with a powerful woman in his business dealings. It must rattle his cage."

"*Bien sûr.*"

Mommy smiled but suddenly looked troubled, guilty.

"I think I've told you more about myself than I've told anyone, maybe even Morgan."

"I'm grateful for your trust," Nattie said. "It's a rare thing to enjoy these days."

"Likewise."

They stared at each other a moment and then hugged. It set them off talking about their childhood experiences again. After almost everything

Nattie described, Mommy kept saying, "I wish I had parents who would have done that."

Once more, I felt like I was watching a movie, trailing along like an almost totally forgotten puppy.

Mommy sent me to the hall closet to get my blue denim jacket. I put it on and followed them through our patio doors off the living room. The patio had a white-cushioned love seat and two matching reclining lounge chairs. Nattie took a chair, and Mommy and I sat on the love seat. The three of us decided to use the blankets.

At Nattie's urging again, Mommy gave me a sip of the liqueur. I liked it and probably drank it too fast.

"I remember that winter has a way of sneaking in here in upstate New York," Nattie said. "Often very much the same in Paris."

"Spring, too. All the seasons sneak in these days. Little different scenery for you right now, I imagine," Mommy said.

We were looking west out over the row of evergreen trees at the partly cloudy sky. I saw an airplane approaching.

"Daddy," I said, pointing. They looked.

"Yes, he's probably talking to the pilot right now," Mommy said. She didn't say it proudly; she said it as if she was jealous that he spoke more to the pilots than he did to her. Maybe Nattie didn't hear it in her voice.

"I don't know how they do it, the concentration," Nattie said.

"Oh, he can do it. Like I said, tunnel vision."

"I imagine that was the way he was when he saw you. He couldn't take his eyes off you."

"He never actually said that, but I like to think it."

"Some men are shy, but somehow I don't think Morgan is."

"No. You don't need to prod Morgan for his opinion when he is determined to give it. Whenever I push him to express it, I usually regret it. Sometimes it's better to leave things unsaid."

"Well, when you're in the State Department, you appreciate people who come right out and say what they believe. Some feel it's a weakness, however. It's not unlike showing your hand in a poker game."

"Yes. Morgan could be a good diplomat. The enemy would never leave the room confident they know our country's thoughts. Maybe that was one of the qualities that attracted me to him," Mommy said. "He can turn his inscrutability off and on like a faucet. He comes from a world in which men control their emotions: the military."

"Yes, inscrutability is important in business and war."

That sounded okay, but Mommy didn't go on to describe how magical it was with Daddy like she did when she told me the fairy tale.

They looked at each other, and there was a long silence that seemed strange to me. It was like they didn't know what else to say.

"They met in the bank," I said, expecting that would start the story, but my mother said nothing more about it except to add, "My father's bank."

"Sounds appropriate."

"Somehow, that word doesn't seem at home with romance," my mother replied.

"*C'est vrai*."

She didn't translate for me, but Nattie began to talk about the Paris night, the lights, describing the cafés and the people, dinner on the Seine River, and the music. I sipped my drink but put it down and leaned against Mommy, who tucked the blanket tighter around me. Nattie's voice and their laughter trailing off into the darkness slowly led me into a comfortable drift. I had no idea how long we were out there. I think it did grow much colder, and at one point I vaguely felt myself being nudged.

"Time for sleep, Caroline."

I *was* asleep, I thought. Maybe it was a result of the wine I had drunk. I rose, groggy. Mommy kept her hands on my shoulders, and we walked to the stairway. I heard Nattie right behind us.

Mommy took my pajamas out of a drawer and even started to help me undress. I pushed her away gently, embarrassed. After all, I was a junior high student by now.

"Brush your teeth, honey?" Mommy said, pulling back the blanket on my bed. They both watched me wash up. They were laughing at my efforts. When Mommy tucked me in, Nattie kissed me on the forehead and said, "*Bien dormir, ma chérie.*"

She kissed me again on the forehead. Mommy kissed my cheek, and they seemed to fade through the bedroom doorway, their voices softly disappearing as if they had boarded a boat and were floating away. Contented, I quickly fell asleep.

Later during the night, I woke abruptly because I heard Mommy and Daddy talking. He had just returned from work, and they were coming up the stairs, Mommy telling him how much she had enjoyed the dinner with Natalie Gleeson.

"She's really had wonderful experiences you'd enjoy hearing about, Morgan."

"Maybe," he said. "I'm tired of some of the travel experiences I hear about at the airport. Everyone thinks he's Columbus."

I could hear in her tone of voice how displeased Mommy was with Daddy's reaction, telling him it was far from the same sort of thing as someone bragging about some travel.

"And by the way, she's invited us all to have dinner with her," Mommy told him. "First night you're available."

"Great. I'll bone up on my French, the language of aristocrats," Daddy said. Their voices died quickly as I fell back asleep.

When I woke in the morning, even though it seemed like a dream, I remembered my mother telling my father that Nattie had invited us all to dinner. I expected to hear more about it at breakfast, but Mommy said nothing, and when Daddy came down, he didn't mention it, either.

"Looks like you two put away some wine," he said, gazing at the bottles in the garbage bin instead.

"You really missed a good one," Mommy replied. "A favorite of the ambassador's." She held up the empty bottle. "She brought it from Paris."

"I bet, but you know I've never been a wine drinker."

"I'm not giving up on you," Mommy said.

He grunted.

"So when is she returning to Paris?" he asked, getting a cup of coffee.

"She's not," Mommy told him, and explained.

He listened, but as if she had just said something casual about the weather or something she wanted done outside, he started to talk about his work and a close call. I knew Mommy hated it when he ignored what she had said and especially when he described those things involving potential airplane disasters, and I knew he knew she hated it.

Mommy told him it gave birth to nightmares.

"Don't be like my father and bring your work home," she had pleaded.

He had said that he wouldn't.

Why was he doing that now?

And with such glee?

3

I was troubled by the way Mommy and Daddy were behaving toward each other lately. I spent more time alone in my room, especially when I heard one or the other say something that was going to lead to an argument. The bubble that had always protected us from all that was dreadful out there was being punctured. All the magic seeped out with the sound of a long gushing breath like when you blew between your almost-closed lips.

"People often drift apart in small ways," Mommy warned me. "Sometimes through no fault of their own. They change in small ways that eventually make them feel more like strangers."

"Even husbands and wives?" I asked.

She touched my cheek lovingly and smiled.

"Yes. It just takes longer to realize it, but don't worry about that. We love you. Very much."

Would that be enough to keep you happy? I wanted to ask, but didn't.

A few times I was awoken by their harsher arguments, their voices louder than ever, but I was too tired to really listen. Or maybe I was afraid to. Now I was desperately trying to make sense of it all: the tone of their voices when they spoke to each other even when they weren't arguing, Daddy eating more often at the airport when his work ended just before dinner, and Nattie coming over to talk to my mother behind closed doors. I knew Daddy was so angry that he would even forget his good posture and stoop as he walked through the house. With his eyes and his avoidance, he was accusing Mommy of something serious, but I had no idea what it could be.

She continued to explain what she meant about people drifting apart, speaking to me with a weak and nervously fluttering smile, but like so often now, she looked like she was talking more to herself, convincing herself of something.

"People, married people, stop doing what to anyone else would look trivial, what they might think of as meaningless little things: a hug here, a touch there, even a smile becomes rarer, faster, and mechanical. A kiss on the lips can become a kiss on a cheek. You find yourself looking away more often. Your conversation turns into small talk, words just to shut out the silence leaking in."

She stopped and looked at me with a frightened expression on her face as if she had done something she hadn't wanted me to know she had done or said something she hadn't wanted me to hear. She looked sorrowful, like someone who couldn't stop herself.

She put her hands on my shoulders and knelt so she was looking straight into my eyes, something she always did when she wanted what she was saying definitely heard and understood.

"I don't want you to blame your father. Right now, he looks dark and gray and very angry to you. He is not at all upset with you, and you must never ever blame yourself for anything. That would break my heart."

But wasn't her heart already broken over how cold Daddy was acting toward her? I wondered. I probably never looked more confused. She paused and took a deep breath. Even though she was talking to me, she stood and raised her eyes toward the ceiling like someone falling into deep thoughts—thoughts that seemed to lift her out of her body. I could feel the struggle to find the right words, to keep herself and me from crying.

"Sometimes . . . sometimes the world we knew for so long . . . changes, but that doesn't mean it has to be worse."

She took my hand.

"We have resilience, you and I, the strength to overcome any sadness and look for good things, because there are a lot of good things waiting for us no matter what."

She smiled, but I didn't feel strong and hopeful. I felt more like I was falling and Daddy wasn't there to catch me. I had slipped off his radar screen. He used to say that was like someone dropped into the ocean who did not know where he was, what direction he should swim. He had to fight back the urge to panic or he would drown.

"I know this all seems hard to understand right now, Caroline, but you will. That's the only good thing I can say about it."

What was harder to understand was that while all that was happening and the world between Mommy and Daddy was crumbling, the opposite was happening between Mommy and Nattie. I wasn't aware of it at once, but I began to feel it more often as Mommy and Nattie grew closer. Eventually, I would think that if Mr. Gleeson hadn't died and Nattie hadn't come back for his funeral, none of this would have happened. Little did I know that I would have plenty of time, too much time, to review each and every moment and continually come to that conclusion, and then realize that maybe because of what had happened, this had happened to me: nothing less than imprisonment at Sutherland.

I think back.

Daddy had agreed to go to dinner two days after Nattie had come to dinner here, but he didn't sound very happy about it. It was like he had to get a vaccination or do something you had to do in a hospital. Nattie was taking us to one of the fancier restaurants, Le Grand Restaurant, one we had never been to, which was what mostly made him want to go. It was famous for its lobster dinners.

Leaving the people behind us waiting, the maître d' herself escorted us to a table that gave us a view of the whole circular room. It seemed to me that everyone was looking at us. I felt important, like the star of a television show, even though Daddy chanted, "Posture, posture."

Nattie sat across from Daddy at our small square table, Mommy on his right and I on his left.

I knew it was very expensive, not only because of how beautiful it was and how dressed up everyone was, but also because of what Daddy said when he looked at the menu, shaking his head: "You'd have to either be the ambassador or work for him to eat here. I don't know if I'm reading altitudes or prices."

"Oh, please," Nattie said. "Don't worry about the cost, Morgan. I appreciate how nice you both have been to my parents. It really is my pleasure."

Daddy lowered his menu and narrowed his eyes with the look that made me think he could see right inside you.

"When was the last time you visited them?" Daddy asked. "I don't recall you being here since we bought the house."

"Well, there were some overnight trips from Washington, D.C., but as to spending quality time . . . I'm ashamed to say."

"Then don't," he said, shrugged, and looked at the menu.

Mommy reached under the table and took hold of Nattie's hand. Daddy didn't see it, but I did. She held it for a few moments before the waiter came, and Nattie, Mommy, and Daddy ordered drinks and Mommy ordered my Shirley Temple.

"This is an elegant place," Mommy said, looking around. "I love the way they utilized those mirrors with the lighting and those drapes . . ."

"Big overhead, big prices," Daddy said. "Approximately sixty percent of restaurants fail within the first year of operation, and eighty percent fail within the first five years."

"How do you know that, Morgan?" Mommy asked. Her slight smile with her eyes practically closed told me she was annoyed with what he was saying. She was making it sound happy and fun, but as she often accused him of doing, he immediately added what she called a "shovelful of rocks." That was really my grandfather's expression for voicing a little annoyance, but I never heard her give him credit for it.

"I spoke to your father once about investing in a restaurant."

"I could easily have guessed. My father loves to be asked his advice . . . about anything," Mommy told Nattie. "And nine times out of ten, he'll be either cynical or negative. Whenever he hears something new to do, he starts with the 'why nots.'"

"It hasn't hurt his bottom line," Daddy said.

"No, just someone else's," she fired back.

My father's eyes glinted and then he looked at the menu. It was one of those silences that my mother said "could swallow you."

"This place has been here a long time," Nattie said quickly, "despite the overhead and those statistics. I'll admit I was surprised that it was still here. There's a smaller version of it in Paris, but of course the food is different."

"Probably not as expensive," Daddy muttered, still looking at the menu.

"Oh, no, not true. With the euro and the dollar now . . . and Paris can be quite pricey. Most cities are, here and in Europe. You get so much more for the dollar in the countryside everywhere."

Daddy looked at her, his cheeks taking on a crimson tint. I knew he hated being wrong.

"Right," he said, and quickly looked at his menu again to stop her from saying any more.

"Is that a 75?" I asked when the drinks were delivered.

Mommy and Nattie laughed, but Daddy smirked with disapproval.

"What does she know about that?"

"Oh, I made them for Nattie before dinner the other night and Nattie explained it to her."

"Very popular in Paris," Nattie said.

"Yeah, well, my parents drank plain gin and tonics. I never knew anything else. I don't think we had anything else in the house except beer."

"But you've been to Paris," Mommy reminded him.

"Yeah, but my father's ways, likes and dislikes, were baked in, no matter where we were. We didn't pick up local customs as easily as some do. My father's blood is red, white, and blue."

"Your father was military, wasn't he?" Nattie asked.

"Still is, retired," Daddy said. "If you've had a career in the military, you're always military, even in assisted living."

"Yes," Nattie said. "Of course. Sorry to suggest . . ."

"Yeah, well, it is what it is. Old soldiers never die. They just fade away."

"MacArthur's farewell speech," Nattie said, smiling. Daddy looked surprised. "We have to know history to be in the diplomatic corps."

"Right," Daddy said.

"I don't know what everyone's eating," Nattie said, "but this 2014 Fleurie Cuvée du Chaos is very good with either fish or meat." She pointed to it on the menu.

"I don't drink much wine," Daddy said. "You two go ahead and choose. I'll just have a beer."

"That wine sounds wonderful," Mommy said.

Nattie ordered it to be served with our dinners and asked Daddy which beer he preferred. He told the waiter. I had the feeling he didn't want her ordering for him. He always told the waiter or waitress what we wanted, even what Mommy wanted before she said it.

After we had ordered our dinners, Nattie asked Daddy more questions about his growing up, but it seemed like Mommy was answering most of them for him. I was surprised he didn't ask Nattie more questions about herself. Two servers brought our dinners and made such a show of it, I was sure everyone was convinced we were very special people.

While we ate, Mommy and Nattie were talking to each other as if Daddy wasn't even there. Suddenly, he put down his silverware and sat back so sharply and dramatically that everyone stopped eating.

"So you really are resigning your position and pursuing a real estate agent's license here?" he asked in the tone of Captain Bryer.

Nattie held her smile. "Yes. Basically taking over my father's business. I've already spoken to some of his old associates. I must say, they were all quite happy about it and very helpful."

"Isn't this quite a comedown from what you're doing now? Paris to Colonie, New York? I don't even think we have a museum."

Nattie smiled again. "Depends how you look at it. I suppose right now it looks more like a come *up* to me. My job is sensitive to the political winds. I'm sure I can get another posting in the State Department, but I think I had better spend more time with my mother first and kind of feel the ground beneath me. I grew up here. I like being around real people for a change, too. You lose sight of all that sometimes. It's like a breath of fresh air," she said, and smiled at Mommy.

"Besides," she added, "I recall something called the Shaker Museum nearby, right?"

Daddy stared at her a moment. He glanced at me and then he nodded and sat forward.

"Being around 'real' people? Who are they?"

"I just mean people who have nothing to hide, no agenda lost in complicated ideas. I've been navigating that river for quite a while now. 'False faces must hide what false hearts doth know' sort of thing."

"Yeah, well, I guess no one really knows what someone else's life is like."

"*Oui.* To think otherwise, *c'est fou.*"

"What's that?" I piped up.

"Crazy," Daddy said, and went back to eating, only now as if he was in a rush to go home.

No one wanted any coffee after dinner, but Nattie wanted me to try a dessert, a dark chocolate soufflé. While I ate it, she asked Daddy more about his work, why he had chosen it. I never had heard him say, so I paused to listen.

"It chose me," he said. "I was going to be a pilot but decided I was more of a homebody than I thought. Maybe because of how much we moved around when I was younger."

"That makes sense."

"Yeah, well, I guess we're all amateur psychiatrists."

Nattie laughed. "Guilty. But the profession you chose . . . you have such responsibility in your work. Such stress requires dedication. I admire that."

Daddy seemed a little embarrassed by the compliment, his cheeks reddening again.

"Every day I hope I do well. Correction, I *expect* to do well. I wouldn't go otherwise. If you don't have a passion for what you do, you're just treading water."

Nattie nodded. "Well, you're lucky to have found your purpose. Some of us . . . wander a bit."

"Wander? Yeah, I guess you could call it that. It's become a country of wanderers. Who knows what we'll be in ten years? It's like watching Rome crumble."

"You're talking to my father too much," Mommy said. "He could turn Santa Claus into a pessimist."

Pessimist? I wondered if I really understood the word. "What's a pessimist?" I asked. I knew, but I just didn't see how it could fit Santa Claus.

"Nowadays, someone who sees the truth," Daddy said.

Mommy looked down.

"Well, let's hope we can change it while there is still time," Nattie said, smiling at Daddy. He didn't respond.

It seemed like no one had anything else to say. Daddy was uncomfortable when the bill came. Mommy and I could see it in his face as Nattie took out her credit card.

"Really, we should share," Mommy said, eyeing Daddy.

"Oh, no, no. This makes me so happy. My mother is very pleased about it, too. Thank you."

"Well, it was a very special evening. Thank you," Mommy told her. She turned to Daddy, expecting him to add something, but he looked like what he accused me of looking like sometimes: someone with ants in their pants.

When the waiter returned, Daddy glanced away while she signed the credit card slip. I could see he felt uncomfortable about her paying for us. When I asked Mommy about it the next day, she told me, "Your father doesn't like a woman being in control. Now you know why he gets along so well with my father. Captain Bryer and the general," she muttered.

We had all come to the restaurant in Daddy's car. Nattie and I sat in the back seat and practiced French, Nattie giving me the words for things in the restaurant and me practicing pronouncing them. After we dropped her off at her house, a deep silence fell. Neither my father nor my mother said a word to each other or even to me. After we pulled into the garage and entered the house, Daddy said, "I'm tired. Need help with anything?"

"No, Morgan. It's all fine. I hope you enjoyed the dinner."

"Food's pricey, but it was good," he admitted.

"I wasn't talking only about food," Mommy said.

"Yeah, well, it was okay," Daddy said. "I'm tired. We're breaking in two new controllers, one male and one female, and it's a lot on me."

"Oh. You mentioned that. How is she doing?"

"Better than the guy," he said.

"You sound angry about it."

"He's probably not going to last. Complains a lot. Not a job for a namby-pamby. I'm going up."

"Okay. I'll be right there. You're yawning, honey," Mommy told me. "We should just get to bed."

I didn't realize how tired I was until we started up after him. I think I was half asleep, but even so, I could see the tension in my mother's face, her lips stiff and her eyes dark, with their lids narrow.

The next day I felt that the chill between my parents continued. When he was leaving for work, Daddy kissed me goodbye and then kissed Mommy, but he kissed her on the cheek. Even before Mommy had explained what that meant, I had felt a little jolt of fear like the time I stupidly put my finger in a lamp socket.

As soon as Daddy had left, Mommy told me we were going shopping with Natalie.

"Got to show her around, don't we, sweetheart? She's been away too long. We'll help her shop for food and get things we need, too, okay? Help me make our list of what is missing or getting low. You remember where everything is in our favorite supermarket even better than I do. Nattie will depend on you. So will I."

She took out the notepad she kept in her purse and we began to make the list. She had almost forgotten Daddy's beer. I saw there was only one bottle left.

"Yes," she said almost in a whisper. "He's been drinking more of it than I realized." She wrote it down.

Shopping was more fun than ever. Nattie said she had forgotten what an experience an American supermarket could be. I helped her find everything she needed. She said in France people were expected to pack their own groceries in their supermarkets. She couldn't keep herself from assisting, and soon I was, too. Afterward, I helped her carry her things into her house while Mommy went home to take ours in. When I got out, she said, "Be sure you say hello to Mrs. Gleeson, Caroline. I'll come back for you."

"Not necessary. I'll bring her home," Nattie told her.

I carried one of the smaller bags for her, embracing it as if it contained the most valuable things in the world. When I put it on the kitchen table, she said, "My mom, *ma mère*, is in the living room."

"I always help Mommy unpack and put everything away."

"It's all right. I'll be right there—*dans une seconde, d'accord?* I'll just put away the stuff that has to be kept cold or frozen."

Timidly, I walked to the living room door. Mrs. Gleeson looked so lonely and so much smaller to me. With a light pink blanket around her shoulders, she was sitting on the dark gray settee, across from the big-cushioned black chair I knew her husband had favored. It was as if she still saw him lying back, reading a book. I stopped and stood quietly until she turned and realized I was there. It had taken her longer than I had expected. I almost ran back to the kitchen to get Nattie because when Mrs. Gleeson finally looked at me, she looked like she didn't know who I was. She gasped the way she would if I was a stranger, and then, as if she had turned little windshield wipers on in her eyes, she smiled.

"Oh, sweetheart," she said. "You are such a surprise. How nice of you to visit me."

I flushed a little with guilt, knowing that my real reason was to help Nattie with her groceries so I could continue being with her. Before I could speak, I felt Nattie's hand on my shoulder.

"She's helped me with our groceries, Mère. She knew the supermarket like the back of her hand."

"That's nice of you, Caroline. Come tell us what's new, what you've been doing," Mrs. Gleeson said, patting the space beside her. "How's school?"

I glanced at Nattie, who nodded slightly, and then I hurried to the sofa.

"Nattie said she's going to help me learn French. She's been teaching me words and sentences like '*Ça va?*' which means 'How are you?'" I said as soon as I sat.

"Oh, is she?" She looked at Nattie. "She calls you Nattie?"

"Yes," Nattie said. "They squeezed that out of me."

Her mother laughed. *We certainly didn't squeeze it out of her*, I thought.

"So what else have you been doing, Caroline?" she asked. I thought her mouth looked a little crooked and her skin looked like old chalk with that yellowish tint, the wrinkles in her face deeper and her eyes glassy like they floated in tears.

I told her about our dinner at the restaurant and described my wonderful dessert. She seemed to regain energy and insisted on making me one of her famous homemade lemonade drinks. Nattie explained the different spelling in French and how to pronounce it.

"She's brilliant," Mrs. Gleeson said when I repeated it perfectly.

"I'll do it," Nattie said. "Don't get up, Ma."

Mrs. Gleeson started to insist she would make it but stopped as if her legs said no to standing. She sat back, her eyes closing. She looked like she had fallen asleep in a second. I was afraid to speak or move. When Nattie returned with my lemonade, she nudged her mother and helped her up.

"You should rest," she told her, helping her stand and start walking out. Mrs. Gleeson never even turned back to say goodbye. It was as if she had forgotten I was there. I sat, sipped the lemonade, and waited. It was so quiet that I could hear the miniature grandfather clock tick.

"I put her to bed," Nattie said. "She doesn't realize how tired she is. I'd better get you home."

Nattie decided we should walk to my house. I saw some neighbors pausing to look at us. I waved to Myra Grayson, who was in my class. She had come to my house with her mother but was friendlier with other girls. She barely waved back; however, she did look curious. I pretended not to care and refused to look at her again.

Nattie held my hand and told me how grateful she was that I had spent time with her mother, despite how short it was. "Tomorrow she might not remember that you were there, but when people get older, we do things that are important to them for the moment and not have them worry so much for their future. Do you understand?"

"Because they forget what's happening tomorrow and only think about what's happening today?"

"That's right." She smiled as if she was as proud of me as my mother could be. "You're quite the young lady already, Caroline. Your mother is doing a wonderful job."

I wondered why she left out Daddy, but I didn't say anything. Hearing her compliment me was too important to criticize in any way. Nattie raved about me to my mother, too, almost as soon as we entered the house.

"I am proud of you. So grown-up already," my mother said, hugged me, and started to prepare lunch. "Ham and cheese on that French baguette?" she asked Nattie.

"It's so tempting, but I should get back," Nattie said. "My mother will get herself up and put everything I put away back in the places she was used to for sure. She'll start cleaning the kitchen again, too."

"You should let her, Nattie. Keeping busy is the only antidote to grief."

"*C'est vrai*," Nattie said, smiled at me, and translated. "Which means 'That's true.' But her sorrow has aged her overnight, Linsey. She is so fragile. I think we avoid our parents when they're older so we can remember them as they were."

"I know that's why Morgan avoids visiting his own. He hasn't been there for a few years and made it practically an overnight trip so Caroline and I didn't go. My parents don't change," Mommy said regretfully. "Age softens fruit but makes the fruit trees brittle."

I couldn't tell if they were both terribly sad or terribly happy about what Mommy had said, but then, with her eyes suddenly tearing, she hugged Nattie. They held on to each other, both with their eyes closed. I felt funny just standing there and staring at them. *Should I be hugging her, too?* I wondered.

"I'll make your sandwich, Nattie," I volunteered, desperately wanting them to be happy, but mostly wanting to have them remember I was there. It was as if they could both step in and out of the world, but not take me along.

Mommy wiped the tears off her cheeks and smiled.

"Well, since you're preparing my baguette, I'll stay," Nattie said.

I concentrated on it as if it was to be a cherished work of art, which made them both laugh. It was as if a storm cloud had been pushed out the window. They had wine again. Every once in a while during her conversation with my mother, Nattie would pause, point something out, and give me the French word. She'd correct my pronunciation, but most of the time, she said, I had a pretty good ear for language.

"She's a good student," Mommy agreed, reaching to brush her fingers through my hair. "She has the patience to learn new things. Always on the honor roll."

"Your husband's concentration, perhaps."

"Yes, I'm sure. I barely scraped my way to my college diploma, thanks to my roommate, who did my homework as well as her own half the time."

That got Nattie talking in more detail about her experiences at the Sorbonne, and once again I felt more like a fly on the wall, spying on a private conversation. So quickly and so easily they could forget I was there. But it didn't bother me to be ignored as much as I thought it might. I enjoyed listening to them now that I had heard them so often. They seemed more and more like old friends. Each would finish the other's sentences, and sometimes, because they were so excited, they would start to talk at the same time, pause, and laugh and hug.

After we ate, Mommy made coffee. She had bought the espresso Nattie liked, and our lunch—really, their lunch—went on longer than any lunch I could remember. Suddenly, Mommy looked at the clock.

"Oh, I forgot to take out the frozen chicken Morgan expects to have tonight. I was going to make the stew he loves and let it simmer for hours. We plan our menu for the week. Actually, he does, and we stick to it unless his shift takes him too late."

"What happens then?"

"He eats at the airport or I wait up and warm up his food usually, but lately he decides more to eat at the airport because it's more . . ."

"Efficient?"

"Exactly," Mommy said. "He would say that. You know him already. It's another way he resembles my father, measuring time as if we all had meters running on our backs. I grew up feeling guilty for daydreaming. I'm surprised my father didn't give out parking tickets."

Again, for a reason I didn't understand, Nattie thought it was necessary to reach for Mommy's hand after she had said that. She held it a moment while they stared at each other, and then she glanced at me and let go as if Mommy's hand had become too hot.

"Oh, my mother must have thought I got lost or went off to the park with Caroline."

"That would be nice!" I quickly said. They both laughed.

"I think the ducks are still here," Mommy said. "Caroline enjoys feeding them. We could go tomorrow. Caroline's school is closed for a teachers' meeting."

"*Matin?* Say about ten?" Nattie asked.

"'*Matin*' is 'morning,'" I said.

"*Oui. Tu apprend vite.* What do you think that means?"

I looked at Mommy and thought. Daddy used the word *vite* sometimes. I already knew what *tu* meant.

"You listen fast?"

Her eyes widened with her smile.

"You *learn* fast, not listen. But it was a very good guess. *Très bien.*"

She rose. At the door, Nattie turned to Mommy and said, "I feel I'm to blame, taking up so much of your time. I could return to the supermarket and pick up a fresh chicken for you."

"Oh, I'll do that. You're not to blame. I enjoyed our lunch as much as you, if not more, and you want to get back to your mother."

Nattie kissed her on both cheeks, paused to smile at her, and then did the same to me.

"*À bientôt,*" she said, and left. Mommy closed the door slowly.

"She didn't tell me what that meant," I said.

"It means 'See you soon.'"

"Oh. *Très bien,*" I said, and she laughed and hugged me.

"C'mon, we're going to do just what she suggested and get that fresh chicken."

We hurried out and drove back to the supermarket, but it was different from the earlier time. Now the parking lot was nearly full. Mommy found an empty spot, parked, and took my hand as we started for the store. The sky had turned gray and overcast.

"Looks like it's going to rain soon. Maybe we'll miss it if we get in and out quickly. We just need the chicken," Mommy said, walking fast, but there were long lines at the meat counter and then the checkout places. Nevertheless, she picked out a chicken, and two people in one line were nice enough to let us go through before them.

"I have just enough time to make this," Mommy mumbled as we headed for the car. Light rain had started. It grew harder after we hurried to get in.

"If your father finds out about this, he'll give me the third degree."

"What does that really mean?" I asked. Now that Nattie was teaching me language, words and expressions had become more important to me.

"Battering someone with a million questions," she muttered. I knew that meant I was to keep a secret. It wouldn't be the first, although I was never comfortable doing it when it came to Daddy.

Mommy turned on the windshield wipers and began to back out. She screamed when she hit the front side of another car that had moved from the right and was unexpectedly behind us. The accident stopped us with a jolt. Mommy lowered her head to the steering wheel. "Oh, no."

"Are you all right, Mommy?"

"Yes, yes. I couldn't see it. He came out of nowhere." She put her hands over her eyes and took a breath.

"Mommy?"

"Just sit there," she said, and got out of the car.

The rain was steady now. The driver of the car she hit was an elderly man in a pair of dark blue shorts and a white T-shirt. He combed his fingers through his thin gray hair as he stared at his car's damage, not even caring how wet he was getting or how wet Mommy was getting. I didn't hear exactly what he said, but he was very upset, swinging his arms and pointing to his car. Mommy kept apologizing. She turned and hurried to my side, opened the door, and went into the glove compartment.

"Your hair is wet, Mommy, and so are your clothes."

"I'll survive, but this will take a while," she said. "There was some damage, so I have to give him insurance information and my driver's license. Let the insurance companies fight it out. Just stay put."

I turned and watched through the rear window as the elderly man sat in his car and copied information from the cards Mommy had given him. She stood in the rain waiting, her arms crossed over her breasts and her shoulders hunched up. Surely, she was getting cold, too. Why didn't he ask her to wait in the car? Some other shoppers with umbrellas watched as if it was the most exciting thing that they had seen all day. Finally, Mommy took her cards and returned to the car. She sat staring ahead in silence for a long moment, so long that it frightened me. Her clothes were soaked and her hair looked like it was leaking off her head.

"Mommy? You're drenched!"

"What? Oh." She looked in the rearview mirror. "Unbelievable. He's still out there. I don't know what good it is doing him to stare at the damage in the rain," she said. "That won't make it go away."

I looked back. Why didn't he care how wet he got? He was blocking us, but Mommy didn't want to scream at him. Finally, he got into his car and started away. Mommy backed up extra slowly. She didn't even pause to wipe the rainwater off the side of her face. It just ran off her chin. I was afraid to say anything, but to me it looked like the rain was mixing in with her tears.

"Don't say anything later to Daddy," she said. "I'll tell him."

Another secret.

"He'll be mad, huh?"

"It doesn't take much to make him mad these days," she said, then pressed her lips together tightly as if she wanted to be sure she didn't say anything else.

Both of us were surprised to see that Daddy's car was in the garage and he was already home. Mommy even said, "Oh, no. Of all days for him to come home early."

She wiped her face and got out of the car slowly, straightening her clothes even though they were clearly damp through and through. I carried our chicken and walked in behind her.

"Why are you home so early?" Mommy asked as soon as we entered from the garage. "Something wrong?"

"Nothing's wrong, Linsey. Those were my hours today. I was doing a favor substituting for someone whose wife was having her gallbladder removed. He came to work as soon as she was in recovery. I told you before we went to sleep last night, and I marked it on the wall calendar. Somehow, I knew you weren't listening. You have other things on your mind."

He pointed to his schedule on the kitchen bulletin board.

"Oh, right. Sorry."

"Where were you? Why are you soaked? What is Caroline carrying?" She took the chicken from me.

"I forgot to take the chicken out of the freezer, so I went to get a fresh one and the rain started after we got into the supermarket."

"I saw you went shopping earlier," he said, nodding at some things Mommy had not yet put in the cabinet.

"We did. Nattie came with us. I helped her shop, too," I said. "I found everything for her, even the French mustard she wanted, and we helped pack the groceries because people do that in France."

"Is that right?" he said without smiling. "Real people stuff, huh?"

I remembered Nattie saying "real people" at dinner, but I didn't see how that meant packing groceries.

Mommy went to the counter and took the chicken out of the bag.

"Kind of late for that now, isn't it?" Daddy asked.

Mommy stopped and stared at the chicken with her back to us. Seconds passed and she didn't speak or turn.

"What is it, Linsey? You have something more to tell me?"

"I had an accident in the parking lot," she said. She turned around. "I backed into someone."

"Oh. Now or the first time you went with the ambassador?"

"She's not the ambassador, Morgan. No, now. Rushing to get home to make your chicken."

"My chicken? Did the person you hit claim any physical injury?"

"No. It was a fender bender."

"What about your car?"

"Nothing, really. His had a bad dent. I got soaked giving him the information. He wasn't very courteous. If I'd had more time, I would have called the police. I'll put this in the freezer and make some pasta with the eggplant from yesterday."

"I visited with Mrs. Gleeson and she made me a *limonade*," I piped up, saying it the French way. I was hoping that would make Daddy happier and he would forget about the accident.

"*Limonade*, huh? Went there on your own?"

"When I helped Nattie take in her groceries."

"I see," Daddy said, but again he didn't smile the way I had hoped he would. "Everything for Nattie these days."

"I'll get out of these clothes and start on our salad," Mommy said, ignoring him. "You can help me," Mommy told me.

"What else did you do today that distracted you and caused you to forget our dinner?" Daddy asked her.

"Can we talk about it after I change? Caroline, wash your face and hands and change into the blouse and your jeans hanging on your closet door."

"I'll check your car," Daddy said, and went into the garage.

The rain grew harder, what Grandfather Sutherland called "raining nails." I followed Mommy up and hurried to my room. I knew when Daddy was extra mad, but I wasn't sure why he should be. He should feel sorry for Mommy, I thought, but the air felt like there were Fourth of July sparklers all around me. Mommy and I came out at the same time. She smiled and reached for my hand.

"Daddy's really mad," I said. "Just like you thought he'd be."

"He'll get over it. Men. They're quick to forget their little mistakes and love to point out ours. My father could be the pope."

"Why would he want to be the pope? He's not religious, right?"

"Let's do the salad," she said. I could see she was running out of patience, even for me.

As soon as we sat for dinner, Daddy clutched his hands with his elbows on the table and looked at Mommy.

"What?" she asked.

"Did you look at the backup camera before you started to back out in the parking lot?" Daddy asked.

"I was just stupid, Morgan. In a rush and in the rain. There's no excuse."

"Yeah, well, I don't depend entirely on the backup camera. Look at enough screens all day. So what else did you do today?" he asked, beginning to eat his salad. She told him about the long lunch with Nattie and more about Nattie's time in France, how she had gotten into the diplomatic corps and achieved the position with the ambassador, at times quoting her exact words and even using some French.

Daddy just looked at her as she talked. I was surprised at how she went on and on, barely letting him say a word.

"Sounds like you won't come back to earth until she actually starts working," he said, "if that really ever happens, getting a real estate license."

"I should think someone with her accomplishments could get a real estate license, Morgan. I told you how well she did in college, her awards."

She brought the pasta to the table and started to put some on my plate.

"Your father called me today," Daddy said.

Mommy froze.

"When?"

"I spoke to him after I left the airport, on my way home."

"And?" she said, continuing to serve the pasta.

"He has an investment he thinks we should make."

She sat but didn't pick up her fork. She looked down like she often did when she was trying not to be mad or was about to say something she knew wasn't going to please Daddy.

"I thought we said we'd never get involved in his business schemes, Morgan."

"Hey, you can't lose with a winning hand. He advised us to buy this house, didn't he? And helped out with the down payment. Very wise decision. Its value went up more than twenty percent after the first year. He has something else he's doing in real estate and—"

"Do what you want," she said sharply, and began to eat. "Start eating, Caroline."

"Used to be you wanted more for us, too," Daddy said. He moved his salad plate and began to eat the pasta and eggplant. "You'd think your sophisticated friend would inspire you."

"Okay, okay. Just be wary of my father. He likes people being indebted to him."

"I can handle your father," Daddy said.

"Yes, you knew real generals."

Everyone ate quietly for almost a minute. I kept looking from him to her and her to him.

"So your car . . ." Daddy began, like someone who had just remembered something.

"What about it?"

"Your bumper is dented and your taillight is seriously cracked. The bulb is dead. It will have to be brought into the dealership tomorrow. Sometimes they can't repair a dent on a bumper and have to replace the whole thing."

"It's that bad?"

"Bad enough, and it's a leased car. We'll pay for it now or later when you turn it in. You didn't just bump him. You were probably backing out too fast."

Mommy stopped eating and lowered her head to her open palms.

"I'm just saying, if you had your mind on your driving, especially in the rain . . ."

She raised her head.

"It's not easy living with a saint, Morgan. I should know. I was brought up by one, if you can call it any sort of bringing up. I thought you at least appreciated how difficult all that was for me. If you didn't, you did a good job of acting."

Daddy just nodded. I knew that his doing that was worse than him yelling.

We ate in silence, and then Daddy put his fork down as if he knew the exact spot it should be.

"I don't want any dessert or coffee. Finish your dinner, Caroline," he told me, and went into the living room.

Mommy just stared down at her pasta.

"Mommy?"

"It's all right," she said. "Daddy's right. Finish eating, Caroline."

I ate as much as I could. I didn't have any dessert, either. When I went into the living room, Daddy turned to me and asked, "So what did you do while they were having this long lunch, Caroline?"

"I just listened to them talk about things."

"Uh-huh. Like what?"

"When they were younger. In college," I said. "Boyfriends they didn't like."

"I can just imagine," he said. "The untouchables."

"What?"

Mommy was in the doorway.

"Don't use her like that, Morgan," she said sharply.

"Use her? She's thirteen, Linsey, soon fourteen. I hope she wasn't hearing inappropriate things. I know how liberal-minded the ambassador's girl is."

"She's not the ambassador's girl. She's not going to say things that are inappropriate in front of Caroline. She's a highly educated, sophisticated woman who has had wonderful experiences and has a lot to share. She's a little lost now and just needs a good friend. Calling her that in front of Caroline is what's inappropriate."

"Uh-huh."

"What is your problem, Morgan?"

"I have no problem," he said, and turned on the television. Mommy walked up to my room with me to help with some of my weekend homework, something she said she liked to do not so much because I needed it but because she did. She said it helped her remember some of her cherished school days. Her favorite thing was my literature assignments. She especially liked to read the poems aloud.

But I couldn't listen as well when she did this time. Her voice was too sharp and correct and she read faster than usual—read as though it was the only thing keeping her from bursting into tears.

Afterward, I heard nothing but Daddy's footsteps, doors closing, and the house creaking as the wind played it like a piano.

The silences, I thought, seemed to be getting deeper.

Even I knew they could get too deep.

We could all drown in them.

4

Daddy didn't have to go to work until late in the afternoon Monday. He forgot that I didn't have to go to school because of a teacher conference, and he at first thought Mommy was deliberately keeping me home for some reason, something perhaps to do with Nattie. After Mommy had explained the reason, he looked apologetic. I think he was also feeling bad about the things he had said to Mommy about the accident in the supermarket parking lot, because the first thing he told her at breakfast was that he would take her car to the garage.

"Thanks, Morgan."

"Yeah, those guys take advantage of women," he muttered, "who don't know how to haggle over the cost of repairs as well as they haggle over clothes and shoes."

She stared coldly at him for a moment before saying, "My father couldn't have said it any better."

Daddy laughed this time.

"You know, I think he did, and I remembered it."

"Parroted, you mean."

He lost his smile.

"A lot of people quote my father," she added, maybe to make what she had said sound less terrible. "I'm used to it."

"Yes," Daddy said. "And for good reason. Why, from time to time, I've even heard Caroline quote him." He smiled at me, but I looked at my mother. Would she be happy about that? She didn't smile.

"We should never have let him help us with the down payment on this house," she said. "He never misses an opportunity to remind me."

"We'll pay him back. He never mentions it to me, but you can get a job with that as its purpose if it bothers you so much."

"Right," she said. "I'd like that. Might take a drop of smugness out of his smile. And don't say it," she quickly added. "He's never smug with you."

Daddy shrugged.

"Families are complex," he admitted.

"Complex? You don't have to get a degree in psychotherapy to figure out my family: Daddy rules. His family are his servants," Mommy flared back. "You used to say the same about your own."

The crests of her cheeks seemed to redden and then fade. Daddy avoided looking at her and then just rose and left.

I didn't understand what Daddy meant about families, but I didn't want to ask Mommy any more about it. Whatever Daddy had meant annoyed her enough to have her snap at him. Her cheeks reddened again. She battered the pans, glasses, and dishes about as if she wanted to lash out at the kitchen.

Not long after Daddy left to bring Mommy's car to the garage, Nattie showed up to go with us to the park. I had been anxious about it because of how hard it had rained, but the rain had stopped late at night and there was a partly cloudy sky. It was cooler for a late September morning, so we bundled up more than usual, Mommy buttoning my frayed pink tweed coat to the top.

"She's a big girl, Linsey," Nattie said. "She can do that if she's cold."

"Once a mother, always a mother," Mommy told her.

"Now that you mention it, mine was doing stuff like that even after I started college."

We started out for the park. I carried the bag of food for the ducks cradled in my right arm. I could see some of our neighbors watching us as we headed down the street. They probably knew Nattie had worked for our ambassador to France. *Maybe they won't call us the Robot Family anymore*, I thought.

As we walked, Mommy told her about her accident in the supermarket parking lot.

"I'm so sorry. I feel responsible staying so long for lunch. If you would have remembered to take the chicken out of the freezer . . ."

"If Adam wouldn't have listened to Eve . . . C'mon, Nattie. There's no way you're to blame for this."

"Everything has a consequence. If Adam hadn't listened to Eve, there'd be no clothing industry."

They both laughed, hooking their arms together. Mommy reached for my left hand, but I felt like I was invisible. Neither said a word to me the rest of the way. They were too involved in their conversation and laughter. Sometimes they deliberately bumped shoulders after saying something they both thought was funny.

By the time we arrived, the sky had cleared even more and we could feel it was getting warmer. Mommy loosened my coat and told me to start feeding the ducks. I was so intent on it because of how quickly all the ducks came to me that I didn't notice she and Nattie had left my side. It was maybe a good ten minutes before I finally realized it. I glanced back at them.

While I continued to feed the ducks, Mommy and Nattie sat on the grass, watching me and talking. When I looked at them again, I saw that my mother had lowered her head and Nattie was holding her hand with her other hand over the top of it in a comforting gesture. Whatever my mother was saying was upsetting her, and she looked so sad. I thought she was about to cry if she wasn't already. I stopped feeding the ducks and started toward them. Nattie said something to my mother, warning her I was approaching. She sat up quickly, letting go of Nattie's hand and smiling.

"Hungry today, weren't they?" Mommy asked, quickly wiping away any evidence of tears on her cheeks.

I nodded. Her eyes still looked teary. What had disturbed her so much? She patted the space beside her, and I sat and leaned my head back on her lap to look up at the sky. My mother combed her fingers through my hair.

"She's going to look more and more like you. I can see it. It's like looking through a telescope into the future," Nattie remarked.

"She has Morgan's eyes and often the same intense look I see in them, especially if she is upset with me."

"His concentration, certainly," Nattie said.

"Yes. I guess that's good. It's only when we're distracted that we're vulnerable."

"We know she's a quick learner."

"Lately, she's been just as precise as Morgan can be about where she places her things, too. I think she's looking for his approval."

"Don't most daughters look for their fathers' approval?"

"I suppose. As a result, I have the neatest daughter in daughterdom."

"I bet. Some obsessions aren't so bad."

Mommy laughed.

"Morgan would agree. Half the time she makes me aware of my own sloppiness. But I like that better than Morgan reminding me. I keep expecting to find the demerits posted on our kitchen bulletin board."

"'And a little child shall lead them.'"

"Where exactly is that from?"

"Isaiah. Old Testament."

"You are one impressive woman, Natalie Gleeson."

"My father liked to read the Bible to me."

"I don't think my father has one. He has Adam Smith's *The Wealth of Nations* instead. He quotes from it like a priest quotes from Scripture."

They both laughed. And then did that thing they were doing more and more: pausing and staring into each other's eyes.

"I should tell Caroline more from the Bible," Mommy said. "Read her some of the important stories and verses. It helps with studying literature, too. Both Morgan and I have neglected that. For different reasons."

"I think I have a book of Bible stories for young people. My parents gave it to me when I was about ten. I'm sure Caroline will like it. I'll dig through my things at the back of my closet. My mother never threw out anything of mine."

"Oh, she'll like it. Especially if it's coming from you."

Mommy paused. I could practically feel her thinking, feel a strange sadness.

"I could be a better mother."

"Oh, stop. You're doing a wonderful job with her. Your father surely sees that, if he's as critical of things as you say."

"I'm sure I get ten percent and Morgan gets ninety."

It was odd hearing them talk about me as if I wasn't there, but I was also fascinated. I hated to admit it, but I was sure it was Grandfather Sutherland who told me, "You can't see yourself as well as others see you. Impression. Think about making an impression. The first one usually sticks."

"Sometimes, when I look at myself and see my father in me, it makes me cringe and retreat, and then other times it fills me with confidence," Mommy said.

"'Do I contradict myself? Very well then, I contradict myself. I am large, I contain multitudes.'"

"I know that. Don't tell me. Whitman. Walt Whitman."

"*Très bien.*"

"When I remembered quotes or facts like that, my father would tell me unless I went on *Jeopardy!* it was worthless."

"Then self-satisfaction is worthless," Nattie said. "Your father, from what you tell me and from what I've learned about his success, should know that."

"He has his own peculiar sense of it."

I was fascinated, holding my breath so I wouldn't miss another word while they were talking about Grandfather. Despite how many times I had seen him and Grandmother Judith and despite the things Mommy had told me about him and her life at Sutherland, he remained as mysterious as the small statue of Buddha Mommy had in the backyard. She told Daddy she had bought it because there was a place to put a flower in front of it. But sometimes, especially lately, she would stare at it for minutes and not even hear me when I spoke to her.

"I'm almost tempted to have you meet him. I think you might be more than he could handle. Although he would never admit it. He believes humility is for the weak."

Nattie laughed. I had my eyes closed, but I could sense how close together they were sitting. When I looked, Nattie's leg was touching my mother's.

They're always touching, hugging, kissing, I thought. Was I jealous? For a moment I wondered which one I wanted to hug me more. Nattie's hug felt like she was congratulating me for something; Mommy's was more like she was saving me from something, protecting me. Maybe that was what all mothers' hugs were: protection first, love second.

They stopped talking for a few moments. I opened my eyes and glanced at them. They weren't looking at me or anything else. It was a different kind of silence, a silence in which eyes talked and a gentle touch of a hand, of an arm or even a cheek, spoke louder. Out of the corner of my eye, I could see that they were holding hands, just between them and behind me as if they didn't want anyone else to see.

Then Nattie sighed.

"What?" Mommy asked.

"It's beautiful just enjoying the weather and the free time, but I've got to start preparing for that real estate license," Nattie said. She laughed. "Morgan doesn't think I'll do it, does he?"

"No, but he doesn't think I'll do most of what I say I will, either. It's in his nature to begin with skepticism. You could tell that from dinner at the restaurant. 'Start with doubt and you'll be more successful.' That's his motto. Maybe it's necessary for an air traffic controller to believe that. I wish he was able to leave his distrust at the airport and not bring it home."

"Was he like that from the start?"

"Not as much. Or maybe I didn't notice it as much. I don't remember where I read it, but some author in some novel wrote that love begins with forgiveness. I suppose I was too forgiving."

"Don't worry. I'll make him a believer. In fact, his skepticism makes me more determined. The only way to upend a skeptic is to prove him wrong. My boss says the hardest words to swallow are your own."

Mommy laughed.

"Morgan? Swallow his words? I'll help you get your real estate license, then."

"And maybe incidentally you'll be able to get one yourself."

"You think so? Morgan did suggest that I think of getting some part-time work while Caroline goes to school."

"There you go," Nattie said. "It would be perfect for real estate. We could work together."

"My doing what you're planning on doing wouldn't surprise him," she said, making it sound like something hurtful.

"Oh? Well then, you should seriously consider it. So he can say he was right about you, at least."

Mommy laughed harder.

"You do know him. Maybe I will."

The distant sound of music on someone's radio got them talking about their favorite songs. They started singing some, each finishing the other's lyrics. One song reminded Nattie or my mother of another, and they were singing again. I think they lost track of time. I know I dozed off, mesmerized by the sounds of them singing and the murmurs of other people talking as they walked by. Suddenly, my mother shook me awake.

"We have to go, Caroline. Daddy should be back from the garage and leaves for work in less than an hour."

I stood up. My mother gently pinched my cheeks to get me more alert. She took my hand, and we all started back to our street. Before Mommy and Nattie parted in front of our house, they made plans for dinner, having pizzas delivered to our house. They held hands for a moment, and then Nattie let go, but slowly, as if she really never wanted to. For a moment we watched her walk off, and then we entered the house.

When we entered, it was obvious that Daddy had been standing by the living room window, looking out at us.

"The long goodbye. Looked very dramatic. Does that mean she decided to return to Paris?"

"No, Morgan. She's determined to stay and do what she said."

"We'll see. Like your father says, the only thing cheaper than talk is more talk. So, where were you?" he asked. "I called to get you to pick me up in my car. I hate waiting for them to transport me, usually having to drop one or two others home as well. Didn't you have your mobile phone?"

"Oh, no, I'm sorry. I didn't think of that. We took Caroline to the park to feed the ducks. She remembered it."

"Who? Caroline or Mademoiselle Gleeson?"

"Nattie," Mommy said. "We've been there many times, Morgan, even with you. Remember the ducks? Caroline wouldn't have forgotten."

He nodded. I could see Daddy was avoiding an argument.

"They won't have your car ready until late tomorrow. Maybe your new friend will run you over there. I have the same schedule tomorrow." He looked at his watch. "I've got to get back to the airport for the late shift."

"Do you want some lunch?"

"Not that hungry right now. I'll pick up something for later. I have worked out an extended weekend, Friday off, to make a good three days. If you can tear yourself away from French lessons, we'll go up to Lake George."

"We'll be taking Caroline out of school."

"For a day. She can handle it, Linsey. What do you say, Caroline?"

I shrugged.

"I'll just get my homework ahead of time, right, Mommy?"

Daddy liked that, but I thought Mommy wasn't going to answer. Her face was tight, her lips pressed hard enough against each other to make the lower lip practically disappear. She looked like she had swallowed whatever she was really going to say. Then her whole body relaxed, her shoulders lowered and her face softened. She nodded.

"That sounds nice, Morgan. I think we both need a change of scenery. I'll talk to Caroline's principal."

"Well . . . good," he said, looking happily surprised. "I'm glad you realize it."

He started away, then stopped and approached to kiss her, not on the cheek this time. I was happy even though it was a quick touch of her lips with his, like the snapping of fingers. He patted my head.

"The ducks know when to duck, Caroline. Take a lesson. It's more important than French," he said, poking me softly on the forehead. "See you later." He went toward the garage. Maybe things were going to get nicer, back to the way they always had been, I thought.

"I'll fix us some lunch," Mommy said.

About five o'clock, Nattie called to say her mother wasn't feeling well.

"Well, if you still want the pizza, we can come to you. I know you have what we need for a salad," Mommy said.

When she hung up, Mommy looked thoughtful, even worried.

"What's wrong, Mommy?"

"What? Oh. We're going over to the Gleesons' for dinner," she said. "You can wear a pair of jeans and that blue shirt and sweater with sneakers. Mrs. Gleeson is under the weather, so Nattie wants to stay close to her tonight."

"What's wrong with her?"

"Could be a lot of things, especially when you're an elderly lady."

"Maybe she misses Mr. Gleeson too much and doesn't want to wait," I said.

Mommy stared at me with a soft smile as if she wasn't sure I was being serious.

"Well, don't say that too loudly," she said, still smiling. "But I'm sure you're right. It's not easy to be alone after so many years. It's a good thing Nattie decided to stay and not return to Paris."

Just before we left to go to Nattie's house, Daddy called to say he had booked the Lodge for our trip to Lake George. It was a hotel we had been to. He said like last time, he had rented a boat and had made dinner reservations at the restaurant he liked. I listened to them talk. Mommy didn't sound as excited about our trip as she had in the past, and she didn't tell Daddy where we were going for dinner. She did say Nattie had agreed to take her to the dealership tomorrow to retrieve her car. Whatever he said at the end made her smirk and nod as if he was standing right in front of her.

"Let's go," she said abruptly, the way someone who wanted to get away might.

She took my hand as soon as we stepped out the door and began walking faster. I practically had to skip to keep up. I knew she was upset, but I wasn't sure why.

She slowed, paused, and took a breath.

"I hope when you get married that your husband at least consults with you before he makes a decision that will affect you. I was not crazy about that restaurant and he knew it, but he probably forgot or maybe only cared about what he likes."

We started walking again.

When I get married? I thought. Not in my wildest dreams had I yet imagined it. Sometimes I thought, maybe even believed, that nothing would ever change—that I would always be this age and my mother and father would stay as they were forever and ever. Of course I knew that wasn't true, but what Mommy was saying seemed as far away as a star. Once in a while my future might blink at me, but it felt more comfortable and even safer not to think about it. I did remember Nattie saying growing up could be painful.

I found myself more alone than I had anticipated at the Gleesons' house. We ate pizza and a salad Nattie had made before we arrived. Mrs. Gleeson was only served some chicken soup and remained in her room. Nattie and Mommy decided I should not go in to talk to her until after she ate so that I didn't disturb her eating. After dinner, we had started to watch television when suddenly they were talking about clothes they wore as teenagers. Nattie gave me a dish of ice cream, and they went to her room to look at what she still had "deep in my closets."

Once in a while, I thought I heard them laughing, but most of the time they were quiet. I peeked in at Mrs. Gleeson and saw she was fast asleep. I tiptoed in to get her soup bowl. She had hardly eaten any of it. I thought she might hear me and I could talk to her, but she had her face turned away. When I looked back at her, I thought her eyes were closed as tightly as those of someone in pain. Maybe she was having a terrible dream, I thought.

I brought the bowl to the kitchen and returned to the living room. Mommy and Nattie were still not there. I was about to go find them when Mommy appeared. Her cheeks looked flushed, and her hair was down.

"Time to go home," she said.

Nattie appeared, smiling.

"We didn't forget about you," she said. "Your mother and I can be like teenagers. I don't think I've giggled as much since then."

"I know I haven't," Mommy said.

"Mrs. Gleeson is still sleeping," I said. "She looks like she's having a bad dream. I was about to go get you." I didn't realize I was angry, but maybe I sounded like it.

"Maybe she is," Nattie said, more in her mother's direction than to me.

"I brought the soup bowl to the kitchen. She didn't eat very much."

"That was nice of you," Nattie said. She looked at my mother. "She hasn't eaten a thing all day. I might need to take her to see her doctor."

"Oh, then don't worry about taking me to the garage tomorrow. I'll get an Uber."

"I'll let you know. Thank you for looking in on my mother, Caroline. That was very thoughtful. I'll see you tomorrow, okay?"

I nodded and rose. Nattie kissed me goodbye, and we left. Mommy didn't say much as we walked, but she kept her smile all the way home. I thought she was remembering happy thoughts and wished she'd tell me about them. When we arrived, she followed me up to go to bed herself. I woke a little while after I had fallen asleep. I could hear Mommy talking and got up to see if Daddy had come home, but she was only on the phone.

And talking to Nattie.

The first thing that occurred to me was that she was worried about Mrs. Gleeson, but then I heard her laugh. Her voice lowered, and she came out of her and Daddy's bedroom, perhaps seeing me in the hallway.

"Why are you up?"

"I thought Daddy was home," I said.

"Well, he's not. C'mon. Get back to bed. You'll see him tomorrow."

She tucked me in again and returned to her bedroom. I listened hard.

She was still talking to Nattie. They had just seen each other. What had they forgotten to tell each other? Maybe they really were acting more like teenagers. I fell asleep to the low murmur of her voice and her soft laughter. I slept a little later than usual and quickly rose to wash and dress. The house was so quiet. I wondered if everyone was asleep, but I found Mommy sitting in the kitchen, sipping her coffee and so deep in thought that she didn't hear me enter.

"Oh," she said as soon as she realized I was standing there. "Sit, and I'll get you your juice. Want scrambled eggs?"

I nodded. There was something about the way she moved and smiled to herself that told me she was happier than usual this morning. When she brought me my eggs, she sat and talked about how happy she was at the way I had begun junior high.

"There are still some new things you need. I don't know where my mind has been. You need new shoes and new sneakers. I think we should look for a bigger book bag, too. We've got to update stuff."

She seemed more excited about all I would get than I was. She saw the surprised look on my face as she listed one thing after another and laughed.

"Don't look so surprised. Every mother relives her youth through her children, Caroline. You will, too."

Here she goes again, I thought, describing me in ways I either couldn't or wouldn't imagine. Me? A mother?

"Where's Daddy?" I asked.

"He came home very late," she said. "I didn't want to wake him."

Nevertheless, Daddy came down for breakfast before I was finished. Mommy prepared him some scrambled eggs, too, and listened as he described his work and ranted a bit about the new male controller's "stupid mistakes." I was waiting to hear Mommy tell him about Mrs. Gleeson and us having pizza with Natalie, but instead she surprised him by telling him she was going to study for the real estate license with Nattie.

He sat back and stared at her a few moments.

"You're serious about that? Real estate?"

"Why not? It's sort of in the family blood, isn't it? Maybe Daddy dearest will be proud of me for a change. A few good sales, and I could chip away at the loan my father gave us. Just like you suggested."

He nodded, but he didn't look happy she had taken his suggestion.

"Did you make a note to call the garage?"

"No, but I won't forget, Morgan."

"Probably those are the most famous last words anyone has ever said," he said.

"About tonight . . ." Mommy began.

"I'm not home for dinner. Remember? I'm working extra time to get the three-day weekend."

Mommy just nodded. After he finished, he went upstairs to shave and dress. I helped Mommy clean up. She seemed so lost in thought. Then, as if she had forgotten I was getting ready to go to school, Mommy called Nattie. They didn't speak long. All I heard her say was, "Oh, no, Nattie."

Daddy hadn't yet come down.

"What is it, Mommy?"

"Nattie had to take her mother to the hospital."

"What happened?"

"The doctor in the ER said she suffered a stroke and they're not sure of the damage. They need to keep her under observation."

I simply stared at her. Because of the look on her face, I wasn't sure I wanted to ask any more questions.

I hated the possibility that I had been right.

Nattie's mother didn't want to wait to see Mr. Gleeson in heaven.

5

Mrs. Gleeson passed away in her sleep on her third day in the hospital. Mommy had been taking Nattie to the hospital once she had her car back from the shop. I wanted to go one time, too, after school, but Mommy said I'd just be sitting there in the waiting room. I said I would do homework, but she said it wasn't a good place for it. She always returned in time to make dinner. Daddy was home only once for dinner during the three days. Oddly, he did most of the talking, describing what happened at work, avoiding any suggestions of near tragedies, and then went into his detailed plans for our weekend trip.

When I returned home from school on that third day, I knew almost before I saw Mommy sitting in the living room. I could sense it in the silence, but mostly because Mommy hadn't turned on a light on this overcast afternoon.

"She died in her sleep, at least," she said when she looked up at me. She didn't even preface it with *Mrs. Gleeson has passed away*.

I started to cry and sat beside her, both of us hugging and rocking a little.

We were both still sitting there when Daddy returned from work.

"I expected it," he said. "It's not so unusual for a spouse in a long-term marriage to die shortly after the other does. I'm anticipating that for my parents. It's called the widowhood effect."

Daddy had entered so softly that I didn't hear him come in. I don't think Mommy heard him, either. She still had her eyes closed until he said what he said about widowhood.

She cleared her throat and began in a voice so cold that it was almost unrecognizable to me.

"Don't start giving me your statistics, Morgan Bryer. Citing charts and reports won't make what happened to Nattie's mother any less horrible."

"Whatever," Daddy said. "I'm just telling you what I know."

"What you know," Mommy muttered. She let go of my hand and embraced herself.

Daddy stared at us for a few moments. Mommy lowered her head as if she wanted to avoid looking at him. I couldn't help but hold my breath because neither of them was talking, and I knew by now that deep silences between them usually occurred right before something nasty.

"Well," Daddy finally said in a calmer voice than I had anticipated, "maybe she'll return to Paris now and forget about this real estate nonsense."

Mommy looked up sharply.

"What?"

"She said she wanted to spend time with her mother. She can't now, so . . ."

"That's cold, even for you, Morgan. I'm sure she's not thinking of Paris. She just buried her father. They haven't even put up his stone yet or finished paying for his funeral costs, and now this."

"Devastating, I'm sure, all of it being so close to home. The gloom on this street will be so thick that you can't breathe. That's all anyone around here will talk about, and because they see you constantly with Ms. Gleeson, they'll treat us like mourning family. Ironically, the Lake George trip has come up at the right time."

"Lake George?" Mommy grimaced. "I'm not going to Lake George now, Morgan. How can you even think that? Nattie will need us more than ever. I'm going over to her house in an hour or so. You don't flee to vacation when your friends suffer tragedy. You help them get through it. We are the same as mourning family!"

"Flee?" Daddy remained calm. "You hardly know her. She's not a lifelong friend or something. What's it been, a few weeks? You just have an infatuation with someone who had a high position in the State Department and lived in glamorous Paris. In a month she'll put the house up for sale and leave. You'll forget about her."

Both of them simply stared at each other for another long, silent moment. Mommy appeared more shocked than angry. She took a deep breath, looked away to gather her strength, and then turned to Daddy with more fire in her eyes.

"It doesn't take a lot of time to make a good friend if that's what someone is, Morgan," she said, surprisingly quietly. She sounded more like she did when she told me not to do something, her anger held down like boiling milk under the lid of a pot. "It's not an infatuation. I've never been a celebrity freak. I was used to important people coming to see my father, but a real friend is someone you recognize quickly." She relaxed. "There's an energy that exists between you from the beginning, a very positive energy, and—"

"That's romantic slop. Everyone wants something from somebody. A friend is simply someone who disguises that well."

Mommy looked like she was smiling, but she wasn't.

"You never really did have a best friend, did you, Morgan? You never told me about anyone in particular, and even now, these men you call your friends . . . they use you to get on my father's golf course or tennis court. Not everyone is like that, Morgan. I'm just sorry you've never truly experienced it."

"Please, spare me all this analysis."

"I wonder whose childhood was worse, yours or mine."

Daddy's face flushed redder than I had ever seen it.

"Now, you listen to me, Linsey. I made all these plans, fixed my schedule, and called in a few favors. What good is my having an extended weekend off?"

"We'll do it another time," Mommy said firmly. Now she was the one who sounded like Captain Bryer. "I'm not going to desert Nattie when she needs me the most."

Daddy started to speak but stopped. He turned to leave, then paused and turned back to Mommy.

"Well, I'm taking my well-earned time off. I need relief from the pressure I work under, too. If you want to help with another wake and a funeral, go to it," he said, waving his arms as if he was chasing away mosquitoes. "I'll leave early in the morning. If you're not going, maybe I'll even leave tonight."

He marched out. We heard him going up the stairway, each step like a hammer that probably made the whole house shudder. I was too shocked by my father's outburst to speak or move. Mommy looked stunned as well.

"Mommy?"

"If you want to go to Lake George with your father, you can go, Caroline. I'll help you pack your things."

"I want to be here for Nattie, too," I said. I started to cry.

She smiled and hugged me, holding me longer than usual, holding me as if she thought I might break apart.

"Okay," she said. "We'll go over to the Gleeson house as soon as Nattie calls. No matter how smart and accomplished you are, you're not at your best at times like these. You depend on the kindness and assistance of your friends. And that's who we are, Caroline, Nattie's friends."

She looked at the doorway as if she expected Daddy to have changed his mind and be there, but I could actually hear him opening and closing drawers upstairs. He was packing his suitcase. However, I knew he wouldn't leave until he had taken a shower and had a shave. I could almost feel his rage raining down on us.

What if he did ask me to go with him? What should I say? I wondered.

Nattie called before he came down. She was home.

"We'll be right there," Mommy told her. I looked at the stairway and then at Mommy.

"Let's just go," she said. "He'll figure it out. This isn't the time for arguments."

I followed her to the front entrance. She put my coat on me and put on her own. I kept expecting Daddy to appear because he had thought about it and had changed his mind, but he didn't, and Mommy opened the door without calling up to him or even looking toward the stairway. We went out and started up the street. When I looked back at our house, she tugged my hand.

"He's not coming. When your father makes up his mind, he's like my father. There's no pause button. 'Reconsideration' is another word for weakness."

I still couldn't help glancing back. Once, my mother had liked my father's determination. She had told me many times that he made her feel safe because he was so sure of himself. Self-confidence was a power. Vaguely I wondered if Nattie had changed my mother's mind about Daddy, maybe changed her mind about many more things, too. As we rushed along the sidewalk that day, I remember thinking my father was falling back instead of us going forward. He was severed like the first stage of a rocket ship I watched being launched on television, and he wasn't going to get to the stars with us.

When Nattie opened the door, her face looked like it had been soaked in tears for hours. Her lips and cheeks were pale. The brightness was gone from her eyes. She was trembling so badly that she swayed. Mommy stepped up quickly to embrace her. Nattie held on to her tightly, as tightly as you would hold on to someone when you thought you were drowning.

Neither of them spoke or moved for so long that I wondered if we would go into the house or just talk to her from the entrance. I glanced backward to see if anyone on the street was watching us, but it seemed no one was home anywhere. Maybe all of them had heard about Mrs. Gleeson and didn't want to come out to see such sorrow. Maybe Daddy was right about that: gloom like a cloud full of tears would hover over our street and homes, and everyone would look at us with pity.

Later, Mommy would tell me during a quiet moment together that every time someone you love or someone you knew well died, it was another second toward the end of the world. Everyone felt it and hid from it.

Finally, we went in and to the kitchen, where Nattie was making some coffee. She described in detail what had happened at the hospital, speaking quickly like someone who was afraid she would be interrupted or someone who couldn't stand holding the words inside her. When she paused to catch her breath, Mommy said, "Maybe we need a drink instead of coffee."

"Yes," Nattie said, putting the coffeepot down so hard that I thought it would break. Mommy didn't reveal that she had already had two drinks while she and I had been sitting in the living room, waiting for Daddy. Nattie told me to go to the refrigerator and take out anything I wanted. There was still lemonade, Mrs. Gleeson's lemonade. When they both started crying, I started to cry, too. Nattie realized it first and quickly embraced me.

"You shouldn't have to see all this sorrow so young," she told me. She kissed me on the forehead and then told Mommy, "It's like a replay. I still have all the contact numbers. There are still flowers in my mother's room. It's almost like the undertaker is on speed dial and the hearse was kept running."

"I know. Let me help you with everything," Mommy told her, and they returned to the kitchen to make calls and discuss arrangements. I wandered out and gazed into Mrs. Gleeson's bedroom. Her bed looked like she had just risen from it. I half expected her to appear from the bathroom, smile, and say, *It's all been a horrible mistake. Go tell them to stop crying, Caroline.*

Later, when we were all in the dining room, eating some toast and jam and some eggs Mommy had quickly made, she told Nattie about Daddy, their argument, and that he might have left for Lake George. At first Nattie said she understood. "Morgan's work is stressful. I'm sure he needs quite a few breaks."

But when Mommy raged about Daddy's indifference to what had happened to Mrs. Gleeson, Nattie was quiet.

"It's that military thing: never show emotion on the battlefield. Unfortunately, for Morgan, the world's just one big combat zone."

The phone began ringing because many of the Gleesons' friends had found out what happened to Mrs. Gleeson. With Mommy at her side, Nattie spoke to at least a dozen people while we were there, promising to get them all the details. She had a paper in front of her on which were listed all the people who had been contacted after her father's death. She said her mother had made up the list and had asked her to call each one.

"Talk about déjà vu," she told Mommy, and my mind immediately went into translation mode. A few minutes later, Nattie had another drink and Mommy called to see if Daddy had really left. When he didn't answer at home, she called his mobile. I drew closer to hear what she was saying. He was really on his way to Lake George. She mostly listened, so I knew he was still raging mad. When she did talk, all she said was "I'm sorry you feel that way, Morgan."

After she ended the call, she looked like she was going to cry again. Nattie rose quickly to embrace her. Now Nattie was comforting her.

"I hate to leave you alone with all this," Mommy said as it grew later, the shadows darkening and thickening. I didn't keep track of time, but I knew we had been here for hours and hours.

"And I hate to leave you alone with all that dissension at home. I know how empty the house will feel, how you can still hear the words you regret," Nattie responded.

"I didn't say anything I regret."

"Oh, Linsey . . ."

The two stared at each other for a long moment, and then both began the same sentence with "Maybe you—" They stopped and laughed. The sound of laughter was so unexpected and immediately felt wrong, but I sensed that it gave them desperately needed relief. They laughed until they started to cry again. Then they hugged, and both took a breath.

"It might be better for you to come to our place," Mommy said. "Get away from that phone until you've had some rest. I'll make us a light dinner. All the details for the services can be confirmed tomorrow."

Going home sounded very good to me. I was getting uncomfortable being in Mrs. Gleeson's house. My eyes wouldn't stop looking toward her bedroom every once in a while. And I really didn't know what to do with myself. At least at home, in my room, I could distract myself with books and even do some of the homework I was supposed to do over the weekend in Lake George.

And besides, what if Daddy called later? We should be there.

Nattie nodded.

"I'll put some of my things together. I'll drive. I don't want to look like I'm running away from home or something."

"We'll wait and drive back with you. You're right. We don't need to parade before these neighbors right now," Mommy said, which surprised me. What did she mean by "parade"? Was it the same thing Daddy had said about the people on our street?

Night came so much faster now. By the time we all got into Nattie's car, it was about as dark as it would be before sunrise. Maybe because of how we all felt, especially me, it seemed a lot colder suddenly, too. I half anticipated snow flurries even though we were only days away from October and the earliest snow I could remember wasn't until November. I wondered if Daddy would be a lot colder up in Lake George and if maybe now he was regretting driving there. I really hoped he would call us tonight.

"Time takes the pain out of a bee sting," Grandmother Judith told me once when I pinched my finger in a door at the mansion. She didn't offer to kiss me or suggest some remedy. She said there was nothing else to do but wait. Mommy moved quickly to soothe me, eyeing her mother as though she was some sort of alien creature.

But Grandmother Judith wasn't wrong this time. That was all I could do about Daddy: wait.

"Make yourself something to drink," Mommy told Nattie as soon as we entered the house. "Caroline, wash up and change your clothes. Put on one of your nice new dresses for dinner," she added, smiling.

"Which one?"

"I'll let you decide."

What if I make a mistake, I thought, *and put on something too festive?* It didn't seem right to look so happy right now.

"Why don't I help you?" Nattie offered. "I have to keep busy, too."

I had the oddest sense of fear. She could suddenly think about her mother and start crying in my room. What would I do? It was always hard to watch adults cry and not cry, too.

I looked at Mommy to answer for me.

"Sure," she said. "You two go on. I'll start preparations for our light dinner."

Nattie smiled at me. I hoped she didn't see any of my fear. I was ashamed of it. When she held out her hand, I took it quickly, and we went to the stairway.

"I'm very grateful that I have you as a friend," she said when we started up the stairs. "You make all the sadness easier to bear."

I wondered if she could read my thoughts, especially my hope that she wouldn't start to cry. We went right to my closet.

"Which one do you think you like the most?" she asked, shuffling through my dresses, blouses, and skirts. "I think this is very fashionable."

She plucked out the dress Mommy had recently bought me for the start of school. It was what the saleslady called a floral jersey T-shirt dress. Nattie looked at the label.

"And a Ralph Lauren, too!"

She waited for my nod. If she liked it, I surely would.

"That was easy," she said, and handed it to me. I took it gingerly and set it on the bed. When I turned back to her, she was staring at me in such a different way. It was more like she was looking through me.

"Remember when I told you growing up could be painful, too?"

I nodded. I was afraid of the sound of my own voice right now, afraid it would start me crying and then she would cry.

"Well, this is one example. You can't be a child when there is tragedy. We'd all like to hide in our youth, be babies again, sucking our thumbs, but life doesn't let you. That's what I meant about how growing up could be painful. Understand?"

"Yes."

If I ever wished I wouldn't get older and things would never change, I surely did now. Truthfully, I didn't want to understand. I wished Mommy could do what she did when something unpleasant was happening on television: turn it off and tell me there was time before I would have to face all that, time before I would have to face all this. Adults could argue, adults could be terribly sad, but I could retreat to my room and my dolls and live in a different world. I could be that turtle. But it was too late. In the darkest, saddest places of my heart, I knew. It was too late.

"Good. Now," she said, softening her smile, "what we have to do is help your mother, too. When you're sad, it helps to help someone else who is sad as well. It helps her and it helps you. You don't have time to be sad for yourself. *Comprendre*, Caroline?"

"*Oui*," I said, and she widened her smile. She reached out to embrace me.

"*Merci*," she said. "Let's all keep each other from being sad for a while. We'll leave it waiting outside the door. I'd better get down and help your mother while you wash and dress. She'll probably make us too much to eat. It would be exactly what my mother would do."

She turned and left. I looked at my dress.

I had to choose the right shoes to wear. Even Daddy would appreciate that.

I thought about him again all by himself up in Lake George. He was at work so often and at such odd hours sometimes that it almost didn't feel much different if I didn't think about how angry he was. But the sound of his steps on the stairs and the opening and closing of his bureau drawers still echoed.

I took my time washing, dressing, and brushing my hair. Maybe if they were surprised at how well I had done, they would be less sad. I paused at the top of the stairs when I was ready to go down. It was so quiet that for a moment I thought they might have gone out or maybe back to Nattie's house to get something.

I tiptoed down the stairs. I don't know why I was so quiet, but it just seemed the right way to be. When I looked in the kitchen, I saw they weren't there. Where did they go? I listened but heard nothing, so I walked slowly to the living room, where I found them on the sofa. Mommy was sitting, and Nattie was lying with her head on Mommy's lap. Mommy was stroking her hair the way she would mine when I would lie on her lap. Neither realized I was standing there in the doorway, gazing in at them.

Despite Nattie's sadness and what had happened, I couldn't stop the pang of jealousy moving up my spine and into my heart. I couldn't imagine my mother comforting anyone else in the special way she comforted me. Mommy finally saw me.

"Oh, how pretty you look, Caroline," she said. Nattie turned her head slightly and smiled. I immediately felt guilty for being jealous.

"That dress looks beautiful on her. All the girls will be envious when she wears it to school," Nattie said. She didn't move to sit up, and Mommy kept her fingers entwined in her hair.

I said nothing, surprised at how my coming didn't get them to stop what they were doing.

"Hungry?" Mommy asked.

I nodded because I didn't know what else to say. Nattie finally sat up.

"We were both just suddenly tired," she said, maybe finally feeling a little embarrassed, especially because of the way I was looking at them. "Everything hit us at once, but I'm a little hungry now, too. Your mother made a nice salad, and she has linguine and cheese ready to go. She said that's one of your favorites. I'll make it one of mine."

I said nothing. Did I want to share my favorites, too?

They both stood, and we all went to the kitchen. They decided to have wine with their dinner, again gave me a taste, and almost finished a second bottle before we were done. As they had promised each other and me, nothing was said about Mrs. Gleeson's dying or Daddy's running off. They talked about food and wine, and as usual Nattie had stories about the restaurants she had discovered traveling outside of Paris, describing the smaller mom-and-pop restaurants she discovered in the smaller villages.

"I'll do the dishes," Nattie said almost as soon as we put down our forks. "Maybe Caroline will help me."

That was always something I did with my mother, I thought, feeling a little resentful. Then I looked at Mommy. She did appear very tired. I thought she even swayed, until she opened her eyes wide.

"I will," I said quickly, regretting that I'd had even a second of doubt.

"I'll tend to some things," Mommy said, and left us.

"You okay?" Nattie asked me. I nodded, thinking I should be the one asking her.

While we did the dishes, she talked again about her growing up, about school and friends. I didn't think she even stopped for a breath. Talking seemed to be her defense against crying, and it was fun to hear about the things she had done as a little girl. She repeated some of the things she had told Mommy, things I would have thought she knew I had heard, but I didn't interrupt her the way I would Mommy sometimes. I had yet to have those social experiences.

Just after we had put things away, Mommy appeared in the doorway, dressed in her nightgown.

"I don't know about you two, but I'm exhausted."

"If I think about it, I get even more tired," Nattie said.

"We should all get an early night," Mommy said, turning to me. "You can read or even watch television until you're tired enough to sleep. Okay?"

I nodded but thought, *What about Daddy? What if he calls?*

She held out her hand, and I joined her and went up to my room. She had my cover down and my pajamas out, having done all that while Nattie and I cleaned up after dinner.

"You can take it from here, can't you, Caroline?"

"Of course, Mommy," I said. I wanted to add, as Nattie often did now, *I'm not a child anymore.* But it sounded cruel to say that. She looked so broken, so vulnerable. I almost asked, *What about Daddy?* but kept my lips tight. I was afraid of the things she would say, things that would give me nightmares. She kissed me good night and went off to her bedroom.

I was more tired than I had thought, maybe because of all this thinking and crying inside. I washed and, almost asleep already, put on my pajamas and got into bed. I was going to read, but my eyes welcomed my closing them.

I vaguely heard Nattie's voice before I went to sleep.

When I woke again, the world I had known, the bubble I had imagined would protect us even now, exploded.

And in an instant, it was gone, and forever spring along with it.

6

It was nearly morning. Whenever I woke before I had to and just lay there thinking about the things I would do or remember a dream I just had, the dim streak of light from a peekaboo rising sun would bounce off a cloud. It would begin to lift the darkness from my windows, urging me to get up to start the day. The birth of light fascinated me. Mommy always left my curtains open so I could go to sleep looking at the stars or the moonlight when it was there. She told me that when she was my age, she always found comfort at night while gazing out her windows at what was beyond Sutherland. I came to realize what she really meant was what was beyond her father's control.

I began thinking about all that had happened yesterday. The weight of those memories seemed to settle on my chest. More than ever, I wanted to be the turtle Daddy had predicted I could become, at least for a little while. I wished the sun would stop, stay dim, and delay the start of the day. Mommy had so much to be sad about, so many reasons to cry. Although being with Nattie kept the death of her parents bright and alive, my mother didn't want to leave her, even for a minute. Last night we had put the dark cloud away for a little while at dinner, but it was seeping back into my mind every ticking minute, crawling along with the rising sun. Surely, both my mother and Nattie would wake up with tears already on their cheeks.

I could feel those tears being born in my eyes, but before I could reluctantly sit up to get dressed, I heard what sounded like a large rock hitting the wall of our house just outside my room. Then I heard Daddy booming almost as loudly.

"I KNEW IT! I KNEW WHAT SHE WAS FROM THE MOMENT I SET EYES ON HER. AND I ALWAYS HAD MY SUSPICIONS ABOUT YOU. THE TRUTH IS, SO DID YOUR FATHER. I HOPE YOU'RE HAPPY TOGETHER! I'LL BE BACK FOR MY THINGS. MY ADVICE IS NEITHER OF YOU BE HERE WHEN I RETURN FOR THEM."

I heard his footsteps on the stairs. He never went down them so fast and so hard. The stairway shook and made the whole house tremble. I could hear him leave below, sounding like he had torn the door off its hinges. The slam was like the popping of a balloon. The house was so silent immediately afterward, as silent as it had been when I had fallen asleep. Was I awake? Was all that a nightmare?

Rising quickly now, I hurried out, not even pausing to put on my slippers. No one was in the hallway. I stopped the moment I saw the hole Daddy must have punched in the wall near the door to his and Mommy's bedroom. I started to touch it but hesitated, actually afraid it might be too hot. Mommy and Daddy's bedroom door was open. I stepped up to it slowly, still not hearing a voice, a sound. When I looked in, I saw Nattie beside Mommy in bed. They were both sitting up, and Nattie had her arms around her. Mommy had her head on Nattie's shoulder. They were both naked. I stood there staring, utterly fascinated with how dearly Nattie was kissing Mommy's neck and shoulder, until Nattie saw me and whispered something to Mommy, who instantly pulled up the blanket and turned to me. Nattie lay back quickly.

"Oh, honey, I'm so sorry that happened. I had no idea he'd come home this soon."

"What happened? There's a big hole in the wall."

"Just go back to your room, honey. Go on. I'll be there as soon as we get up and put on our robes, okay?"

"Why did he punch the wall?"

"Just go to your room, honey. I'll explain everything," she said.

I hesitated. They both were staring at me so fearfully that I turned and ran back to my room. My legs were trembling as I sat on the bed and waited. The sun was fully up now. The rays seemed to shatter the window, scattering every shadow, erasing every place to hide. The morning had begun. I think I had the vague realization at that moment that, as Daddy sometimes said, this was the first day of the rest of my life.

Mommy came in slowly and sat beside me. She took my hand in hers.

"I wasn't expecting your father to have regrets about going to Lake George and then come back overnight. He must have woken up from sleep and . . . so he surprised us," she said as softly and as calmly as she could.

"Why was he so angry?"

"Nattie didn't sleep in our guest room; she slept with me."

"Because you wanted her to feel better," I said, nodding to help her defend herself. How often I had crawled into bed beside her to feel better, feel safer.

"Well, yes, but it's more than that now," she said. She blew air through her lips as if she had just run a mile. "This is almost as much a surprise to me as it will be to you and was to your father, despite what he said about himself and your grandfather knowing things about me."

"Why? What things?"

I knew the answers, but I didn't want to hear them or reveal that I was even thinking them.

She took another deep breath. As she spoke, her eyes avoided mine. It almost sounded like something she had rehearsed for days.

"Nattie and I discovered that we have feelings for each other, stronger feelings that make us more than just friends. They are the kind of feelings I thought I had for your father and he had for me, feelings men and women who marry are expected to have for each other. I know I described the beginning of all that to you as if it was something magical, but I think I described what I wished and not what was. It's my fault, and I know that will be a big reason for your confusion. I wasn't lying; I was dreaming. My father is right about me doing far too much of it. We lie to ourselves because we can't face the truth."

"Why can't we?"

"It's too painful. It's as simple as that . . . sometimes."

The truth? Daddy always said that avoiding the truth always led to pain and disaster. Even lying to protect someone you love would eventually bite you like a snake. Mommy never disagreed.

I didn't know what the expression on my face was like, but whatever it was, it was enough for her to let go of my hand and hug me, laying her forehead against my head for a long moment. The silence between us was roaring in my ears. She sat up firmly again, mother-firmly.

"I don't expect you to understand all this quickly, Caroline. I know it's such a surprise. Maybe my father did say something to your daddy about me. It's not unusual, but when it involves people in a marriage, people have a different, or let's just say bigger, reaction. Lots of surprise, I guess. Truthfully, I might have felt this way before with someone, a girlfriend in college, and maybe my father saw that, but it's the first time I let my feelings speak. I smothered them then, probably because I had the weight of my parents' shadows lying over me like some iron blanket. Now I let myself go along with those smothered feelings, let them breathe and blossom. And I'm not sorry," she said, mustering all the defiance she could. "I'm happy Nattie has come into my life, into both our lives."

Iron blanket? Smothered feelings? Her words just seemed to fall like teardrops into my ears. I knew that the affection you had with a best friend was strong, but how did that change into the way she had felt with Daddy? Of course, I understood that being a wife and being a best friend had to be different, although I recalled Daddy telling me that husbands and wives had to be best friends for their marriage to work.

My mother could see that her words were just weaving the web of confusion thicker and wider over my face. Didn't we have magic in this home? Weren't we called the Robot Family because we were so perfect? How could it all have been only what she had wished and not what was?

"It's going to take time for you to understand all this. I know, and I know you might even be very mad at me because of it. That's why I'm so sorry this happened before I could explain it and properly prepare you."

Now my feelings and thoughts were really tangled up. Should I be angry at her? Even at Nattie? I felt the way I did when I had first put on ice skates, my legs going in opposite directions from the rest of me. I remembered Daddy getting impatient and ripping me from Mommy's arms, saying, "She has to fall down or she'll never get up." That didn't make any sense, but after a while I did stay up and even began to skate a little.

"See? Being afraid to fall is what makes you a better skater," he had said. "That's a lesson to remember for everything in your life. Fear is not a bad thing, Caroline. Without it, we'd all go crashing into each other and everything else. The key is simply knowing how to use it and use it well."

I had fear now, and I had no idea how to use it.

"All right, let me explain it to you this way," Mommy said. "You know how Daddy and I used to like to kiss and hug, hold hands, and snuggle in bed, at least in the early years of our marriage? You would crawl in with us, remember? It seems so long ago," she said sadly, and then she took another deep breath, this time like someone who was going underwater. "Well, that romantic feeling between us has been gone for a long time.

I thought I could ignore it and stay in a marriage that had lost its spark, but when Nattie came into our lives, she reminded me how much I love feeling that spark. How much magic there is in romance, and falling for someone."

I know that, I wanted to say. *I just didn't know, or even suspect, it would be true for you.* The words were there, but I couldn't say them.

"You're just starting to have these feelings, I know, sexual feelings. Romantic feelings! We've talked a little about that. Now we have to talk about it a great deal more. I expect that soon you will have your menarche, your first menstruation. The sexual part of you is awakening, just as it did for me and does for all women."

She brushed back my hair.

"I don't want you to be afraid of it or, maybe worse, ashamed of it or anything feminine because of me. Oh, I know you're so confused. I know how terrible that must feel."

"So you don't love Daddy anymore?" I asked, even though I immediately thought it was a child's question.

"I'm not so sure I ever did. Not in the way any woman should love the person she is married to. I think I've said it in so many different ways. Nattie's made me quite aware of it, too. Your daddy has been more of a father figure for me than a husband. I respected him; I let him control our lives."

"So now you love Nattie the way you tried to love him," I said. I could almost feel the child in me crumbling. Age doesn't make you an adult; events do.

"Yes," she said without hesitation. "That's exactly it."

In my heart of hearts, I knew that truth was there almost the day she and Nattie had met. I felt it when I watched them become more than just best friends: holding hands, hugging, and kissing each other hello or goodbye. Surely Daddy had been realizing it, too. Maybe both of us were looking away. This morning there was no way he could. Was my mother aware that he knew? Was she looking away, too?

"Did Daddy know before?"

"Yes, I think your father suspected this for a while. I almost think that's why he pulled this surprise. He's a very clever man. He wanted to catch us," she said, looking more like she was voicing a thought that had just occurred to her. "Yes," she said, nodding to herself. "I'm sure of it."

She paused for a moment, and then, as if she suddenly realized she was with me, she widened her eyes and turned to me.

"I was hoping to do this break with him in a more civilized, smooth way, making it less painful for all of us, especially you. I guess that was another pipe dream. Linsey the Pipe Dreamer. Even Nattie says that's surely been my problem: always seeing the wild rose in a garden of weeds." She sighed. "But the truth is that was how I managed to survive, by sipping on pipe dreams."

She took my hand again in both of hers.

"Your father is not going to want to stay with me now," she said. "And I think that is all right for me. And it will be for you, too."

"Why wouldn't he want to stay with me? Is Daddy mad at me, too?"

"No, I wouldn't call it mad. He just isn't equipped for raising a daughter alone. It irked him how much you liked Nattie, too. You knew that, right?"

"Yes. But I was hoping he would change."

She smiled.

"'Change' is a word that isn't in your father's vocabulary. Once you think of yourself as being perfect, any alteration, no matter how minor, is either a mistake or a result of some weakness, and you know how your father feels about weaknesses."

I didn't know what to say. I knew it was true, but I didn't want to say it. It seemed more wrong than ever to say anything bad about him. In fact, in the back of my mind I was thinking that none of this was really his fault. I felt anger, too, but I knew if I showed it, even a little, my mother would cry and everything would get worse.

"This is all too much to know at once. It's like overeating," she said. "Let's take it all a step at a time. I promise to be sure you have answers to any questions, ever."

She stood up, clasped her hands, and talked more to the floor than to me.

"Here's what I can tell you now. Daddy will want to divorce me, and there'll be some arguments about whom you stay with and when. What he saw, what he apparently suspected, is not something a man like him can tolerate. He'll want it, me, out of his mind as fast as possible. Your father was brought up even more conservatively than I was. It's like growing up in a box with your eyes always facing forward. You're taught to ignore the things your parents and their close friends think are wrong, evil, and just too different. If you don't ignore them, you're taught to openly reject them, even condone violence against them."

"But Daddy doesn't hurt people. He saves people from being hurt."

She laughed tightly, not a laugh of joy or humor.

"Strangers, true. Look, it's all too much for you to understand right now in one gulp. It takes time for all of us to learn to live with the truth. Which is another reason so many don't. Including me," she added under her breath. She looked at me again and smiled. "We'll be patient, and we'll always consider your feelings. I hope you will always believe that I would never do anything to hurt you. You believe that, don't you, Caroline?"

I nodded, but it was still so gray and smoky, like being in that place between a dream and awakening. I could feel it threading through me to tighten its grip around my heart: the ugly truth. There would be no more pretending to help me feel better. I really was going to have to grow up . . . today. All the good lies were being swept away with the bad. There would be no pipe dreams for either of us, maybe ever again.

"Your father won't stop being angry at me, honey, but as I said, that doesn't mean he will leave you completely or stop loving you. You'll see him. Everything will be arranged. Right now, it seems too horrible for you to imagine, but in time . . . in time things will settle down. We'll be fine."

Nattie appeared in the doorway. She was wearing one of Mommy's bathrobes and a pair of her slippers.

"Need any help?" she asked Mommy.

"No, I think we have enough to digest right now." She took my hand again and smiled. "Little by little, she'll understand. Our girl is too bright not to understand."

Our girl?

I looked at Nattie, who was smiling.

"For now, let's all concentrate on what we have to do for your mother's final arrangements. Caroline wants to do that, too, right, Caroline? We have to think about Mrs. Gleeson and about Nattie, right?"

I nodded, but I didn't see how that would help me forget about Daddy, and truthfully, I didn't want to think about anything else. Maybe it was mean and selfish, but I was more worried about myself than I was concerned about another funeral. Didn't something just die here?

"We'll all get dressed, have a little breakfast, and go back to Nattie's house to do what has to be done. You can take things to read or any homework. I know it will be hard to concentrate on anything else, but we'll be there all day."

She leaned over to kiss me.

"Let's all get dressed. We'll have some breakfast first."

"When will Daddy come back for his things?" I asked. "I heard him say he would."

She raised her eyes toward the ceiling and covered her upper lip with her lower one before she blew air.

"He'll come back after we leave to go to Nattie's, for sure," Mommy said. "But he won't stay here, Caroline. He'll take what he needs for now and stay somewhere else."

"Where?"

"I don't know."

She looked at Nattie. "My guess is he'll be calling my father. He knows I won't call to explain anything before he does. That's not going to be very pleasant, either."

"Maybe we should have—" Nattie began.

"Don't say it," my mother said, putting up her hand. "As they say, the die is cast. Maybe this was the best thing, the best way it could have happened."

"Are you absolutely sure, Linsey? There are ways to work back, marriage counselors . . ."

"No," Mommy said. She pressed her clasped hands against her heart. "We talked about it and I know this is right. In one way or another, for one reason or another, he'd be punching other holes in our walls. He's different; I'm different. If anything, I have a sense of relief. You understand," she said firmly.

"Of course."

"Good. For now, let's do what must be done for your mother. There will be plenty of time to deal with the fallout of all this."

"Okay," Nattie said. She smiled at me and started back to Mommy and Daddy's bedroom.

"Wash up and get fully awake before you get dressed so you don't put on different-colored socks or something," Mommy said. It was what she always said, but I couldn't imagine being any more awake than I was now. "I'll make those mushy scrambled eggs you like."

She kissed me again and left.

I looked back at my bed. If I could be granted a wish magically, it would be that I would still be asleep and this would all be just a terrible nightmare. The sun would wake me again, and the world would be as it was.

But I knew that would never be. I didn't have to go too deeply into my heart or mind to know that was true. What I didn't envision, could perhaps never envision, was what it all would mean for me. I just had no idea how terrible it would all become.

By the time I dressed, Mommy and Nattie were downstairs, preparing breakfast, with moments of silence that were deeper than any I had heard in my house, even the silence that had fallen between my mother and my father. They seemed intent on talking about simple things when they did speak. Truthfully, I thought they both looked a little frightened.

"Do you want more salt for your eggs?" Mommy asked. "More coffee? I could make more toast. I do have some bagels in the freezer."

"Linsey," Nattie suddenly said, reaching for Mommy's hand. "I could just leave, and you might—"

"Would you really like that?" Mommy asked quickly.

Nattie shook her head.

"But I feel more like a home breaker than—"

"You tell me," Mommy said. "Was it broken before you came or not?"

"I know, but what a time to choose for this," Nattie said, shaking her head and smiling.

"Maybe we didn't choose it. Maybe things choose themselves."

"I might slip into the pipe dreams alongside you," Nattie said, and they both finally laughed the way they usually did with each other.

However, now it was difficult for me to listen to them and eat. My stomach still felt like I had swallowed a twisted ball of string.

"You should eat," Mommy said, noticing how little I had eaten. "We have a lot to do today."

I tried. She saw how I was struggling and just smiled and took my plate. Then she started to clean up. Nattie helped her, and even though there was still more to do, Mommy just stopped.

"Let's just go. There'll be plenty of time later to attend to all this," she said. "And he's right. We don't want to be here when he comes back."

She had me put on my light blue leather jacket and gather the books and things I wanted, and then we walked out. I immediately looked for

Daddy, but he wasn't waiting in his car anywhere on the street that I could see.

"Where's Daddy?" I asked as we turned to walk to Nattie's house. "Where did he go? How will he know we've left?"

"He'll know, and he'll be here to get his things. He is like a rocket launched into outer space when he decides to do something. Remember how he often says, 'Hesitation is dangerous'?"

"But—"

"We'll talk about it all later, Caroline. We'll talk a lot about it. I promise," Mommy said. And then, lowering her voice, she said, "Probably for a while we won't talk much about anything else."

I looked back, but I still didn't see him. How would he know when we had left? Was he hiding near a neighbor's house? Would news about us spread quickly? I paused to watch from Nattie's front door, and then Mommy urged me inside. It felt like I was closing a book, one I would never again read.

Once we were in Nattie's house, I considered sitting near the front window so I could look down the street and maybe see Daddy come home. I wondered if Mommy would be angry if I ran out and to him, pleading with him not to go away. Maybe Daddy would take me before Mommy had realized it, and she would be even angrier. I heard Nattie and Mommy talking, heard Nattie on the phone, but I didn't really listen. Instead, I inched up to the front window.

When I saw Daddy arrive, I rushed to tell Mommy. Both she and Nattie stopped doing whatever they were doing and simply looked at me as if I had said something so important that the whole world would pause. Mommy's mobile phone rang. She just looked at that, too. Then she picked it up, saw who was calling, and shut it off.

"The general?" Nattie asked.

"Champing at the bit to go at me for sure," Mommy said. "He won't be able to concentrate on anything else until he does. I don't have many weapons, so I'll enjoy what I have. Let him stew a little, not that I expect it to soften him. But I've never been more ready for a confrontation with him."

Nattie smiled. "I'm—"

"Don't," Mommy warned her. She kept her smile, and they embraced.

I don't think I've ever felt more alone. *She should be embracing me*, I thought.

I left them and again sat by the window. When Daddy emerged from our house, he was carrying two suitcases. He put them at the side of his car and returned to the house. Moments later, he came out with two more and began putting them all in his car. *He's taking so much*, I thought. *There might be nothing left of his, nothing he cares about. When we go back, it will really feel like he is gone.*

Before we returned, Mommy and Nattie went to the funeral parlor to complete the arrangements for her mother. Nattie gave me the Bible story book she had promised, and I waited in the car for them. When they came out, Mommy was embracing Nattie. It looked like she was keeping her from falling. It was obvious she had been crying, crying hard. I stopped thinking about myself and Daddy and felt sorrier for her.

We returned first to Nattie's house. She packed some of her things, telling Mommy she didn't want her to be alone. They were telling each other the same thing. But Mommy wouldn't be alone, I thought. She'd have me. How could she forget?

When we returned to our house, I hurried up the stairs and looked in Mommy and Daddy's bathroom. It was what I feared. Everything of his was gone from his counters. While Mommy and Nattie were still downstairs, I went to Mommy and Daddy's bedroom and looked in his closet. All his pants with their perfect creases, his shoes, and his shirts were gone.

I heard my mother calling for me and went to the top of the stairway.

"We're talking about what to do for dinner tonight. You and I might go out for some groceries while Nattie takes a rest. I'll need your help," she added.

I just stared down at her. Didn't she realize?

"Daddy took all his clothes and all his things from the bathroom."

"I'm sure he did," she said. "Leave no stone unturned."

"What?"

"Get ready to go to the store," she said.

She walked away. I continued to stand there looking after her. Why didn't she look more upset, so upset that she couldn't do anything? So much was ending. No matter what, shouldn't we feel sad about that? It was how I felt. Nattie appeared with her overnight bag and small suitcase. She started up toward me.

"You want to help me unpack my things?" she asked, smiling.

"No, I have to go shopping with my mother," I said, and hurried down past her.

Mommy was standing by the phone in the kitchen, just staring at it. She didn't realize I was there. She lifted the receiver, dialed, and waited.

"If you start shouting at me, I'll hang up," she said when someone answered. I felt sure it was Grandfather Sutherland. She listened and said, "I am who I am. Sometimes it takes longer to find that out." She listened again and said, "Actually, you're the one who lives in a dream world, Father. You're living in a different time. You can control everything and everyone who depends on your money, but people don't tell you what's true; they tell you what you want to be true. I'm no longer one of them."

She lifted the receiver away from her ear and then put it back to say, "You're screaming. Morgan and I will work out what we have to work out. I'm not worried. Nattie Gleeson connected me to a very good lawyer friend of hers, one you would call a high-powered attorney yourself."

She listened, her left hand on her forehead, the palm pressed against it.

"Okay, Father. Do what you want with your wills and your money.

Should my mother feel any differently, she's welcome to call me. . . . Yes, I don't imagine she will, either. Well, have a nice rest of the day," she said, and hung up.

For a long moment she stood there looking down. I thought she was pushing back the urge to cry, but she took a deep breath before I could run to her to embrace her and turned to me, smiling instead.

"Now, let's make our grocery list," she said, as if nothing in the world had changed.

7

Despite how sure of everything Mommy sounded about Daddy being gone and their marriage coming to an end, I was still surprised and disappointed that Daddy never called or returned to our house after he discovered Nattie and Mommy in their bed. He had taken out his rage on the house, punching the wall, but Mommy assured me that his rainfall of anger would not splash over me, too. I didn't see any reason why it should, so if the phone rang, I expected her to call for me to tell me that he wanted to speak to me. I held my breath with the expectation, but she never did.

After he was gone for almost a week, I overheard her tell Nattie that she didn't want to say anything to me about his ignoring me and not being concerned about my feelings. "I know she's wondering about her father. It seems cruel for me to ignore it, but if I said anything, it would just make her feel worse."

Nattie agreed, but I recall thinking that maybe because I wasn't asking more about Daddy, I was becoming the turtle he foresaw. Was he expecting me to come out of my shell, go looking for him, sneak away and go to the airport? I had no doubt that was something he would do, even as a little boy.

I thought about doing it, but I was afraid of how much worse it might make Mommy feel if I did. Would she think I cared more about Daddy than I cared about her? And what if he refused to come down from his tower to see me? I had no idea why he would refuse. He might be busy, but he would tell whomever to ask me to wait. However, just the thought of his refusing and telling me to go home and envisioning myself alone at the airport were enough to make me shudder so much that I was afraid I would have a nightmare about it. In it a stranger would see me crying in a corner and ask, "Whose child are you?"

What had the Robot Family become? If we were no longer perfect, what were we? I didn't know everyone in every house from the beginning of our street to the end, but as far as I could tell, there was no other house besides Nattie's without a daddy in it. There were two students in my class whose parents had divorced, but their father was at every school activity and even occasionally brought them to school or picked them up. Would mine?

Nattie brought more of her things over to our house. Her car was in our garage where Daddy's car used to be. She had her toiletries in the bathroom where Daddy's once were. Basically, she was living with us now. The following week, I even heard her mention selling her parents' house, the house that had become hers.

"It could be my first sale as a real estate agent," she said.

Mommy thought that was funny, but to me it felt like all her family memories would go poof and be forgotten. Was that what it meant to be an adult? Put all your sadness in a drawer and close it? Nattie wasn't crying anymore; she hardly ever mentioned her parents.

In the evenings after dinner and sometimes during, she and Mommy had long discussions about things they were going to do to get over all the sadness and go on with their lives, one of them being all of us going to

Paris, maybe for Christmas. I remembered how Mommy had described her Paris family trip unhappily and how beautiful and exciting Nattie's descriptions were. I think talking about it was their biggest distraction from all else that was happening, the main thing being Mommy's divorce proceedings.

She had already met with her lawyer, Mr. Milton, Nattie's friend. Most of the time, Nattie and Mommy would go off to whisper about it, avoiding talking about it at dinner. But I couldn't stop thinking about it. It loomed over our heads like a pending storm. Never again would there be an anniversary celebration or a time they would give each other birthday presents, and because Daddy was so angry, he might never be here at Christmas or even attend my birthday party this month. Would I be able to go to his? Questions like that burned on my tongue, because I was afraid to ask them and bring back the sadness and tears. Most of the time, I felt like I was tiptoeing around the house. To me every window was frowning, every curtain was sagging.

And then it came, maybe because my body knew that I couldn't be a child anymore. I woke up with the cramps my mother had described as being associated with periods. For the first few moments, I forgot that it could happen, and I thought something else was wrong with me. It was certainly the wrong time to get sick. Then I went to the bathroom and saw the blood on my underwear. Although my mother was downstairs in the kitchen already, she heard my scream. Actually, Nattie heard it first and was there before her.

"I think you'll have to stay home from school on the first day," my mother said.

Nattie agreed, and then both of them, one trying to outdo the other, it seemed, began to describe their first time. The big difference was Nattie's mother was there for her; Mommy's wasn't. She'd had Mrs. Lawson.

"Who was as sympathetic as a bag of thornbushes. She made me feel so dirty, I remember, thrusting things at me and standing at arm's length as if what was happening was contagious."

In the back of my mind loomed the thought that maybe Daddy would find out and want to see me to be sure I was all right, even though the slightest mention of it before he and Mommy parted sent him off, criticizing Mommy for discussing such a thing in his presence.

Later that day, Nattie and my mother went to my school to get my homework assignments. My cramps were more severe than either of them had anticipated. I was practically bedridden, so my mother thought I might be out another day or even two more. I wondered if Daddy would have been as sympathetic. Was this just another challenge to meet, another obstacle to overcome? Would he say, "Nonsense, bite down hard and go to school"?

There above my desk, pinned to the bulletin board, were his instructions for my first day in junior high. He had written it all out himself and had me pin it up.

> *Never forget your pen and pencil.*
> *If you know the answer to a question, try to be the first to raise your hand.*
> *If you don't understand something, raise your hand and ask about it. Ignorant people are those who don't ask questions.*
> *Be neat at lunch, and don't let your friends get you to do something wrong. A friendship based on do's and dares is worse than no friendship at all.*
> *When you're given a challenge, don't regret it, enjoy it.*

As it turned out, I did stay out of school for another day, and both Mommy and Nattie insisted they drive me, even though it was only a short walk. By now, almost everyone knew about the divorce and Nattie.

Many of the students in my class saw me get out of the car, but no one in my class actually asked me any questions. Even so, I could see the words in their eyes. *Does your mother really have a girlfriend instead of your father? What is it like for you? Did you see them kiss? What else do they do?*

Worst of all, I could feel how those who were my friends were not as eager to talk to me and be with me. Obviously, their parents were talking about us. If anyone mentioned her father in my presence, all eyes would swing to me as if they were all connected. There was that pause full of expectations. Would I say anything? Would I start to cry? Of course, I didn't say or do anything, but I could feel myself step away, drift into my own thoughts.

I think this emptiness, this loneliness and isolation, since Daddy left was something my mother must have felt, too. For a while it seemed like everyone and everything else in the world had just floated away. The neighbors weren't waving hello, and the phone hardly rang with calls from old friends. Most of them were wives of Daddy's friends anyway. And those who were the mothers of other children in my class or school might have thought they would be contaminated or something.

"The thing about neighborhoods like ours," Mommy said one day at breakfast, "is that everyone knows everyone else's business without anyone bothering to call you or visit to ask questions. It seeps out."

Nattie laughed. "Both here and there, and surely at the airport."

"No, I doubt that Morgan is saying much at work. He doesn't want the attention or anyone's words of pity, but you're right. There are too many people involved now and—"

"I haven't actually been sneaking in and out," Nattie said. "My car is in your garage. Two and two is still four, even for the mathematically disabled."

Mommy laughed. Who were they talking about, exactly? Our neighbors or everyone? How could they be laughing about it? When was the last time I laughed for real?

"I'm sure we're the center of attention. There's not another gay couple on the street."

"Maybe for the surrounding half mile," Nattie said, and they laughed again.

Again, I wondered why this was at all funny. It was the first time I had heard them mention the word, a word I would hear whispered almost from that first day after the news was spread. Nattie and Mommy didn't avoid talking about it. In fact, they wanted to have some discussion at dinner or right after almost daily. I knew they were worried more about me than about themselves.

The conversations were as intimate as I could imagine them to be. Neither wanted to avoid reality. Little remarks like "Two women can be satisfied as much as a man and a woman" floated past me. Despite all their explanations, it still felt like a mystery. Another, probably more important to me, was the mystery of Daddy not coming to see me or even calling me. Didn't he even want to know how my days at school were going now? He used to be so interested in my schoolwork and grades. Mommy's answer when I finally began asking about it was simply "He needs time to digest it all. We'll see."

What were we waiting to see? I wondered. Was all this going to end like a bad dream? Would Nattie just get up one morning and return to her job in Paris? Would Daddy come home with his four suitcases? All my questions seemed to be dangling in the air like broken spiderwebs.

The answers came after Mommy had her first face-to-face with Daddy and his attorney at her attorney's office. Nattie and I waited for her at home. She finally had been studying for her real estate exam. Mommy said she would, too, but not until "all this other business is settled."

After this very important meeting, I hoped Daddy would start calling me and come to see me or take me places with him, but I didn't tell Mommy or Nattie about my hope. Although neither of them harped on how bad my father was for running off and basically forgetting about me,

I sensed that my wishing for him to want to talk and be with me was not something they really wanted to hear every day, or any time, for that matter, especially now, now that the argument was in the open. At times I felt like someone who had put her clenched fist in her mouth to stop herself from screaming.

When Mommy came home from her meeting with Daddy and their lawyers, Nattie and I were waiting for her in the living room. Nattie looked as tense and nervous as I felt. With a strange smile on her face and a curious little laugh, Mommy stepped into the doorway.

"I have a lot of breaking news," she said, and dropped herself into what was always Daddy's chair.

She looked exhausted. Seconds passed, but she wasn't rattling anything off. I was afraid she would say nothing in front of me. She would send me up to my room because she and Nattie had something not right for young ears. It would all end up in whispers behind the closed bedroom door.

"We're listening," Nattie said, smiling at me. She put her pamphlets aside and folded her hands on her lap. I closed my math book and tucked the notebook between the cover and the first page.

Mommy sat up, anger obviously fueling her with new energy.

"I had forgotten how prim and proper he could look with his perfectly knotted black tie and his close shave and military haircut. You could be cut by the crease in his pants. I felt like a slob, the haggard, evil wife. I could have done more with my hair, my makeup. I'm sure he was pleased."

"Stop it. You looked very pretty when you left here," Nattie said. "Don't tell me he and the attorneys didn't notice."

Mommy shrugged. "Morgan can be inscrutable, as good as any CIA agent. What he was at that table was so proud, like he would be if he beat me in Ping-Pong in front of my father at Sutherland."

"Ping-Pong? Why was he proud at the meeting?"

"Morgan has an ego that rivals my father's. For me to be tossing him over for a woman is worse than if I were having an affair with one of his friends. He would do everything, anything, to avoid embarrassment."

"Ah," Nattie said. "And so? What did he do?"

Mommy looked at me before answering. I had already told myself I would be grown-up and not cry about anything. Maybe she saw that in my face. I never had much doubt that she could read my thoughts as if the words were rolling across my eyes.

"He's been seeing someone, or at least he claims it's been going on long enough for him to call it a serious relationship. Imagine? Like ours was a form of comedy."

"How long was it going on?"

"If I believe him, months. Months before your father died, in fact. He emphasized that it became more serious after you and I became friends, however. His subtle little insinuation, blaming me for his indiscretions."

"He said this in front of his lawyer and Mr. Milton?"

"Casually, like, 'Oh, by the way, I bought a new car.'"

"Won't that complicate things for your father, Morgan carrying on an affair while you were still married?"

"My father will rationalize it. I can practically hear him saying it," Mommy said, and then she imitated Grandfather Sutherland, her head tilted back a little and her voice a little nasal. "'Obviously, Morgan wasn't getting the womanly devotion he was supposed to be getting,'" she said, then lowered her head and in her own voice added, "especially because of my time with you, so naturally it was expected Morgan would seek it elsewhere. I'm sure that rationalization is something my father has used to defend himself, especially to himself, never mind my mother.

"By the way . . . how's this for fatherly love? Morgan has my father's attorney. I suspect my father is even paying for him."

"Oh, Linsey. Paying for him? Your mother would put up with that?"

"Don't even go there. The last time she came to my defense, he nearly drowned her. You'll also notice that my brother hasn't called me, either, not even to ask what happened. My father issued an edict, for sure. He's doling out justice, Sutherland justice, which has his thumb on the scale."

Nattie laughed, but nervously. "But doesn't this weaken Morgan's or your father's attorney's arguments? I mean, why own up to adultery now?"

"As I said, ego, and . . ." She paused to look at me. "He's not arguing for any sort of custody, at least not in the traditional sense."

"Oh?"

Nattie looked troubled suddenly.

What was Mommy saying?

"We'll settle whatever money we have, but there might be an issue with the house."

"Meaning?"

"Daddy dearest's bank could foreclose on it. I can't justify a new mortgage. Unemployed at the moment."

"John Milton won't force him to maintain his child's residence? I'll give him hell and tell him I'm sorry I recommended him to you."

"It's not that. There are some codicils in the mortgage I never knew about. They even surprised John. It's my own fault for being so mandependent, but I'm sure my father had much more to do with it than Morgan did. When the time came, I signed whatever Morgan told me to sign, even though I was so angry at the time, because he took a down payment from my father, who even paid for some new furniture and insisted on paying for our honeymoon. Where we would go was presented to me like a multiple-choice question. My father surely provided each possible suggestion."

"I'm sorry. I didn't realize the extent of his control over your marriage, right from the start, using his money like . . ."

"I know what you're thinking. It sounds almost as if . . ."

"As if your father paid him to marry you?" Nattie asked quickly.

Mommy smirked. "He'll deny that, of course, but now . . . when I look back on it all . . ."

"It's ridiculous, Linsey. You're far from someone men would overlook or have to be coerced to date and marry."

"I don't know what I am right now in the eyes of men, especially Morgan. Maybe all his compliments were rehearsed and first approved."

They were both silent, staring at each other.

"Are you suggesting that your father didn't think you'd find a man for other reasons—reasons you've made clear now?"

"Possibly, but I have no regrets," Mommy quickly added. "I mean it, Nattie."

She smiled. "Neither do I."

They were both so quiet. Did they mean it?

Nattie slapped her knees and rose.

"None of this matters anyway. Let him foreclose. We'll have fun redoing my house," she said. "I won't put it up for sale. We'll move Caroline's room inch by inch, thread by thread, into mine. She'll never know the difference."

"What does that mean?" I finally piped up. Until this comment, I hadn't heard my name mentioned. I was really feeling invisible now. "What are all these things you're saying about Daddy and Grandfather Sutherland? And my room?"

Mommy nodded at Nattie, one of their unspoken messages to each other. That was something I thought only Mommy and I had, those unheard words, those telegraphing eyes and smiles. I knew that Daddy was jealous. He felt left out, just like I did right now.

Mommy gave me a fluttering smile that brought me no comfort. When I didn't change my expression, her eyes skipped guiltily away. *There is so much she's hiding*, I thought, *so much both of them are hiding*. School and help with my homework, shopping and dreams of future happiness discussed at dinners—none of it drove the gloom away. If it was beautiful outside, there were still heavy clouds over our house and me! I felt like I was ready to explode. I think Nattie saw that first.

"I'm going to do dinner tonight. One of my French specialties," Nattie said, then gathered her real estate material and left for the kitchen. I watched her leave, my heart suddenly beating faster when I looked at my mother.

"What happens now," Mommy began as soon as Nattie left, "is the legal paperwork for our divorce is drawn up. One of the things that looks like it will happen is we won't live here anymore."

"We'll be moving to Nattie's house?"

"Yes, but not immediately, and although it seemed like she was joking, your room will look the same. You saw her room: it's bigger than yours and has nicer windows. I think her bathroom is nicer, too. That will all be yours. The Gleesons always had the nicest house on the street."

"Who will live here? Will Daddy live here?"

I was hoping for that, at least. If he was close by, he couldn't avoid seeing me.

"No. The bank will put it up for sale, and someone is sure to buy it right away. It will feel strange for both of us, but let's not think about that right now. We have lots to do. We'll be so busy that we won't have time to feel sad. You'll see."

"When will Daddy come see me? Did you tell him about school, how well I was doing?"

"I don't know when he'll see you, Caroline. He didn't ask anything, nor did he say anything at the meeting or afterward. It's not your fault. He's not blaming you for anything. You know him. He's just focused on what he thinks he has to do. Maybe soon . . . when these things calm down . . ."

She sighed and looked down. This was what she meant by him needing time? Didn't he worry that I would slouch or go to school with my clothes not perfect, brush my teeth too quickly, or stay up too late? How could he not ask questions about me?

I sat back. This was too much to understand. I felt like crying, but I didn't want to cause my mother to feel worse than she was feeling. She rose and came over to sit beside me, taking my hand.

"Look," she said. "I don't like to or want to get you to dislike your father. I'm not going to tell you all sorts of bad things about him so you'll love me more or anything, but a big reason he's so angry at me is just like a puppeteer would be angry at his puppet for no longer needing his strings. He's not the kind of man who can tolerate that, and his frustration and rage about it . . ."

"Spills over on me, too," I said, nodding. Telling me it didn't would just be a way to make me feel better, keep me in the fairy tale.

She smiled softly and brushed my hair.

"You are so smart, Caroline. Unfairly, yes, it does at the moment. I think he was always a little jealous of how close we are. He just doesn't expect you will see his side of things. I'm sure he'll get over it and realize how important you are to him, too."

"But you told Nattie he is with someone else. Who is that? Does she have a daughter?"

She sucked in her breath like she was about to go under the water at Grandfather Sutherland's pool. "That was stupid of me to blurt, but I was just angry. When you're angry, you almost always do the wrong thing. I don't know everything about it; I didn't want to hear it, either, even though . . . even though, under the circumstances, he has a right to find his own happiness. What I think is he's been seeing the TSA agent he was helping to train at the airport.

"Sometimes, when a marriage splinters like cracked glass, both people keep secrets. It makes them feel better. Oh, this is so complicated," she said, turning away as if there was someone else with us and she needed more help explaining things to me.

"But is there another daughter?"

"I don't know very much about it. He should really be the one to tell you."

"When?"

"When he wants to, Caroline. I can't force him to do it."

"Maybe Nattie can find out more. She has important friends, right? She got you your lawyer."

"Oh, Caroline. We can't ask her to do that. You wouldn't want her to feel like a sneak, right?"

"Right," I said, but with disappointment.

"Meanwhile, everything will be fine," she said. "I promise. Nattie will keep teaching you French. We'll take more trips on weekends and shop, shop, shop. Nobody will be pacing the halls impatiently, rushing us. I'm going to start studying real estate with Natalie. You'll help me with that, too. We'll be redoing the Gleeson house, an entire makeover. We'll have lots to do."

Lots to do? I thought. But what should I do to stop from crying every time I saw an airplane coming in to land or one taking off? I bit down on my lip. Mommy hugged me. My arms were limp at my sides. Whenever I looked back at our house after we moved out, I was sure I'd see us three, the Robot Family, laughing and singing in the magic ball with snowflakes floating around us.

I wished I could truly share in the excitement Nattie and Mommy seemed to feel. They skipped over the sadness and anger easily. In an hour we'd be having dinner, and all these terrible thoughts would be put in a closet. Just today, Nattie told me the story of the Three Musketeers and said that's who we'd become. "We'll do everything together," she promised. "Everything to help each other. One for all and all for one. Okay?"

I didn't say okay. Didn't she understand? The more we did together, the further away my father would drift from me. I knew that. I was sure both Mommy and Natalie knew it, too. They would just ignore it, push it aside like one of those dangling spiderwebs. Maybe they wouldn't see them after a while, but I knew in my heart that I always would.

8

A little more than a week later, we began to move into Nattie's house. My mother had made it sound like we wouldn't leave that soon, but she received a letter from Grandfather Sutherland's bank, and whatever it said made her and Nattie so angry that they both ranted about the power men had over women. I heard Nattie call Mr. Milton and raise her voice when he told her that he was unable to do much about the bank's decision.

"But break his balls about something, John!" she shouted, and hung up. I would swear I saw smoke stream out of her ears. She and Mommy went right to the bar to have a drink. They didn't ask me to join them, and I was afraid to go near them. Nattie was rattling off stories about times she had been mistreated in the diplomatic corps.

After a while they calmed down and just laughed and hugged. How could they be so angry and then so happy? I wondered, and went off to my room, not to pout so much as to think deeply about what was happening to me. My father was gone, and my mother seemed to enjoy Nattie's company more than mine. Other things were disappearing, like the hours we had spent together reading to each other aloud. Whether he was pretending or not, I thought Daddy had enjoyed hearing us. However, even the work we would do together around the house dwindled. Before we left, we still had early fall leaves to rake, and many of the windows needed washing.

"Why leave things so nice for the bank?" Nattie said, but except for doing some specialty cooking and helping to clean up in the kitchen, she didn't like to do any housework.

More than once I had heard Daddy say that Nattie, being in the diplomatic corps, had everything done for her, especially in France. Mommy told him that when she was growing up at Sutherland, she did, too. She had told me so many times, but she didn't sound like someone bragging about it. In fact, I wondered if that was why she wanted to do everything for our home herself. She tried to make it all be different, even how our house was cleaned.

But lately, she also blamed Daddy for her housework, telling Nattie, "He wanted to keep me locked away so I wouldn't develop an independent career, just like my father stifled my mother's attempt at any independence. She couldn't even write a check! And if she tried to change anything, even move an ashtray in his office, he would go into a tirade, ranting about how it was upsetting for him to not have things in their proper place."

For a moment I thought about Daddy and how intent he had been about where his things were, especially in the bathroom. Lately, when Mommy talked about him, she made it sound like Daddy instead of Uncle Martin was Grandfather Sutherland's son.

"Some men are like that," Nattie agreed. "It's part of their DNA. Even now, with all the progress we've made, there are still areas in this country where women are treated like possessions and not people." But she did add, "Caroline benefited by your being here. Don't belittle that." Then she laughed and said, "I often wished I had a reason like her to stay home."

"Really?" Mommy asked, looking a little skeptical.

"Really. I even considered adopting at one point, but then I realized, with my life, I wouldn't be much of a mother. Nothing like you are," she added.

"I guess everyone thinks about being someone else at one time or another," Mommy said. She wasn't wrong. At this moment, I was.

Thinking about wishes usually turned Mommy and Nattie silent for long moments. Were they regretting, dreaming, or just out of things to say to each other? I was certain no other girl my age watched and listened to her mother as much as I did mine. Of course, few had as much of a reason. So much of what Nattie and my mother had done had changed and would change my life.

It wasn't long after Nattie had called Mr. Milton and I had retreated to my room that my mother came with the first empty carton. There were many stacked in the garage in anticipation of our moving. They had ordered some and brought some home from stores while I was at school. This one was filled with Bubble Wrap.

"We're not going to rush moving to Nattie's house despite my father's bank, but we'll do a little every day so it won't seem like such a big move. We're not taking any furniture other than your bed," she told me, and set down the carton.

"How fast will we move?"

"There's a lot to do at Nattie's house as well as our packing. We'll do all the things that are most important to you first," she said, "and wrap them carefully so nothing gets broken or chipped."

She illustrated what she meant using my first doll. It was a baby doll in a pink outfit, with a matching hat and booties. It lay on a soft blanket with the baby bottle and pacifier. The pacifier had been my real one, saved along with my first baby shoes. As she talked and wrapped all of it, I couldn't help but remember how my doll had been so important to me. I recalled how I would imitate my mother, even trying to match her voice.

I stared at the carton but didn't leap to help. I knew she was waiting for me to jump right in, but this was the beginning of saying goodbye to my room, despite her and Nattie's promise that they would move it inch by inch into Nattie's house and what had been her room. It was going to be one of the saddest things to happen since Daddy left. Hadn't Nattie told me how important your first room was?

I couldn't stop the rush of sorrow threatening to drown me. My mother paused when she saw my lips trembling and the tears soaking my eyes. They were poised to explode down my cheeks. I quickly closed my eyes to shut them in.

"Oh, Caroline, please don't be unhappy. We're going to have so much fun duplicating your room. Because it will now be bigger, we'll have to get you more shelves and clothes to fill all the extra space, including new shoes. That's exciting, isn't it?"

Was it? Could it ever be? It was almost like saying, *Daddy's gone, but we'll get you a puppy, something you always wanted.* At this point, I bet I could get her to buy me anything I wanted. But that would be like trying to fool myself, I thought. Things didn't really heal; they didn't even plug holes. They just distracted for a moment.

Although it hadn't occurred to me to wonder about, she added, "Money is not going to be a problem for us. Daddy will still be giving us money, and we will have what is ours, but Natalie has inherited a lot and has always earned a good salary, saving a lot.

"I don't want you to believe that money solves every problem, however. That's my father's philosophy, not mine. Yes, it will make things easier, and we'll always be able to buy you what you need. We'll be able to travel and go to restaurants. We won't have to worry about anyone else telling us what to do or not do. We won't be silly, of course, but we'll be . . . more than safe.

"But real happiness comes from having love and being satisfied with yourself, not from your bank account or your stock portfolio."

She was avoiding the real question, I thought.

"Doesn't Daddy love me anymore?" I asked, seeing the hole to charge through. I had thought about it often during the past few weeks. He still hadn't called or come to see me. The legal work was done. What reason could he have?

Mommy pulled her hand away and even took a step back as if she had come too close to a fire.

"Yes, yes, of course. He's just confused and angry right now. It will settle down, and he'll wake up one morning crying for you. I'm sure," she said.

I swallowed back my sob and nodded, but I wanted to ask, *Why isn't he crying for me now?* How could I be expected to care about new things? Our lives were changing, drastically and so dramatically that the word *Daddy* was becoming unspeakable in our house, and painful for me even to hear in school. She stared a moment and then moved to hug and hold me.

"I need you to be strong for us both," she said. "I want to cry, too, but we can't."

Why do you want to cry? I thought. *You have Nattie, and you never say anything that indicates regret over Daddy's wanting a divorce and our life changing. You aren't even upset about how angry Grandfather Sutherland and Grandmother Judith are. You don't cry about Uncle Martin and Aunt Holly having nothing to do with us. You rant and rave about it all, but you don't cry, not like I cry.*

She released me, and I tried to smile because I knew that was what would make her feel better and not let her believe that I was angry at her. I suppose I was, just like she had predicted I might be, but I tried not to let her see it, and I tried hard not to let myself feel it.

"We'll wait a little longer to start the packing," she decided. "I know what to do instead. Help me make your favorite cake for tonight's dessert. You'll mix the flour and the chocolate icing, okay?"

"It won't be French," I said, and she lost whatever hopeful smile she had. A flash of rarely seen anger toward me flushed her face for a moment. I guess I sounded a bit sarcastic, like Daddy.

"It'll be us, Caroline. That's more important," she said, almost in a stranger's voice. Then she smiled again and held out her hand. "C'mon, let's get to it."

I know I had sounded more like my father than like her, and it had been like a stab to her heart, but I couldn't help it. Shouldn't I sound like him? Ever? Daddy was never going to be out of me, even if Mommy and I were gone from his life. Despite what Mommy just promised, I couldn't help but wonder if I inherently knew the real reason Daddy was avoiding me. Wasn't it possible that when parents got divorced, they hated the way their children resembled their ex-husband or ex-wife? These thoughts bounced around in my head like the little ball in the small pinball toy Daddy had bought me three years ago for my eleventh birthday.

Would we Bubble Wrap it carefully, too?

I tried to forget all my questions and help make the best vanilla cake with chocolate icing ever. Natalie said it was wonderful and kept giving me compliments, but I couldn't help but believe much of what she said was meant to prevent me from being sad, keep me from missing Daddy, and convince me to be happy I was in a new kind of family. I didn't like her less since all this had happened, but it would be a lie to say I liked her more.

For the next few days, while I was at school, Nattie and Mommy were busy replicating my room in Nattie's house. They had the walls painted the same shade of warm pink and somehow found a crystal chandelier identical to the one that hung in the center of the ceiling. By the time it came to actually bringing my things over, my collectible dolls, the plane

Daddy had given me, all my clothes, Nattie's room had been made over to mine. Almost a week later, Mommy announced at dinner that tomorrow the movers would bring my bed and that would be the official first day in our new home.

That was also done while I was at school. Mommy and Nattie decided to pick me up, their faces full of excitement, both eager to surprise me. Nattie said it was like an inauguration or something, and driving into her driveway was something special this day.

"We just think we should all be together when you see it," she said.

I don't think any ride from school felt stranger than this one, because this time we drove past our house and pulled into Nattie's driveway. That was why they wanted to be with me, for sure, I thought. There was room for Mommy's car in the garage. Nattie had sold her parents' car right after her father had died.

When they brought me to look at my room, I know I didn't have the reaction they were both hoping to see. I knew from the way their smiles faded. I couldn't help it; it was all just unreal, almost like a very strange dream. In it I was being lifted out of my old body and placed in a new one. All this that they had done was an effort to have me believe nothing had changed for me.

But everything had.

That night my mother knew what I felt; I didn't have to lie and pretend I was happy, that all was okay. She sat with me until I fell asleep. She never stopped talking, describing how they, we, were going to change Nattie's house continually to feel more like a new house, our house. All of Nattie's parents' clothes and shoes, even some of their jewelry, had been donated to charities, and she and Nattie had already shopped for new furniture, again giving the old to charities.

"You won't even recognize it from what it was," she promised, offering me this stream of optimism with a weak, fluttering smile. I knew she wished she had a magic wand to wave, but I was too tired and confused to be hopeful about anything. I was sleeping in my same bed, but I wasn't having the same dreams. Even the stars visible through the bigger windows didn't look like the ones through my old windows. They seemed farther away and less bright. I felt more like I was being swallowed by the new darkness.

Mommy was there when I woke in the morning. For a moment I wondered if she had been there all night. She smiled and helped me choose my clothes for school as if I were years younger.

"You should show off some of your new things," she said.

I knew both of them were working so hard to be cheerful at breakfast. I couldn't change what they saw in my face, not this soon. I even closed my eyes when we drove past our old house on the way to school that morning, as if I was afraid it would look angry.

Whenever I returned from school during the next week, there was always something different, something replaced in Nattie's house. But every time I went to school, I avoided looking at our old house, imagining Daddy at the front door, glaring out angrily at me or working on the grounds, looking upset that Mommy and I had not done it.

I never saw him.

Days later, on the weekend, when I returned from grocery shopping with my mother, I winced when I saw that the FOR SALE sign had gone up. Mommy averted her eyes and immediately started to talk about how we were going to celebrate the holidays. We were obviously not going to Sutherland for Thanksgiving, where Grandfather put on a big celebration, lighting up the property and having a very big Christmas tree and a fancy turkey and ham dinner with white-gloved servants. Mommy said she had never liked it even as a child. "And when Christmas came, my and my brother's gifts were always too practical. Toys and dolls and games were all a 'waste of money.' My mother had to talk our father into getting us bikes!"

Somehow, because of her divorce, my mother was more vociferous about criticizing her father and even her mother. She brought up things I had never heard her mention. It was as if she had opened some door to her childhood memories and they were spilling out in a flood of stored-up rage. No wonder she didn't mind being sent off to private school and was so eager to go to college. What was more surprising probably was that she came home at all. But really, where was she to go? What was she to do? It was like the shoes didn't fit, but you had to wear them or go barefoot.

She and Nattie had decided we would spend Christmas in New York City. "We'll see all the lights and store windows and the biggest Christmas tree in Rockefeller Center. We'll stuff your stockings until they burst."

The final divorce papers arrived four days before Thanksgiving. Mommy told Nattie it was Daddy's last Christmas gift. Even if there was a slight feeling of regret or sadness, it was quickly smothered with talk of a celebration dinner. "Guess where we're going," Mommy said later. Of course, I had no idea. "Le Grand Restaurant," she said. She turned to Nattie and added, "There. Eat your heart out, Morgan."

They both laughed. But I didn't. I didn't laugh at many things they thought were funny. What was funny or strange was how their laughter, their private jokes, and even their hugs caused me to feel even more alone. I kept waiting for Mommy to notice. Maybe she did; maybe she didn't want to.

That week we had our first snowfall. It started lightly enough for us to think it would stop and melt away almost immediately, but Nattie explained that some front had stalled and the snow would continue all that night. In fact, school was canceled. When it stopped, the two of them decided they would do all the shoveling, even clear the driveway. They said I didn't have to do it, but I went out with them to help. Almost immediately, the memories of Daddy, Mommy, and me frolicking in the snow when I was very little returned. From the way she was looking at me, I thought Mommy knew what I was recalling.

Her cheeks were glistening from the cold air, but she didn't look cold until she gazed at me, my hand out, catching the snowflakes.

Then Nattie went, "Wow!"

Mommy turned, and we all looked down the street at our old house. The FOR SALE sign had a small one hanging beneath it. It read SOLD.

It was like a clap of thunder.

We were really gone. Someone else, maybe even another little girl, would be sleeping in my old room. Whoever the new owners were, I was sure they'd never be called the Robot Family.

"Just think, I could have sold that if I was ready," Nattie said, and Mommy laughed, but nervously, her eyes still on me. I continued to shovel snow. Did Daddy know our house was sold? Where was he going to live now?

Maybe because Mommy gave her a look, Nattie didn't mention the house again in front of me. Whoever bought it was taking their time moving in. I looked for signs of them the next day. I even walked up to it quickly. All the curtains were drawn, the shades down, so I couldn't see inside. Maybe the new owners were making it like Mommy and Nattie had remade Nattie's house, I thought, and I ran home before my mother knew I had gone to see.

Two days later, Nattie got her real estate license, and then she and Mommy invited people who worked in real estate to our house for our Thanksgiving dinner. There wasn't even a mention of Grandfather Sutherland's fancy holiday dinners. I couldn't help but wonder if Daddy still had been invited there. My head was always full of questions that I dared not ask for fear of bringing sadness in the front door. With a few words, I could drive smiles underground. And it was obvious: everyone who saw us expected me to look and sound happy.

Not long after we saw that our house was sold, Nattie brought some shocking news home from work. Mommy saw it in her face when she entered the kitchen. I was setting the table.

"What?" she asked.

"Your house was bought by one of your father's shell companies."

"Pardon?"

"There's no family moving into it. Not right away, that is. I think . . ." She paused to look at me. "I think your father just wanted us to see that SOLD sign as soon as possible."

"I'm not surprised," Mommy said. "I imagine he knew we'd find out what he had done. Sick," she said, and returned to preparing dinner.

I wasn't completely sure what that all meant. There was no family moving in? There would be no one sleeping in my room? Ever? I didn't want to ask questions about it. They both avoided mentioning it at dinner. What I did sense was that they were both a little fearful. Grandfather Sutherland was a very powerful man. Who knew what he might do next?

There was a "next," but it wasn't Grandfather Sutherland's doing. It was Daddy's.

It happened ten days after Thanksgiving break. It was flurrying and quite cold. Mommy picked me up at school. Nattie was already working every day, showing houses and condos for sale. Everyone thought it was amazing that she had drawn up her first contract less than a week after she had gotten her license. We all went out to celebrate. We would go out to celebrate almost everything cheerful now. I felt as if the two of them were constantly trying to prove that they were contented, that we were always in high spirits.

Mommy was picking me up alone more since Nattie was working, but this time I could tell something was bothering her; it was the first time in a long time that she looked unable to smile. She would always say, "How was school today?" as soon as she saw me after school. If it was unpleasant for some reason, I would say, "Okay," and she knew something was wrong, but if it was an okay day, I'd say, "Good." Until today, I would never say, "Very good."

What I was eager to tell her was that some of my classmates had become friendlier. It was as if some terrible storm had blown over. There was even a girl who could become my best friend. Her name was Luci, but the other girls nicknamed her Luci-Goosey because of how she kept her dark brown hair and how she waddled a little when she walked. I never called her that, so she began telling me things about herself and her family, the biggest thing being that her aunt, her mother's sister, was married to a woman. She just said it and walked away quickly, not more than an hour ago.

I was going to tell my mother all of this immediately after I got into the car, but before I could, she took a deep breath and said, "Your father is going to Hawaii for the Christmas and New Year's holidays, so you won't see him." She paused, looked away, and then looked back at me sharply. "Actually, he's going for more than just the holidays, Caroline. It's stupid for me to hold back anything now."

I could feel the anger rushing into her face, tightening her mouth and narrowing her eyelids.

"He's moving there with his . . . woman, his TSA trainee," she said, making "trainee" sound like a curse word. "And yes, she was married before and has a daughter a year older than you and a son two years older."

A son was one thing, but a new daughter? I felt like I had just dropped off the edge of the world. I'd had nightmares about this. I never mentioned my suspicions to my mother. I was still at the age when I could believe that if you didn't say something, it wouldn't be true or it wouldn't happen. Mommy had once said, "We all cling to our fantasies for as long as we can." She had smiled and added, "Who really wants to give up Santa Claus?"

Mommy slowed down and pulled off the highway into a sand and gravel road with a sign that read RUNAWAY TRUCK RAMP. She didn't go too far on it before stopping and parking. Then she turned to me and sat back against the door.

"We've always shared secrets, Caroline, and we're not going to stop. It's what mothers and daughters do. We're going to always be able to do that, keep things to ourselves, even from Nattie, which is what I want to do now."

"She doesn't know about Daddy?"

"She knows he's left for Hawaii."

"And his new daughter and son?"

"She knows about them, yes."

"Then what doesn't she know?" I didn't see much of a secret to share.

Mommy took a deep breath and looked up as if she wanted to keep her tears from flowing from her eyes.

"I told you I wasn't going to tell you bad things about your father just so you would love me more during all this, but apparently, I didn't have to plot against him. I didn't have to drive you away from him. He's done that all himself."

"Never calling or coming to see me," I said, nodding.

"Yes, that's what's happened, but you don't know why, and Nattie doesn't know why. I had it out with him before he left. It wasn't a pleasant conversation, not that any have been since . . . since he left us."

She paused. I knew I was holding my breath because my chest began to ache.

"Why?" I managed.

"In his mind, his distorted mind, he thinks we've poisoned you, corrupted you. He thinks that your being with us will change you and maybe has already changed you. He says he knows that's gone on from the start of my relationship with Nattie. He calls us 'man-haters,' but you know that's not true. He thinks you'll never want him, never respect him. I know, I know," she said quickly. "You've done nothing or said anything to give him that idea. It's what's in his mind.

"I think in a sick sort of way this is what he wants to believe to punish me. He wants to blame me and Nattie for the way he thinks you are. He always thought you were closer to me than you were to him, so whatever I do, whatever I say or believe, you'll do, say, and believe. It's complicated, even for me, so I don't expect you to fully understand it. It's all right. All of this will take time.

"I didn't go into detail about our final divorce papers. At the signing, I didn't know everything about him and his plans, but he didn't contest full custody of you. I left the option for him to have you for visits, take you places. He didn't ask for it, but it's there in black and white.

"Someday he might change his way of thinking, but for now, he's made his choices. I'm sorry. I really and truly never intended for this to happen. I did my best with him under the circumstances, but as I said, he's using you to get back at me.

"And back at Nattie," she added, "which is why I wanted to tell you all this without her. It's our secret. If Nattie knew, she would just feel . . ."

"Terrible? Because Daddy doesn't want me because of you and her? She'd feel blamed?"

"Yes, exactly, and he would get what he wants: our misery. He hates that we're happy. He takes it personally, all of it, like it's a stain on his manhood. Can you understand that, understand why this is an important secret for just us?"

I nodded, but I had the strange, contradictory feeling, a Daddy feeling, that part of me I couldn't deny. Would I be so upset if Nattie was unhappy? If she went back to Paris, would I cry? If Mommy and I were alone again, maybe . . . But then I thought about his new daughter as well as a new son and quickly smothered the Daddy feeling.

"Yes, Mommy. It's our special secret. I promise."

She took a deep breath and smiled.

"You are so special, Caroline. Very few girls your age could handle all this. Few adults could handle it," she added.

I wanted to say I couldn't. More important, I didn't want to. I wanted to be just like my classmates. I didn't want only Luci-Goosey as a best friend. I wanted to be popular, too. I knew some of the girls had parties but didn't invite me now. Maybe their mothers and fathers thought like Daddy, thought I might poison or corrupt them.

But I said nothing like that. I swallowed all those thoughts back and asked, "What's her name?"

"Who?"

"His new daughter."

"You know, I don't think he even mentioned it."

"Maybe I'll make up a name for her," I said, and Mommy laughed.

"Okay. We don't want to hurt her, though, do we? No nasty names. I mean, just like you, none of this is her fault."

"I'll still think of a name," I said. "When I think about someone, I like her to have a name."

"Of course." She shrugged. "Who knows? Maybe you'll guess the right one," she said. She reached out to brush my hair and then leaned in to pull me toward her to hold me.

She held me so long I got a little frightened.

"We'd better go, Mommy. A truck might come, and the driver would be very angry. He could even crash into us."

"Yes, yes. You're right. I could get a ticket. Your grandfather would see to it," she said. She looked at me intensely. "Are you okay, Caroline?"

I nodded.

"Let's get a pizza for tonight. We'll surprise Nattie."

She started to back out slowly.

Daddy's new daughter, I thought. I wondered if she had a name that was in a song, just like me. And I wondered if his new son was someone who wanted to be like him.

I tried not to think about any of it, but it was like touching super-glue.

When we got home, Nattie knew Mommy had told me about Daddy going to Hawaii with his girlfriend and her children. She took me aside and told me, "Time will cure all sad things." Maybe that was true for older adults, I thought. Young people my age needed to pretend more, fantasize about themselves, and when reality stopped it, time didn't help.

Minutes and hours didn't silence Daddy's voice or erase the memory of his face. More often than not, I found myself counting steps. I even tried to arrange my bathroom the way he had arranged his. It was truly as if I was looking for ways to defeat time, to cling to memories even when it meant I'd bring back all the sadness.

But now I had so much more to wonder about. What was Daddy doing with his new children in Hawaii, especially his daughter? Was he taking her to the beach, going to stores to buy her things, showing her how to stand straight, and fixing her clothes so she would look perfect? He surely did that with his new son. Did they hate him or love him? None of these questions grew less intense with time. Distractions brought a momentary pause and a flash of a smile, but they didn't cure anything.

It was always worse at night; it was always worse just before going to bed. I was actually afraid of sleep, afraid of the dreams.

How odd, I thought, that there was something I was having trouble remembering: the last time Mommy and I had danced to "Sweet Caroline."

And when I thought about that, I began to make my list of names for Daddy's new daughter. I didn't want her name to be too nice, despite what my mother had said about not blaming her, but the names I found in songs were all good; otherwise, why would any of them be used in a song? I decided to put all the names I found on slips of paper and then put them in a big bowl. I would shake it up, turn it over, spin it, and then, without looking, dip my fingers into it and pluck one out.

I came up with "Lily" and then immediately wished it wasn't her name. I realized that it was too pretty, but I didn't try again. I crunched the paper up and put it in the drawer by my bed. This was a secret I wouldn't share, but I don't think a day went by when I didn't wonder if I had chosen the right one, if maybe it really was her name. Magic could work that way, I thought. Truthfully, I didn't want to know; I didn't want to meet her, and I certainly didn't want Daddy's first call to me to be to tell me about her. For now, and hopefully forever, I wouldn't think about it. It was in my drawer.

I'll just let Mommy and Nattie try to make me happy, I thought.

As it grew closer to the school break for Christmas, Mommy and Nattie worked on the plans for our trip to New York City. After dinner they would spread out pictures and descriptions of sights for us all to review. I had no doubt that they were doing this for me more than for themselves. They had been there. Every time either Mommy or Nattie pointed to something, they would pause to see what my reaction was.

I liked the idea of seeing the big Christmas tree and going to the top of the Empire State Building, but mostly, of course, I liked the thought of shopping in the grand department stores. This week we had shopped for our own Christmas tree and decorated it, just like we used to. I started to wonder if Daddy was decorating a tree with his new son and daughter in Hawaii. I knew Mommy and Nattie could see what I was thinking. They did everything they could to stop me: playing holiday music, singing holiday songs, and dancing.

And they made sure to have me open one of my gifts early.

"You'll need it for our New York trip," Mommy said.

I tore off the wrapping and opened the box to see a watch with a clear strap and a rose-tinted dial.

"Nattie picked it out for you. It shows you world time, time in different countries. Isn't it beautiful?"

"Yes," I said. Mommy strapped it on my wrist.

"Oh, how pretty it looks on you."

"Thank you, Nattie," I said. She hugged me.

"We both paid for it for you. It's a lot like my first watch," she said.

"You'll keep track of time for us in New York," Mommy said. "We can both be so oblivious. We'll need you to watch out for us. 'A child shall lead them,'" Mommy told Nattie.

They laughed. The watch was pretty, maybe prettier than anything Daddy had ever given me. I went to sleep with it still on my wrist. It had an alarm if I wanted to wake up to it. I set it, but I woke up before it went off.

All the preparations were made for our Christmas trip. There were just three more days of school.

I had decided I would become friendlier with Luci-Goosey. I didn't want to beg anyone else to like me as much as she did. We ate our lunches together and walked together to our classes. We were going to share homework and talk to each other on our mobile phones, texting and everything. She really loved my watch. Many of the other girls said something nice about it. Some of them told me I was doing a nice thing being friendlier to Luci-Goosey. They made it sound like an act of charity, which was ironic. Little did they realize that I was getting more out of it than she was.

It seemed funny to think that I was trying harder every day to be happy. Why was it something you had to work at? But that was what I was doing. I was avoiding sad and bad thoughts, just the way you might go inside when a heavy rainstorm or snowfall was starting. *Just go inside*, I thought, *and everything will be all right*. I really began to think so.

But it wasn't going to be. Something more would make sure of that.

Maybe not for a long time.

Maybe not for the rest of my life.

9

The moment our classroom door was opened, my heart began to race. My emotions were on a roller coaster since our wonderful Christmas trip, but this feeling now was more than simply doing the ordinary after so much excitement. This was far darker. Later in my life I would think that I had prophetic powers, whether it was for something good or something bad. It was as telling as someone whispering in my ear, "Beware" or "Be ready to be happy."

Although our teacher, Mrs. Cardin, was trying very hard to keep us interested in the Louisiana Purchase, we were all fascinated with how fast the new snowfall was covering the ground. Occasionally, flurries would streak across our windows. Everyone was anticipating the principal coming on the school intercom system to announce school would be closing early. It was as if the snow paroled us. Our teachers looked as happy as we were with the early releases when they occurred.

However, that wasn't it, not yet. Even though I had never had to see her for anything, I knew Mrs. Mills was the school nurse. She stood in the doorway as if she was going to stop anyone from going in or out, her hand holding the doorframe. There was something about the look on her face that suggested she was the one who needed a nurse. I realized she was keeping herself steady. Her lips moved, but she didn't say anything. Mrs. Cardin stopped talking, and immediately, since they knew each other well and could read each other's faces, she took a deep breath and stepped back as if a gust of wind had come through the opened classroom door. I looked from one to the other. Everyone did. It was that long of a pause.

"Yes, Mrs. Mills?" Mrs. Cardin finally said.

"I need Caroline Bryer," she said. She scanned the room until she saw me. She looked like she was trying to smile but couldn't. I turned to Mrs. Cardin.

"Go on, dear," she said. "Take your books," she added. How did she know I had to do that?

Everyone in the class was staring at me now, questions rippling in waves from their eyes. Was I sick? Why was the school nurse and not the principal's secretary or a student assistant asking for me? Had I missed a required vaccination? I didn't have any more specific knowledge of the situation than any of them had, but I started to cry, my tears pausing on my eyelids. I was, after all, at the center of unusual marriage and family turmoil. Whatever it was, it would put me back into the center of gossip, and the little progress I had made toward becoming accepted and normal in the eyes of my school friends would shatter.

I picked up my books and walked to the doorway. Mrs. Mills put her hand on my shoulder and guided me out to the hallway, closing the door behind her.

"Let's go to my office," she said.

I was afraid to ask why, so I just walked alongside her. Had my father returned? Was he now asking for custody of me? Would I be taken to some courtroom and asked questions like whom I loved better? Should I be happy or sad that my father finally cared? Maybe my mother was here to tell me about the sudden new events. No matter how normal or comfortable Mommy and Nattie were trying to make me feel, there was always an underlying trepidation. Maybe now there was good reason for it. Minds were changed; lawyers were at it again. I'd become the Ping-Pong ball that I had originally feared I'd be.

However, when Mrs. Mills's office came into view, I paused so quickly that I almost fell forward. Actually, I wanted to turn and run in the opposite direction, but my legs felt frozen. In the doorway stood Mrs. Lawson. Although I saw her only when we went to Sutherland and we hadn't been there for quite a while, she wasn't someone easy to forget. She had always looked like an old lady to me. Mommy had told me that she was five when Mrs. Lawson had come to work at Sutherland as her father's head housekeeper. She, too, had always thought of her as being an old lady. She said Mrs. Lawson was only thirty-six at the time, but her hair had begun to turn gray and she didn't do anything to change the color. She always wore it severely pinned back, so severely that it looked like it tightened her eyes and stretched her forehead, a forehead peppered with tiny brown spots, which I thought were faded freckles.

I remembered Mommy asking Daddy, "Why doesn't that woman realize she's making herself look bald in the front, showing so much forehead? She actually is balding, you know, Morgan."

"I doubt she'll ever care to make a fashion statement, Linsey. It doesn't appear to bother your father. He seems to care more about her opinion of things than he does your mother's."

Mommy laughed.

"I used to imagine she was my father's sister pretending to be his head housekeeper."

"Why would she pretend?"

"It was a child's fantasy, Morgan. They're not built on logic. But I imagine yours probably were."

"Yes, mine were more like plans and ambitions than fantasy," he said. He smiled, but Mommy didn't, and she said nothing more about Mrs. Lawson.

After that, I always looked at her hair to see if she had lost any more of it. Often, I studied her so closely that Mommy shook my arm a little and said, "It's not nice to stare at people, Caroline."

I couldn't help but stare at her now. Mrs. Lawson was wearing a long gray raincoat and a shiny black vinyl rain hat, wet from melted snowflakes. She held an umbrella in her right hand. The gray in her hair seemed to have leaked into her face. Her plump cheeks were pale. She never wore lipstick, so her lips resembled dead, dry worms. Despite the plumpness in her cheeks, she had a thin chin that looked like it was being absorbed by the loose skin around her neck.

She was a stout woman, with breasts Mommy said arrived anywhere she was going an hour before the rest of her. Daddy laughed at that. She wasn't very tall, maybe two or three inches taller than I was, but she always seemed a lot taller. Even other servants at my grandfather's house who were six feet tall or so looked like they were shorter than she was. When she spoke, she spoke so low that you had to pay attention. My mother said Mrs. Lawson believed women should not raise their voices; it was unladylike, something that cheapened you. I never saw her laugh, but my mother said Mrs. Lawson always placed her hand lightly over her mouth if she laughed. "Like her laugh would spread germs or something. It always did sound more like a cough to me."

"I've signed her out," she told Mrs. Mills, her voice a little louder and sterner than I recalled. "Where's your coat, Caroline?"

"In my locker," I said. "Where am I going? Where's my mother?"

"Can you get her to her locker," she asked Mrs. Mills, "and have her fetch her coat?" Now she sounded more like my grandfather. His questions seemed always to be orders already suffering from impatience.

"I thought you might want to talk to her in my office," Mrs. Mills said. "I mean, I could be there and—"

"There's no need for that. I'd like to get back to Sutherland before this snowfall gets worse, and there is a lot for me to do."

"Okay. Let's go to your locker, Caroline," Mrs. Mills said. She turned me toward the hallway where my locker was.

"Why is my grandfather's housekeeper here? Why am I going to Sutherland?"

Mrs. Mills stopped and took a deep breath.

"Your mother's been in an accident," she said. "She's taking you to your grandfather, who I imagine will give you the details or whatever. Go on, get your coat," she said, a clear note of anger in her voice.

I saw that whatever she was thinking had put a crimson tint in her cheeks. I moved quickly to my locker. When I took out my coat, I was shaking so hard that it took me three tries to get my hand into the right sleeve. Mrs. Mills was looking down and not at me until she realized I was ready.

"What kind of an accident?" I asked. "Is she all right?"

She put her hand on my shoulder again so I would move along. After we reached Mrs. Lawson, who was standing in the hallway impatiently now, Mrs. Mills turned and hugged me.

"When you return to school," she said, "I will be here for you any time you need me."

When I returned to school? How long was I going to be away?

She stepped back.

"Come along," Mrs. Lawson ordered, and without waiting for me, she started out. I had to walk quickly to catch up. At the doorway, she opened her umbrella. "Just run and get into the limousine."

I recognized Grandfather Sutherland's vintage Rolls-Royce. Daddy always praised it and the way it was being kept up. He said it was a Silver Cloud built in 1961, "but you'd think it was brand-new."

We had been in it the four times Grandfather Sutherland had sent for us to come to one of his special dinners. Daddy said Grandfather Sutherland's driver, Emerson, looked like he had been driving the car since it was built. He was a tall, thin man who had been born in East Sussex, England. He was always immaculately dressed in his uniform and cap. He had a trimmed mustache, as gray as his full head of hair, and dark blue eyes. His face was lean, with sharp creases in his forehead. Ordinarily, he kept his thick lower lip over his upper lip so that it looked like he had only one.

I knew that whenever Grandfather Sutherland went on a trip, especially to England, he always took Emerson along to drive a car. He lived in an apartment above the garage, which my mother said always smelled like fish and chips. She liked him very much, and while she was growing up at Sutherland, she spent more time talking to him than she did to any of the other servants, save the cook, Mrs. Wilson. She told me she would sit and watch him wash and polish the limousine, vacuuming the inside so immaculately he could pick up something with tweezers. While he worked, he told her about his life in England and how he had wanted to be a race car driver when he was younger. Occasionally, she rode along when he had to do some errand. She said he would sing her old English folk songs like "Last of the Summer Wine" and had a deep, melodic voice: "I don't think he ever turned on the radio, but I never cared."

Emerson got out of the limousine quickly as I approached and opened the rear door for me.

"There you go, missy," he said, and closed it. He stood outside in the snow, the flakes soaking his cheeks as Mrs. Lawson took her time walking from the school's front entrance. She looked like she thought she was walking on ice. As soon as she was close enough, Emerson opened the rear door for her, too. I moved to the left. She handed him her umbrella and slipped in, muttering something to herself about all she had to do.

Emerson got in, put the umbrella on the passenger-side floor, and drove off.

"Just mind those roads," Mrs. Lawson told him.

"Aye, Mrs. Lawson. My very thought."

She grunted. And then finally turned to me. I was scrunched back as far as I could be, my legs dangling over the seat. I clung to my books as if they were shielding me from her.

"So here it is, plain and simple," she began. "Your mother was driving on the highway, and an eighteen-wheeler tractor trailer jackknifed the back end, swatting her car like a fly.

"There is some question about the truck driver's sobriety, but whether or not he was inebriated will not change the outcome."

What was she saying?

"My mommy . . . isn't hurt, is she?"

"Hurt?" She grunted a "Heh," sounding like the start of a laugh. "No, she's not hurt. She's dead," she said. "They told us she died instantly."

My whole body seemed to turn to ice and then to fire. I was squeezing myself so tightly that I couldn't breathe. What was she telling me? I wouldn't hear my mother's voice ever again? She wouldn't hold me and brush my hair with her fingers? We wouldn't share secrets and talk about them? That couldn't be true. She was waiting at home for the time to come for me. We were going to bake an apple pie today.

"You're lying," I spat at her. "You always say mean things. Mommy told me."

"I only speak the truth. Some people think that's mean, but it's their fault, not mine. Your grandfather told me to tell you everything before we arrived at Sutherland. He's dealing with the news in his own way. No man has better control of his emotions. Your grandmother, however, as expected, is collapsed in her room and being nursed and treated by the family doctor, Dr. Immerman. Your aunt and uncle have been informed, as well as your cousin Simon. They will all be over tonight to offer whatever comfort they can to your grandmother. Your grand-father will be planning your mother's funeral with his CEO, Franklin Butler. I don't have any details to give you yet. Your room has been prepared."

She recited it all like a memorized speech and then took a deep breath.

The air between us was filled with sparks and crackles. It was too hot to breathe. I saw that Emerson was watching me in the rearview mirror.

None of this could be true. How could my room be prepared? My mother had done something else to anger my grandfather. He was getting back at her through me.

"I want to go home," I said as calmly but as firmly as I could. "I'll tell my mother about this. You're going to be in big trouble for deliberately scaring me."

She did that aborted laugh again.

"You have no home, Caroline, other than Sutherland. You don't realize it now, but you're very lucky to have a place there. There is no other place for you. Your father is gone. He was informed about all that's happened, and he's fully in agreement with your grandfather. I'm sorry, but that is all truth. Call it mean if you want, but it doesn't change any of it."

"Where's my mother?" I cried.

"She's in a morgue, a place for dead people, until we get her body to the funeral parlor to prepare for her funeral. When I was a little girl, my mother fell in our house and banged her head badly. She died, and almost immediately my father told me everything truthfully, as I'm telling you. In fact, he told me much sooner than you're being told.

"There is no other way to tell it. She was in an accident, and she's gone. Waiting any longer to tell you the truth would be ridiculous, es-pecially at your age. Your grandfather will take care of you. Fortunately, he's healthy enough to do it, with my help and the help of others, of course."

I wanted to open the door and jump out of the car. I would run and run to get as far away from what she was saying as I could. Instead, I started to cry, my body shaking with the sobs. I turned away from her.

"Maybe we should pull over or take her to a doctor first," Emerson said.

"A doctor? For what? Grief? Just drive. She'll survive. We all do."

I curled up more so I could press my face as deeply into the corner of the seat as I could. I didn't want to hear her voice. *I know*, I thought, *I'll call Nattie right away, and she'll come and get me and tell my mother what a horrible thing they tried to do to me.*

I turned sharply on her.

"Where's Nattie?" I asked.

"Nattie? Who is that?"

"My mother's friend."

"Oh, that one. She didn't die, but she's in the hospital, and it's doubtful she'll live. If she does, she'll probably be maimed and crippled for life. There will be little she can do for you, little she can do for herself. If I was religious, I'd say God had spoken."

"Lightening up a bit," Emerson said. He was talking about the snowfall, but I thought he might want to stop her from saying any more. Maybe he was really telling her to lighten it up, not that she looked like anyone but my grandfather could tell her what to do.

"Just keep your eyes on the road, Emerson. One accident a day is enough for this family."

I closed my eyes. I could hear Mommy singing along with Neil Diamond: "*Look at the night and it don't seem so lonely . . .*"

I felt myself smile and sink deeper into the seat or into myself.

So this was why Mrs. Mills said when I came back she'd be there for me.

I closed my eyes hard, squeezing everything Mrs. Lawson had said, squishing her face and her words. When I opened them, I saw that the snow had stopped before we arrived.

The main gate, with the name SUTHERLAND looking larger and more golden than ever above it, began opening before we turned into the long driveway circling to the grand front entrance of my grandfather's mansion. With the new snow still firm, everything was glistening in the afternoon sunshine that had broken through the clouds as if someone had turned on a spotlight to dramatize my arrival.

Although glittering, the gray-silver stone exterior and the grand, oval-shaped copper and mahogany doors looked cold and unwelcoming, resembling those of the castles that housed evil kings and princes, witches, and goblins in my childhood fantasy books. For the first time ever, I didn't want to go through those doors.

Emerson pulled up to the front and stopped. He got out quickly to open the door for Mrs. Lawson and then came around to open my door.

I didn't move.

"Best you come out and get warm in the house," Emerson said.

"I'm not standing out here in the cold waiting for you," Mrs. Lawson added. She started for the door.

I still didn't move. Emerson held out his large hand with his long fingers, that blue onyx ring on his pinkie finger. He smiled, but he looked more like he was going to cry, too.

"It's best for now, missy," he said. "I'll walk in with you."

I looked at the mahogany doors again. *If I walk through them, I will be admitting my mother did die.*

"Your mum would want you to be warm and safe," Emerson said. "By going into your grandfather's house, you're just going to do what she would want. She wouldn't want you out in the cold, aye?"

My whole body ached from holding back my sobs. More stunned

than willing, I took his hand and stepped out. Mrs. Lawson was already in the house.

Never before did the entry look so vast and dark to me. All the Christmas and holiday decorations were gone. The peekaboo sun had gone under a cloud, and the lights in the house looked dimmed in mourning. It was so quiet, too. My eyes went to the large portrait of Grandfather's father, Raymond Sutherland. It was high up on the wall at the foot of the stairway. His light brown hair looked grayer and the sharp creases from the middle of his nose to the corners of his mouth looked deeper than I remembered. It was almost as if the painting could age. His eyes had a greenish tint, and because of the height of the portrait and the way his eyes looked down as if he was staring at someone's feet, I always felt a little intimidated and normally avoided gazing at the picture too long. It seemed his eyes could follow me as I walked along the entry or started up those stairs.

He was taller than Grandfather and in the portrait, at least, looked sturdier, with wider shoulders and a thicker neck. There wasn't a crease in the jacket of his satin tuxedo, and the rose bow tie was perfectly tied and set. Mommy remembered him only as an elderly man in a wheelchair, shouting orders like the captain of a pirate ship. She said he had long arms, and although he had lost his balance and his legs were weak, she recalled how he could lift himself straight up, almost into a standing position, when he was angry.

"I don't think there was much loss of love between my father and his father," she once said. "They tolerated each other like employees of a company who were forced to. That's what this family is and always was and will be, a company."

I wasn't sure what all that meant at the time and didn't want to ask. It didn't sound nice.

"You're going to the rear of the house," Mrs. Lawson said.

For a few moments, I didn't know where she was. Her voice came from the entrance to the hallway ahead. She had crossed the large entryway quickly. "I have a lot to do for your grandfather, so I need you to come along quickly," she said.

Why wasn't there anyone else around? Why did her voice seem to echo as if the entryway was empty and there was no one else home? Was it simply because I had never heard her raise her voice like this? I looked up at Emerson. His long fingers were still firmly around my hand.

"Let go of her, Emerson," she ordered.

He did and patted me on the shoulder.

"I'll see you soon, missy," he said warmly. I watched him walk out. *He's not taking me home; he's not telling me it was all a mistake.*

"Where is everyone?" I asked. I was hoping to see my grandmother, Judith. I didn't think about what Mrs. Lawson had said about her having to have a nurse. She always had a smile for me. I looked at the stairway. Maybe she'd appear and ask, "What's going on here? What is this nonsense you've been telling Caroline?"

But no one appeared, not Mrs. Wilson from the kitchen nor any of the maids or other employees. I looked to the right to what I knew was Grandfather's office. His large scrolled oak doors were shut. He must have known I was here, but he didn't come out to see me. Could it be that he didn't want me to see him crying?

"I want to see my grandfather."

"Oh, will you just come along," Mrs. Lawson said, stamping her right foot. "I told you he was occupied. You don't disturb your grandfather. Now," she said impatiently, and poked her index finger at the floor.

I walked toward her, and she turned immediately, practically jogging down the hallway, past the large dining room, the kitchen, the study, and the entertainment room. She reached the corner and waited. As I approached, she turned left and started down a corridor I had never walked. At the end was another set of double doors. Without any windows in this hallway or light above the doors, they looked like they were made of metal. She opened the door on the right and turned. Light spilled out from inside, casting her elongated shadow over the hallway floor. Her head seemed to have shrunken on her large body.

"This will be your room," she said. She clapped her hands. It sounded like gunshots in a movie. "Come along. The bed is prepared. There are clothes for you to wear. You'll take a bath and put on what I lay out for you on your bed. Then you will wait until I come for you. Well, please move along. I told you. I have things to do for your grandfather."

"What clothes?"

She didn't reply. She stepped into the room and waited for me. I stopped in the doorway and looked at the king-size four-poster bed. The posts were tall, with what looked like crowns at the top. They were delicately carved in a dark wood. The shaped headboard resembled two seals facing each other. There were large white pillows and a white comforter with a dull brown blanket folded at the foot of the bed.

The bed was at the center of the enormous room, back against the far wall. There were two fluffy-looking light brown area rugs on both sides. The floor was an otherwise cold gray tile with swirls of darker gray. Matching nightstands were on either side of the bed, with lamps whose shades were a faded yellow color. There was nothing on any of the walls, not a picture or anything.

The matching long bureau was on the right. It had a half dozen drawers. There wasn't anything on top of it, and there was no mirror in the room. In the right corner of the room there was a desk that reminded me of an old-time school desk and chair I had seen in pictures. It looked like there was even an inkwell in it.

It appeared to be a room that hadn't been used for years and years, even though it seemed spotlessly clean. I saw that the black curtains were open and the shades were almost fully raised on the bay window to my right.

"Well, come in," Mrs. Lawson said. She went to the left and opened a door and flipped a switch. "This is your bathroom. All the clean towels and washcloths are there along with shampoo and soap. There is a new toothbrush and toothpaste, the same one I use, actually. You'll find a new hairbrush as well. In time we'll see what else you need."

"Where are my things?" I asked, almost smiling at her. If I was being moved, someone would have brought my things.

"You don't need any of your things."

She crossed the room to the wall closet and opened it to pluck out a dark blue dress. There were other dresses, blouses, and skirts. I didn't recognize any of the clothes.

"Whose clothes are those?"

"They're yours now. Everything was dry-cleaned or washed and pressed. Your underthings are in the bureau as well as socks. You can choose your own underwear and socks; the socks should match your dress, of course. If you're cold, there are sweaters hanging in the closet as well; almost any of them will be appropriate. And there are two pairs of slippers, one in the closet and one by the bed. We'll see about more new shoes later. For now, there is a pair to match your dress."

"What if they don't fit?"

"They'll fit well enough," she said firmly. "After you bathe and dress, you will wait here until I fetch you for the family gathering."

"What about my other things, besides clothes?"

"They've been gathered and donated to charity," she said bluntly. "It's as your grandfather wished."

"What? That can't be. There are things my parents gave me. My father gave me a model plane and—"

"You won't have any need for those things now. They don't come from a good period of your life anyway. In time, you won't think of them at all. It will be like you were reborn, and you will be grateful for it."

"What are you talking about? What does all that mean? How can I be reborn? Why did you bring me here? My mother can't be dead and all that done so quickly."

"When your grandfather wants something done, it's done quickly."

"Why? Why would he do those things?"

"Oh, I just don't have the patience for nonsense right now," she said, and sighed. "Just do what you're told to do, and that will make it easier for everyone, including yourself."

"I don't believe you. I don't believe you about anything," I said.

I turned to run out.

"Don't dare leave this room!" she snapped. Her words were like whips. I stopped. "I'll call your grandfather's security, and they won't be so gentle bringing you back here."

The threat was frightening. I fought back tears.

"Mrs. Mills will tell my mother that you took me here. She knows about an accident. She said my grandfather would tell me more, not you. And I'll go see Nattie if she's in the hospital. She'll tell me the truth."

"Whatever additional details are necessary for you to know will be told at the family gathering."

She started for the door, then stopped.

"Take my advice and do not mention this Nattie person, especially in front of your grandfather."

When she left, she closed the door sharply. It sounded like she had locked it. For a few moments, I didn't move. I gazed around this large room with its bleak walls. Why had I never seen it? Whose was it?

I looked around the room again. It was barren and cold. None of this was making any sense to me. Mrs. Lawson had said the clothes and the shoes that were already here would fit well enough. How could that be?

I knew my grandfather could snap his fingers and get anything he wanted or have anything he wanted done quickly. I didn't doubt that, but this just seemed to be too much.

Actually, it did feel like someone had planned all this. Maybe this was a plan my grandfather and father had concocted. Maybe my mother knew nothing about it. *She'll find out, and when she does . . . Nattie will call someone important, more important than Grandfather, and they will all be sorry.*

I couldn't wait for that, hoped for that.

I went to the bed and held up the dress. I imagined it would fit me, but it was such a blah dark gray color without any style. It looked more like a sack. I dropped it and sat on the bed, staring at the door.

But what if what I hoped was true really wasn't? What if this was real? Emerson wouldn't hurt Mommy or me. He wouldn't go along with a horrible lie. My heart sank. I couldn't pretend it wasn't true.

Why would my father agree to any of this? Why was he so angry and refusing to care about me now? I wanted to hear his voice, to hear him say with his TSA authority that all would be okay. He would take charge, just like he always did. When did I ever need him more? Didn't he realize that?

I took more deep breaths to keep from crying. He had shown me how to do that. "Caroline, when you get nervous or frightened, take deep breaths and think. Tell yourself to stay calm. Go through your checklist. What did you do that was wrong? What could you have done better?"

"I didn't do anything wrong, Daddy. There was nothing for me to do better."

Silence made the air feel heavy and thick. I thought about running out, running away from Sutherland, maybe hitchhiking to get home. But how would I get past the main gate? Where would I go if I went home and found no one there? What would I do? Nevertheless, I got up and went to the door. For a few moments I just stood there listening. I heard nothing.

Was I so far away that I wouldn't, and no one would hear me? I tried to open the door, but as I suspected, it was locked.

Why?

I started to cry again and returned to the bed. I didn't realize how exhausting my crying and cringing had been. *Mommy*, I thought. *I need you. You can't be dead. Please don't be dead.*

I curled up almost as tightly as I had in the limousine and closed my eyes. Maybe if I slept and woke up, this would all be gone.

10

I thought I was dreaming that I was experiencing an earthquake, like the one I had seen in a movie.

But it was Mrs. Lawson shaking me hard, her hand gripping my shoulder so tightly that it hurt.

My eyelids fluttered, and I saw her angry face only inches from mine. Her pale lips were stretched like a rubber band close to breaking in her grimace. I imagined them snapping and curling into her cheeks. Her brown eyes dominated because of how wide with surprise and rage they were. Her bosom barely shook with her efforts, making it look hard and uncomforting. This close I could see what looked like peck marks in her face and little blue veins under her eyes.

"How dare you defy me," she said. "You haven't bathed and changed. Everyone has arrived. They're waiting on you. Are you trying to make me look like a fool?"

My lips quivered. I couldn't think. The memories of what had happened seemed to rush out and bunch up: leaving my classroom, seeing her in Mrs. Mills's doorway, Mrs. Mills's hug, those horrible words spoken in the limousine, and Emerson's look of pity and sorrow. Sleep had only postponed reality. Mommy had died. But how could she? How could someone so beautiful and kind be gone, and this harsh, cruel, and ugly person be left in charge of me? Her fixed scowl shook me inside.

Daddy's words about death came at me like a loud echo: "Most people convince themselves nothing bad will happen to them. Ignoring something, Caroline, doesn't make it go away. Don't believe that junk about turtles living longest. They've got to come out sometime, and when they do, they're not properly prepared. The odds of being hit by lightning are one in five thousand, so unless it's a bolt of lightning, you could prevent it."

He meant it to be a comfort, but also a warning. Why was my mother the one in five thousand? Why wasn't it Mrs. Lawson?

She straightened up. I ground the sleep and disbelief out of my eyes. Despite the surging memories, I didn't know where I was for a few moments. The late afternoon's waning sunshine drove gray shadows through the bay windows. The walls and floor looked even colder and more uncomforting than they had when I had first been brought here. But I was tired of crying, especially in front of her. Tears brought no compassion, no sympathy. It was as though my mother's death had put more responsibility and work on her and that was all she regretted.

"There is no time for you to bathe now. Just take off those silly school clothes and put on the dress and the shoes."

Silly school clothes? These were the clothes my mother had chosen for me and my teachers had complimented.

I stared at her in silence. I didn't know whether I should cry or scream. What I really wanted to do was run out and find my way home. When I arrived, Mommy would be waiting. "Where have you been?" she'd say, and hug me. "I told you she was all right," Nattie would say. I felt myself becoming stronger and even smiled.

"Are you an idiot child? Now!" she said in her fire-ice voice. I winced, but I didn't move. "Did you hear what I said? This is not the time to show that you are dumb and stupid."

"I'm not dumb and stupid."

She shook her head.

"Not dumb and stupid? Do you think I can just walk out this door and leave you wallowing in here? Your grandfather has already laid down specific instructions for you to follow. Your life has changed and will change even more. Your time to be a child is gone. You're not going to be planted in the sunshine and watered like some fragile flower.

"Outside that door," she said, jabbing her forefinger at it, "hard, cold truth stands waiting. Whining, sobbing, regressing back into a baby, will find you no sympathy. Everyone is suffering in his or her own way. Of course we're all stunned. We live very organized lives and fulfill expectations. Fortunately, you have a grandfather who never loses his perspective and composure, despite all your mother has done to this family."

"What did she do?"

"I have no time for this. You will throw some cold water on your face, straighten up your hair, change your clothes and shoes, and walk out with me to be with your family during this time of great need and heavy responsibilities. You will not upset everyone with your tears and cries. You will sit like a young lady and listen to your grandfather's instructions. Then, along with everyone else, you will eat your dinner. Food is always fed to grief.

"We are all keenly aware of how bad your upbringing has been lately, but all that will be remedied as quickly as possible."

Bad? Why would my life need to be remedied? She made it sound like I had been sick and it was my mother who had made me ill. I wanted to scream back at her to tell her how sick she was, sick and terrible. I didn't speak, but I could see she didn't like my staring at her. I was sure she could read not only my disbelief in what she was saying and what was being done to me but my disgust for her. She stiffened and glared back at me, stern, forbidding. She looked like she wanted to slap me or beat me with something.

"Get up!"

She clapped her hands. The sound felt like a punch to my stomach. She stepped forward, looking like she would pull me up by my hair.

I rose.

"Now, into the bathroom. Wash your face and hands, and hang up the towel properly. I will stand right here and wait, but do not dilly-dally. If your mother's death will mean anything to you, it will be to emphasize how important our time is and how idiotic it is to fritter away any of it. As your grandfather says, the clock never goes backward. A minute wasted is a minute lost forever.

"I assume you can take care of your bathroom needs without me supervising, although I'm sure it wasn't uncommon for you, your mother, and her . . . friend or whatever she called herself to parade before each other when you did personal things."

"What? Personal things? We didn't parade."

"Go on," she said, pointing at the bathroom. "Don't argue."

It's really a waste of time to talk to her, I thought. She was right about that. I went in and did wash my face. I was surprised that there was no mirror above the sink. How was I supposed to brush my hair? Nevertheless, I did as best I could, and then I walked back to the bed. She was standing at the bay window with her back to me and her arms folded. Her wide shoulders were hoisted so that it looked like she had no neck.

She turned quickly.

"Oh, will you move," she said.

I didn't feel comfortable getting undressed and dressed in front of her. I thought about it, scooped up the dress, and returned to the bathroom.

I heard her thin, sarcastic laugh.

"I do hope they didn't put a tattoo on your rear end and that's what you're trying to hide," she said. "If they did, we'll have it removed, and it will be painful."

What? What tattoo? Why would Mommy or Nattie want that?

I put on the dress, hating how it made me look. Nattie would call it "dead fashion, like draping a curtain over your body." It was a little too short. However, the shoes fit surprisingly well.

The moment I stepped out, she hurried across the room to grab my hand and practically tug me to the door.

"Remember. No wailing and crying. Just sit and listen when your grandfather speaks."

When she opened the door to the dark hallway, I felt like I was being dragged into a cave, but it wouldn't be the first time I was in the grand living room with its large fieldstone fireplace, its thick gray area rug over the slate floor, to sit quietly while my grandfather lectured everyone like a king or an emperor. For as long as my mother could remember, she said he held court. Only my mother had the courage to disagree or laugh.

It did seem like the perfect room in which to summon the family. It was even referred to as the Sutherland Room. There were more portraits of my great-grandfather and his wife, as well as a painting of a castle. Supposedly, one portrait featured an ancestor who could have become the king of Scotland. There was a scroll in a glass case with the family history written in an old language, Gaelic. Above it was the family crest, which featured three stars. Grandfather used it as the symbol for his company. Contrary to how proud Grandfather was about it all, my mother said it was an embarrassment. She evaded showing it to her friends, avoided even bringing them to the Sutherland Room.

The windows were draped in a lighter gray. My mother said they were drawn open "like theater curtains exactly the same time every morning, as if the world put on a performance for my father."

The semicircular ruby-red leather sofa faced the thick-cushioned ruby-red chair where Grandfather Sutherland sat with his mahogany walking stick resting against his knee. Over the years, I realized that everyone in my family had a specific place to sit on the semicircular sofa. No one ever changed position.

Grandmother Judith always sat on the far right with the ottoman. Mommy had told me she was the only one who was permitted to look relaxed. "I'm not sure she ever is, but she can appear so," Mommy said. Grandmother was there now. A young nurse with black hair and a milky-white complexion was standing right beside her, holding her hand, but closer to her wrist so she could check her pulse periodically. She wore a light blue uniform and looked the most sympathetic when I entered.

My grandmother was a petite woman, just an inch or so more than five feet tall. She had small, childlike facial features, her green eyes being the brightest part of her despite all the makeup and the constant coloring of her hair to keep it that reddish brown. Mommy had said that grooming herself and fighting age were her chief occupations. She did no housekeeping and had nothing whatsoever to do with Grandfather's businesses. Despite how vigorously she maintained her facade, hoping to look younger, she was fragile. "My father's most valuable piece of china," Mommy would say. "She's pretty, delicate, and devoted to my father.

"Almost to the point of worship," she told Nattie.

Grandmother sat in a black silk robe. At the moment, she laid her head back and kept her left hand opened on her stomach, looking as if she was so upset that she might get up quickly to go to the bathroom.

As always, Uncle Martin sat on her left, his hands clasping his thighs as if he was preparing to leap up at my grandfather's command. My mother had said my grandfather's genes had simply bulldozed over Grandmother Judith's when it came to Uncle Martin. There was no questioning whose son he was. He was close to Grandfather Sutherland's height and had the same shade of light brown hair, closer to golden. Mommy said because of Grandfather's shade of gray, any gray strands were almost indistinguishable from his light brown ones. But Uncle Martin was softer-looking to me than Grandfather, who spoke in a deep, booming voice and strutted through the mansion as if he was marching. Neither he nor Uncle Martin had been in the army.

Uncle Martin was chubbier-faced and had a potbelly, narrower shoulders, and longer, thinner arms. Grandfather was lean, with a firm jawline. Although he was narrow-shouldered and more like an elderly movie star, he radiated a sturdiness that made him seem more like a planted fence post. Just like Daddy, he was conscious of his posture. Uncle Martin had a slight stoop and always looked to me like someone who was anticipating being slapped or criticized. He wore a child's fearful look when he was with my grandfather. "My brother always tried to walk in my father's shadow," Mommy had told Nattie. "It's like he always thought he had to be a step or two behind, as if he didn't deserve to walk with him side by side."

Despite the hesitation in his voice when he spoke to my grandfather, Uncle Martin tried to sound more like his father whenever he spoke to other people, including my mother and especially Aunt Holly. My mother would snap back at him, but Aunt Holly would simply smile as if she knew some secret. I wondered if they ate the same food, because she was very thin, with a small bosom and almost no hips. She favored vintage clothing, "almost as if she didn't want to be in this century," Mommy had said. "She's never really gotten over the loss of Annabelle, not that any mother could. So we give her space, understand?"

I did.

Aunt Holly kept her light brown hair cut short, just above the nape of her neck. At the moment, her sapphire eyes didn't look sorrowful as much as frozen in fear. She wore a shade of lipstick so light and faint that it looked more like ChapStick. When my father said something about Aunt Holly's thinness once, my mother said, "She surely has a nervous stomach, living with my brother since their loss. She once told me he blamed her for Annabelle. Most of the time, there's enough static electricity between them to light their home."

Aunt Holly's voice was soft and childlike, even when she reprimanded my cousin Simon. My mother said Aunt Holly would panic even if he only had the sniffles.

"He takes advantage of that," she told Daddy and me.

Simon usually would do what she asked, sit up, not keep his elbows on the table, use his napkin, whatever, but always with a steely glare as if his mother had no right to tell him what to do. Everyone spoke about how highly intelligent he was that I was ashamed I didn't have all As. He was already five foot nine, but it always seemed to me that the rest of his body was still catching up. I knew that he didn't like athletics and spent most of his free time reading, as if he was soon going to lose his eyesight. His eyes were a piercing shade of dark blue and his hair a darker brown. He often had a little arrogant turn in the right corner of his mouth.

However, Simon, more than anyone else, focused on me when I was brought to the living room. He looked like he was searching my face for a sign of a tear, any sign of emotion, so he could pounce with his right forefinger of accusation and declare, "She's not one of us."

But he was often like that, like some alien studying human beings. *When do we smile? When do we laugh? When do we cry?* Mommy was very nice to him, but sometimes he looked like he resented it. I heard her tell Daddy once that what terrified her nephew the most was the possibility of being pitied. Daddy thought that was good because it showed his self-confidence: "He doesn't need false compliments, or any for that matter."

"He doesn't seem to need anything from anyone," Mommy countered. "Often independence becomes arrogance."

Daddy shrugged.

"Most successful people are arrogant because most other people are jealous."

Mommy said nothing then. If anything, she looked saddened,

whereas Daddy looked satisfied. He could be that way: pleased with what he had thought to say.

Mrs. Lawson was right about how my family would react to me. Even Aunt Holly apparently was reluctant to offer me any sympathy. There wasn't a smile and certainly no tears. It was obvious that everyone was waiting for Grandfather to speak. If he said it was all right to be sad for me, they would, but not until then.

Mrs. Lawson brought me to the other end of the sofa. She nodded at it, and I sat. She stood at my side. For a long moment, my grandfather didn't move, didn't even shift his glance to watch me be seated. He kept his gaze on the floor. He was dressed in his usual charcoal-gray vested suit, white shirt, and matching gray tie. His gold marriage band with its tiny diamonds glittered whenever it picked up any light. My mother admitted that she cared about her clothes not because of my grandmother's pursuit of fashion but because of my grandfather's impeccable way of dressing himself. I couldn't recall ever seeing him in anything but a suit and tie with black shoes that looked newly bought.

He raised his head slowly.

"We're not going to make any sort of a show of this," he began, as always sounding as though he was in the middle of a speech. "I don't want the media or those busybodies hovering around this family waiting for something sensational to be said or done. You are to observe silence and make no comments. Franklin Butler will handle the obituary, and all phone calls inquiring will be answered by him.

"Now," he continued, sitting back more comfortably, "we are not going to have a big church ceremony, and we are not going to hold any wake in this house. I'm not going to hire caterers and order dozens and dozens of flowers to fill our grand ballroom. I don't want a tide of strangers washing into our home more out of curiosity than sympathy. Condolences from those people mean nothing anyway.

"We're not going to wait to bring this to a quick end, either. Tomorrow we will have an abbreviated 'religious' ceremony at the family grave site," he said, pronouncing "religious" as if it hurt his teeth to do so. "It will not be publicized. Nevertheless, I do anticipate gossip spies learning about it and being there. I'll have my security team keep them a good distance from us, especially to block any photographer.

"The family name has been dragged through the mud enough because of Linsey's behavior."

He turned slowly toward me and for a moment just stared at me. I held my breath.

"We are quite aware of the collateral damage. Any child growing up in that environment would be corrupted. Arrangements have been made to ensure that this will not continue and that proper and natural decency will be restored. I'm expecting you all to be cooperative, and if called upon to assist in any way, to do so without complaint or delay."

He turned slightly toward Grandmother Judith.

"Do not misdirect your affections, sympathies, or tolerance, or indulge in any rationalization. You will only make this worse and extend the time for the corrections to be made. We don't need that, and I won't tolerate it."

To emphasize his point, he grasped his walking stick and stamped the floor with it. Grandmother Judith looked at me and then dropped her head back again with a barely audible moan.

I glanced up at Mrs. Lawson, who stared ahead as if she had been turned into stone.

"You're absolutely right about this, Dad," Uncle Martin said. "Holly and I were discussing it on the way over, and—"

"I don't want you discussing it," Grandfather Sutherland snapped. "You have servants who aren't deaf, and when you talk too much, you inevitably say something that will only hurt the family name. Understood?"

"Absolutely," Uncle Martin said. He looked at Aunt Holly. For a moment I thought she was going to say something in opposition, maybe defend Mommy or demand more softness and understanding. Her lips parted, but she quickly looked down with a barely discernible shake of her head.

Simon was still staring at me as if he had been assigned the responsibility of watching my reactions. What corruption did he see in my face? Was he waiting for me to wail against all of this? I barely glanced at him.

The eight-foot-high grandfather clock made in France began to gong. Grandfather waited for it to stop.

"We will have our dinner now," he declared. "You are going to sit at the table, Judith," he told Grandmother. "Whether you eat anything or not. I want this family to get used to having one voice on this matter. Unity brings strength."

"This matter?" Grandmother Judith said without looking at him.

"Yes, this matter. This is more than just an accidental traffic death, Judith. You know too well what has been going on. I've told you a hundred times that pretending something doesn't exist or isn't occurring is no solution. If it's anything, it's cowardice to hide from the truth."

"Like a turtle," I said. I couldn't help it; it was as if Daddy had just whispered in my ear.

I doubt if anything could have resembled a bomb exploding in the living room more. Everyone gaped at me, anticipating my saying more, explaining.

"Exactly," Grandfather Sutherland said, his eyes piercing. His lips looked like they were trying to form a smile, but he wouldn't permit it. His eyes narrowed as he gazed at me. "For now and until all of this is over, especially you will remain in your shell."

He stamped his walking stick and stood.

"Everyone to the dining room."

Uncle Martin rose as if his seat had caught fire. Aunt Holly stood and put her arm through his as if they were about to walk somewhere very important and public together. Simon hesitated, that little curve in the side of his mouth deepening. Mrs. Lawson seized my left hand.

"Get up," she said under her breath. I glanced at Simon. He stood. Grandmother Judith's nurse helped her rise. Everyone else began to follow Grandfather Sutherland. I didn't take a step and pulled my hand free of hers.

"I want to know how Nattie is," I said.

Mrs. Lawson's eyes widened with her sparkle of rage.

"If you say that name again, especially now in the dining room, you will be sent to your room without anything to eat."

"I don't care," I said, mustering as much defiance as I could. I took another step back.

She didn't move. She watched everyone leaving behind Grandfather, and then she thrust her hand at me, nearly bowling me over with her grip of mine again. She held it so tightly that it hurt, but my defiance didn't wane.

"I mean it. No dinner," she threatened.

She continued to hold me back.

"I won't stop asking about Nattie. You can't make me stop asking."

"Very well," she said, "then you'll go to bed hungry."

She forcibly turned me back to the dark hallway.

"No!" I screamed, and tried to resist. She had more strength than I thought, and when I stopped walking and bent my knees, she literally dragged me, the pain in my arm and shoulder shooting down my spine.

I screamed again and again, but when I looked back I saw there was no one coming to help me. She flung open the bedroom door with her free hand and then shoved me into the room so hard that I fell to my knees. I heard her close and lock the door behind me.

"MOMMY!" I yelled. My voice echoed in the big, stark bedroom.

And then there was silence. Listening hard, I vaguely heard her footsteps drifting away. I felt like I was sinking, drowning. "Mommy!"

I screamed again. The silence was as good as a large hand pushing me farther down. I curled up on the floor and, like a baby, put my thumb in my mouth.

My grandfather won't leave me here, I thought. They were all waiting for me in the dining room. As soon as Mrs. Lawson told him that she had locked me in this room, Grandmother Judith would cry and all of them would plead for him to rescue me.

Grandfather would send Mrs. Lawson back for me.

I don't know how long I was lying there before I finally realized he wouldn't.

Not tonight.

Not tomorrow.

Maybe not ever.

11

When I began to shiver on the cold, hard floor, I rose and lay down on the bed, pulling the blanket up and around me. Maybe because crying and being frightened weakened me, I did want to have something to eat. My stomach moaned and churned as I began to envision the wonderful meals Mommy had made, one after another, as well as the fun I'd had helping her prepare dinner and setting the table perfectly to impress Daddy and, later, to impress Nattie. I hadn't been here long, not even a day, but already my whole life seemed more like a forbidden dream. Was it? Mrs. Lawson and Grandfather were telling me I had to be forced to forget, to be corrected, to be remade and cured.

Cured of what? A loving mother? A house filled with music? A glitter of smiles? What kind of medicine would I be made to take? Would I be given some sort of vaccination that would cause me to forget everything, including my mother and father and especially Nattie? Would I ever be permitted to return to school? What would Mrs. Mills, the school nurse, say about all this? She was obviously angry at Mrs. Lawson for the way she was treating me. She'd surely be angrier now. Would she come to see me at Sutherland? What about my teachers? Wouldn't they ask questions?

The afternoon sun sank enough for the shadows to grow away from the bay windows and creep toward me. Around me and above me, this huge house had become monstrous, a giant whale that had swallowed me into its darkness. I realized there was so much about it that I didn't know. Mommy had hidden it from me the way she would turn off terrible or ugly things on television. This mansion, the home filled with and reeking of unpleasant memories, was more of a maze than I had ever imagined. She had never let me out of her sight when we were here, and now that I thought more about it, envisioned those times, I recalled the fear in her eyes, the eyes of a mother who worried that her child would go too close to the edge when and if I wandered toward one of the hallways that spiraled from the warmer, lit places.

But I wasn't especially curious now. I didn't want to know where those hallways led and what those dark places were. Something, as it had even when I was very little, warned me not to roam alone. "Great houses, decades and decades old, harbor great secrets," Mommy once told me. Normally, that would stir a child's curiosity even more, but I resisted, even when there was a real opportunity to slip away and explore.

Now I realized that surely one of those secrets hovered and breathed in this cold bedroom with its bare walls. Who could have lived in it? Why was every suggestion of his or her presence gone? Why did my grandfather think it was a good place for me? I know he knew how warm my bedroom was, how it was furnished with bright colors and loving childhood memories. Mommy had wanted him to know. She had enjoyed describing "a real little girl's room" to him. Was putting me here another way to get back at her?

Remembering how they spoke to each other sliced away at my confidence in him being caring and loving when I would need it the most.

I wished these troubling feelings and memories could be locked away again. Darkness had resurrected them from places that even my nightmares wouldn't visit. I felt like I was in a castle dungeon rather than my grandfather's famous home. I wondered where the light switch was, but I realized seeing where I was again would not give me any comfort.

I turned on my back and looked up at the inky black ceiling, imagining ghosts swirling. I was afraid to sleep but hated being awake here. What would cause a girl my age to feel more desperate than the realization that crying would bring no compassion, no relief? There was no one to rescue me. Daddy had left his tower, and Mommy was gone. The Robot Family had come to a complete stop.

I had no sense of time, but I thought surely hours had passed when the door was finally opened. It wasn't, as I had hoped, to bring me food. Although I didn't hear her flip any switch and actually didn't see any, the room exploded in the light rained down from two simple but very bright glass shades that reminded me of school classroom lights. Darkness seemed to cringe beneath it, and for a few moments my eyes stung and my eyelids fluttered. Mrs. Lawson entered and walked quickly toward me carrying a black dress and a black knee-length hooded puffer jacket. She dropped both beside me on the bed as if she couldn't stand the scent or feel of them. She actually rubbed her hand against her thigh as if to wipe off a stain or a smell.

"You will find a pair of black shoe boots in the closet and socks in the bottom drawer of the dresser. Underthings are in the top drawer. Get dressed as soon as you are awakened by a buzzer in the morning."

"Buzzer?"

I sat up quickly. What did this mean? Dared I hope that Mommy was coming for me, that this torturous lesson was over? Was everything going to be all right after all? Bad dreams ended; cold rains stopped. Why couldn't this be over, too? Being a child meant you never lost hope.

That was clearly why Nattie had told me growing up could be painful. Doubt and cynicism, like mold, accompanied age.

Mrs. Lawson's face, a Halloween mask with its hard crust of scorn and contempt, squeezed the possibilities out of me. She hovered, her nostrils going in and out, reminding me of a bull's. I could think of nothing I might have done that would make her so angry. Was it that she simply hated the sight of me? I hated the sight of *her*!

"What buzzer?" I said more firmly. "Is it just for me or for the whole house?"

"The buzzer will wake only you every morning from now on," she said. "Lights will come on, and you will wash and dress for breakfast. Until your grandfather is satisfied with your redevelopment, you will eat all your meals in here, and you will go out only when Dr. Kirkwell believes it will help the process."

"What's 'redevelopment' mean? What process?"

She made a clicking sound with her pale lips, closed her eyes, and continued.

"The buzzer will warn you when it's time to have lunch and dinner as well. The exact timing of all that will be determined by Dr. Kirkwell. The buzzer will also tell you when to prepare for bed. It will be a lot like school. Twenty minutes later, the lights will go off whether you're ready for it or not. That's all you have to know for now."

She nodded at the dress and coat.

"The funeral will start at seven a.m. tomorrow. You will have no breakfast until after the funeral. There will be more adequate and proper clothing brought here during the funeral and hung up in your closet. You'll change out of your funeral clothes. This one time everything to wear for the day will be on the bed, waiting when you return from the funeral. I have already left instructions for that. Then you will have your breakfast. Assuming, of course, that you don't disobey, embarrass your family, or mention that name anytime during the . . . occasion. There is a proper nightgown for you hanging in the closet with slippers. When I leave, prepare for bed. As I said, the lights will go off in twenty minutes, so don't dilly-dally."

She started to turn away but stopped.

"I'll remind you in the morning, but your grandfather would prefer there not be any emotional outbursts of any kind at the cemetery. That includes crying."

"How can I not cry?"

She thought a moment, and for a second the harshness in her face receded. Could it be that she would say something nice, something sympathetic? She could feel sorry for me. After all, if I was to believe everything, my mother was gone. I would never see her again. She would be in a box slowly dropped into the ground. I had to wonder what her headstone would read. Would Grandfather Sutherland let it say *Beloved daughter and mother*? Or would it just have her name and her dates, birth and death? Really, how could I not cry and scream her name?

I also couldn't help but wonder if Nattie was still alive, and if she was, did she know Mommy was gone? Did she constantly ask after me? What would her nurses tell her? Were they keeping everything secret so she wouldn't cry and have a chance to get better? Every day of my life here, I would hope and pray for her to come for me.

How could tears be forbidden? Would my grandfather and grandmother, my uncle and aunt, and even Simon watch my mother be buried and not shed one? Would I be the only one? In the flash of a horrid image, I saw them all turned to watch me, waiting for me to weaken, their faces full of forbidding. Even the priest would pause to warn me with his God-filled eyes.

"I'll tell you how I behaved at my mother's funeral," Mrs. Lawson began in a deceptively warm voice. "I imagined she was stepping aboard a train and I was there to say goodbye and not make her feel sad and unhappy that she was leaving so she wouldn't be sad leaving me. You can do the same."

"My mother would be sad," I said. "She doesn't want to leave me. She would never want to leave me. Maybe *your* mother wanted to leave *you*," I threw back at her, and folded my arms to emphasize my boldness and insolence.

Mrs. Lawson stared at me with her flinty, steely glare. I tried to be continually defiant and stare back at her just as hard and just as angrily, but I had to look away. She had two small balls of ice for eyes. They chilled me to the base of my spine and nearly took away my breath.

"I see you're going to be quite the task, even for Dr. Kirkwell. You're an undisciplined, unbridled child. What else would we expect from a child brought up in a world of sin by people who had no self-respect or concern for their families? But you won't be any sort of challenge for me. I won't be handcuffed by sympathetic and tender psychology. The best teacher in my opinion is the back of my hand. You had better just do what I say and do it when I tell you to do it. The harder you make things for me, the harder I will make them for you. Remember what is forbidden to mention, even suggest. Is that clearly understood?"

"No. Why can't I say Nattie's name? Why can't I know how she is?"

I expected her to start shouting at me again, but she smiled coldly.

"Frankly, you keep convincing me that this behavior is not unanticipated, considering the life you've been having and all the evil, unnatural things to which you've been exposed."

"That's a lie. There was no evil."

"Oh." She sighed as if I was exhausting her. "I'll offer you something to ease your burden. Believe me, this won't be my usual thing when it comes to you. I'm not here to make things easier for you, so be grateful and listen to what I say this time."

"What?" Was she going to apologize? Was she going to tell me when she would let me out?

She smiled that cold, disdainful smile. There wasn't a hint of mercy in it. My hope fizzled and shrank like a punctured balloon.

"The best way for you to think of all this, and it's not my idea, my words, but Dr. Kirkwell's, is to think that you are being buried alongside your mother tomorrow. When you return from the cemetery to Sutherland, you will start your rebirth. In your new life, there is no Nattie, or whatever you call her. In time you will forget she even existed."

"No, I won't. Never."

"Oh, you will," she said with such confidence. "But it's foolish for me to discuss it any further now. Besides, I'm not the expert when it comes to these matters."

"What matters? Who's Dr. Kirkwell? Why is he in charge of me? Is he giving me medicine? I won't take it. I'll spit it out."

"You'll find out what you will and won't do, starting tomorrow. Dr. Kirkwell will be coming in the early afternoon. Your grandfather spent a lot of money researching and found that Dr. Kirkwell is the top expert in this field."

"What field? I don't even know what you're talking about. Who is Dr. Kirkwell? Expert at what?"

"Enough. I won't be cross-examined like some hired help, especially by you. Hang up your funeral clothes. There will be no personal servants assigned to care for your things and your room. Part of your reeducation will be your learning how to care for yourself. Taking personal responsibility is a major requirement in Dr. Kirkwell's program. As I told you previously, your childhood is over. It wasn't much of a childhood anyway. But you will learn all this for yourself, or—"

"Or what?"

I wanted to rush at her and pummel her with my small fists until she stopped her terrible words and let me out.

She looked around, not in the least troubled by my raging anger.

"This room will get smaller; maybe as small as a coffin. That's what."

Small as a coffin? What did she mean? Could these walls really be moved in closer and closer?

I could feel my tears stirring, but I put all my anger into my own hard wall to hold them back. Nothing she was saying made any sense to me. She wanted to frighten me and frighten me. This was all some sort of stupid game that would soon end. I'd make it end.

"I should be given something to eat," I said in as demanding a tone as I could muster. Often my mother told me I sounded like my grandfather or my father. It was time for the Captain Bryer in me to speak up.

She flashed that cold smile again.

"When I told your grandfather you were going to sleep without any dinner and then have to wait for any breakfast until after the funeral, he said he thought it was a good idea for you to look peaked and pale at the cemetery. Perhaps the gossips will take pity on you and not stir any ugly controversies that would continue to stain the family name.

"So . . . in a way you've pleased him with your defiance. I think, from now on, that should be your principal goal, pleasing your grandfather. I'm sure the reborn you will agree."

She nodded at my funeral clothes again.

"Hang up your things. Prepare for bed. You have fifteen minutes now, since you've wasted five. If you don't move quickly, you'll have to stumble about in the dark." She turned to leave.

"Nattie will get better, and she will come for me, and she will tell her important people what you did to me!" I shouted after her. "You'll be arrested and end up in a prison worse than this. That's where you belong, not me."

She turned back to me, her face grayer, her shoulders hoisted like those of someone who had just had an ice cube dropped down her back.

"There will come a time when you will apologize for saying that," she said in a hoarse, low whisper. Then she smiled her icy smile again. "Now you've given me something to look forward to, something to help me tolerate this assignment I've been given: your apology."

"No, never. I'd rather be dead than tell you I'm sorry."

Her smile faded quickly.

"You will be. Tomorrow. Didn't you hear what I said? Think of it as your funeral, too. And then, if you listen and behave, your re-birth.

"Fifteen minutes. No, fourteen now. We don't forgive people for wasting time here. You probably know that. It was a pet peeve of your mother's."

She walked out and locked the door. The sound of metal on metal and the click of that lock echoed. For a few moments, I thought I would never get it out of my mind, never stop hearing that sound.

But I refused to cry or scream. I knew exactly what I had to do instead.

I began to sing "Sweet Caroline" and spent my fourteen minutes of light in this horrid room dancing with my mother.

After the buzzer had sounded, I did stumble about in the dark, just as she had predicted. It was totally overcast outside. There wasn't even starlight to glimmer through the bay windows. Rather than try to do anything, I crawled back onto the bed and lay back against the pillow. I didn't even remember closing my eyes before the buzzer sounded again and it was morning. I scurried quickly to get myself ready, hating the black dress and the clunky black shoes. Putting on these clothes was forcing me to believe my mother was really gone. But this room had no place for any renewal of hope. It looked like Grandfather's servants had washed and scrubbed it out years ago. Even sunlight was reluctant to cross the threshold of these cold shadows.

I had just started to put on the coat when Mrs. Lawson entered. She was wearing a black dress, with the skirt almost over her shoes, and a black bonnet. She seemed like she was growing taller and wider in the doorway with every passing moment, like some ogre.

"Let's go," she said. "The sooner we get this over with, the better. And the sooner you'll get something to eat and start your new life."

She stood back as I finished putting on the coat and walked slowly toward the door.

"Come along!" she snapped, then seized my arm and pulled me forward, even giving me a little push to walk faster down the dark hallway. All the servants were lined up on both sides of the entryway. Everyone was looking at me, but when Mrs. Lawson looked back at them, each looked down. No one was in the atrium, but Emerson was waiting at the front entrance. He was dressed in a black suit and even had a matching black limousine driver's hat. I saw a small smile on his lips, a smile I knew was meant to give me comfort. Mrs. Lawson's glare did not change his expression or cause him to look away. He moved quickly to open the rear door. Grandmother Judith and Grandfather Sutherland were already seated with their backs to Emerson.

Grandmother Judith had a handkerchief in her right hand. She pressed it to her face immediately, making it look like a mask, but I could still see her eyes, and in them was a look of sympathy and sadness I hoped was for me. Grandfather Sutherland stared at me, his eyes moving quickly, sweeping over me as if he was checking for some button undone or thread out of place. Then he sat back and looked through the window on our left. I searched his face for some of the warmth I occasionally felt when we came to Sutherland. I also hoped to see some sadness. My mother was his daughter. We were going to her funeral. As angry as he was about everything, didn't that matter? How would he ever be sad for me if he wasn't sad for her?

No one spoke during the ride. Grandmother started to sob, but a sharp look from Grandfather quickly smothered it under that handkerchief. I saw Emerson gaze at me in the rearview mirror. It was the only warmth I felt in this limousine refrigerator.

I couldn't remember ever being to the Sutherland family cemetery, which was enclosed within an iron fence in an area only a little ways from a big Catholic cemetery on the right. There were oak trees in each far corner and evergreens along the side gated area of the family cemetery. The cemetery looked like it was constantly maintained, grass mowed and trees trimmed. The centerpiece of the Sutherland cemetery was the tall monument over my great-grandfather's grave. His name was etched in large block letters. All the other family members were buried around it under much smaller gravestones.

Off to the immediate right when we drove up, there were at least ten people. They were obviously not mourners because of how casually some of them were dressed. Between them and the family cemetery were six tall men in black coats and hats, glaring angrily at them. They were surely Grandfather's security men, each one stout and tall.

Uncle Martin, Aunt Holly, and Simon were already at the grave site, which had been dug far enough away from the closest family grave as to make my mother look like an outcast. Aunt Holly wore a black hat with a veil down over her face. She kept her head bowed. Uncle Martin had his hands buried in the deep pockets of his black cashmere overcoat. Simon looked uncomfortable in his dark suit and black tie. He tugged at the collar of his white shirt.

The priest, a tall, thin man with thick, neatly trimmed dark brown hair, stood at the head of the grave. He wore a black overcoat, opened, and a black shirt with that white patch over his throat, and black pants.

He clutched the Bible as if he was going to heave it into the grave. He didn't smile. His face looked chiseled in grayish cement. I didn't think he was very old, but he looked like a young man who was forced to look older, because his hair was streaked with gray as if done with a crayon. He wore round-lensed glasses that reflected the early sunlight.

Aside from two cemetery workers, there was no one else at the grave site. Where were Grandfather Sutherland's important employees, especially Franklin Butler? I didn't see any coffin, either. I looked at the road to the cemetery for signs of a hearse, but there was nothing.

"Let's get this over and done with as quickly as possible," Grandfather Sutherland said as soon as Emerson opened the door for us to step out. He practically lunged at it. Grandmother Judith choked back her sob and followed him. Mrs. Lawson nudged me hard, and I got out. I gazed up at the sky. Mommy's favorite "popcorn puffed clouds" were hanging over the horizon as if they were waiting for the funeral to start, too.

Then I turned toward the people standing off to the right. When one lifted a camera, two of Grandfather Sutherland's security men started toward him. He lowered his camera quickly and stepped back. The security men hovered around him. The other strangers stepped closer to each other protectively. Mrs. Lawson moved me faster toward Uncle Martin, Aunt Holly, and Simon. Grandfather and Grandmother went quickly to the other side of the grave site.

The two cemetery workers now with shovels stepped behind Grandfather Sutherland. The sight of the shovels sent a cold shiver through my chest. My heart started to thump. It was all so curious and so different from Mr. Gleeson's funeral.

"Dad had them lower the coffin before we arrived," Uncle Martin told Mrs. Lawson in a loud whisper. "Make it all go faster," he said. He looked quickly toward Grandfather Sutherland, obviously making sure it was all right for him to tell. Grandfather stood stiffly, neither his eyes nor his mouth moving. Maybe he was praying, I thought. Maybe he was sorry now that we were actually here.

"Very wise," Mrs. Lawson said. "The dead don't suffer at their funerals; only the mourners suffer. Why prolong it?"

Uncle Martin nodded, but Aunt Holly didn't look at us. I stood a foot or so to Simon's right.

"Are we waiting for anyone else, Mr. Sutherland?" the priest asked Grandfather.

"No," he said sharply. "Get on with it."

Simon moved closer to me and nodded at the grave as the priest began his prayers. I still hadn't looked down into it, the dark, cold place Mommy would be in forever. Grandmother Judith started to cry, but Grandfather Sutherland rubbed his shoulder against hers and she stopped.

The priest had yet to mention my mother's name. When I looked at Simon, he had that tight curl at the side of his mouth. He leaned toward me to whisper.

"You can look. She's not down there," he said.

The heat rose up from my pounding heart and into my face. My cheeks felt like they were burning.

What did that mean?

I studied him for a moment. He wasn't laughing, but he was obviously waiting for my reaction. I looked at Mrs. Lawson. She either didn't hear him or didn't care about what he had said. I stepped forward and gazed into the grave.

There was a coffin.

What was he saying? I looked at him again with questions rushing out of my eyes. *If she's not down there, where is she? Who is down there? How do you know?*

He stepped back quickly and stared ahead. Mrs. Lawson and Grandfather would get their wish. Now I surely couldn't cry. I couldn't even look sad.

Without mentioning Mommy's name, the priest finished by saying, "May her soul be embraced by the Lord. Amen."

One of the cemetery workers standing behind Grandfather Sutherland and Grandmother Judith stepped forward and handed him a shovel. He dug into the pile of dirt with surprising enthusiasm and strength, lifting a full shovel, holding it above the grave, and then turning it so the dirt fell in. Uncle Martin hurried around to take the shovel from him and do the same, only his shovel looked half-full. Grandmother Judith looked like she was sinking into the ground. Her legs bent, and Grandfather Sutherland quickly put his arm around her and practically lifted her off the ground. Uncle Martin hurried to her side and began to guide her back toward the limousine. Emerson, who had been standing behind me, rushed to open the door.

Aunt Holly and Simon started toward their car. He didn't look back at me. I wanted to shout at him and demand he tell me what he had meant. I might have if Mrs. Lawson hadn't seized my hand and turned me with an abrupt tug. She put her hand behind my head on my neck to march me forward.

"She's on that train," she said. "Get back into the car."

"No, she's not," I said, and pulled myself out of her grip.

She quickly looked toward Grandfather, her face suddenly pale with fear. When I looked at him, at the anger building in his eyes, I felt the same fear and started toward the limousine. Simon was already in his car anyway. Mrs. Lawson remained right behind me. Grandmother Judith looked collapsed in the seat, her head turned, her eyes closed. Uncle Martin stepped away from the car, and we got in, Mrs. Lawson practically shoving me into my seat.

Grandfather came to the door. He said something to Uncle Martin and then got in. As soon as he sat, he turned to Grandmother Judith.

"Satisfied?" he asked her. Her lips trembled, but she didn't speak. "Let's go," he told Emerson as soon as he got in.

Satisfied with what? I waited, hoping to hear her respond, but she just turned her head and closed her eyes. I looked back at the family grave-yard. The cemetery workers were shoveling furiously.

It was as if they thought that whoever was down there might start to crawl up and out.

12

The nurse I had seen with Grandmother yesterday at Grandfather Sutherland's family meeting was waiting for her at the entrance to the Sutherland house atrium, her palms pressed together under her chin as if in prayer. I felt a surge of warmth and hope in her soft, daughterly concern. It was like a flash of love or at least deep affection and not simply obedience. I had looked at Mommy that way so often that it made my heart ache now to think of the way her smile would begin in her eyes and softly move down to her lips. I wanted it to be like that again; I wanted to soak in her smile, draw it around me like a warm blanket, shielding me from the slightest cold and nasty breeze.

I truly envied Grandmother's nurse at this moment. How lucky she was to have someone to care for in this dank world of shadows, someone whose unhappiness could bring her to tears or whose happiness could cheer her heart. All I saw otherwise were angry or fearful faces, servants like marionettes moving from side to side, up and down, according to a look in my grandfather's eyes or a growl in his voice.

Grandmother Judith's nurse practically leaped toward the limousine when Emerson opened the door. She quickly stepped back when Grandfather emerged first, however—jumped back was more like it. It was as if the air between them had become a rough ocean wave washing over her. He paused, turned, and looked back at us.

"See to it that all goes as it is supposed to," he told Mrs. Lawson, then lowered his head and charged into the house like someone angry and frustrated by an unnecessary disturbance.

Mrs. Lawson tightened her grip on my hand so I wouldn't get up until Grandmother Judith's nurse had reached in to help her out, not that I was eager to return. Grandmother paused and looked back at me, just me. I was hoping she would say something to Mrs. Lawson like "Don't listen to him. Bring her to my room," almost anything warm and hopeful, but instead she turned away and leaned on her nurse.

"Grandmother Judith," I said, loud enough for her to hear.

Mrs. Lawson tightened her grip on my hand so much that it hurt. I tried to pull free so I could run to my grandmother, throw my arms around her, and beg her to help me, but Mrs. Lawson was amazingly strong.

"Wait," she said, jerking my arm so that I sat back.

Helplessly, I looked out at my grandmother and her nurse, who led her into the house as quickly as she would have if it had been pouring cold rain.

Emerson stood waiting at the limousine door. When Mrs. Lawson shoved me, nearly pushing me to the limousine floor, I stepped out. She followed instantly, practically breathing down my neck as if she thought I might bolt and run off. The thought did flash through my mind. What better opportunity would I have? I wanted to go home. I imagined Mommy waiting excitedly at the door, Nattie rushing past me and out to "take care of that hateful woman."

But it wasn't so much Mrs. Lawson as it was Grandfather Sutherland who obviously controlled everything here, even when people could smile or cry. She should go after him, bring the *gendarmes*, as Nattie would say. Every time I thought of some French word, I thought of her and then of Mommy and the warm, comfortable, happy world we had for so short a time, even after Daddy had deserted us. As Mommy might have explained, Grandfather had slapped us down, swatted us like a fly. After all, he moved everyone around like figures on a chessboard, didn't he?

In her way, with all her stories and not-so-subtle comments about her father, Mommy had prepared me for the hard, cold man who ruled his family through fear rather than through respect. Everyone, with perhaps the exception of Simon, who hid his feelings behind the habitual inscrutable face of someone who constantly looked to be in deep thought, was obviously afraid of him. Simon was so good at being aloof that Aunt Holly was always almost apologetic about interrupting him to tell him to do something necessary or proper like wash his hands before dinner or keep his elbows off the table. At the moment, I envied him for his indifference. But how did you not care? Not cry?

Mrs. Lawson leaned down to spit her words into my ear.

"The faster you get yourself into the house and into your room, the faster you'll get something to eat."

Emerson heard her.

"You get more with honey than vinegar," he told her.

"Maybe you do. I do just fine with vinegar," she replied, and poked me in the shoulder to walk faster, her right forefinger feeling more like a sharp stick.

There was no one in the entryway or hallways when we entered. I saw the nurse helping Grandmother up the stairway. She was practically carrying her. Grandmother looked like she had aged decades during the minutes it took to get from the limousine to the middle of the curved flight of steps. We had just come from her daughter's, my mother's, funeral, and rushing her in, maybe to keep her away from me, probably didn't help. I was still tempted to yell out to her, even though she could clearly do nothing to help me right now; she couldn't help herself.

I looked to the right toward Grandfather's office. The door was closed. Maybe he was secretly crying. Dared I hope that he might have a change of heart and treat me more like his granddaughter? Should I rush to his door, pound on it, and beg him to care about me?

"Stop gawking at everything. You're wasting time," Mrs. Lawson said.

What time? I wanted to ask. *How can you waste time thinking and mourning after a funeral, especially one that was supposed to be your mother's?* I shouldn't move, I thought. I should be crying hysterically, but I was more in a daze, confused, frightened, and feeling very alone.

We entered the dark hallway. Once again, I had the urge to turn and run. Perhaps the gate wasn't closed yet. I could surely run faster than Mrs. Lawson, and maybe Emerson would refuse to go after me. Mrs. Lawson put her hand on my shoulder when I nearly stopped walking. I had to wonder if she really could read my thoughts.

She leaned down to bring her lips close enough to my ears that I could feel her hot breath.

"You have no other place to go. Your house was sold. That woman's house has been locked by the bank, and it will be that way for some time, off bounds to anyone but the bank's officers. Your grandfather saw to that. As far as your neighbors and your school know, you are completely in your grandfather's control. He's your only guardian now and has made all arrangements. They realize that, and they will have nothing to do with you."

I stopped, my shouts of defiance rising in my throat. Suddenly, she grabbed both my shoulders and spun me around to face her.

"I'm telling you all of this so you will obey all the rules set down and not disturb anyone in this house, least of all your grandfather, especially right now. Understood? Well?"

I was too frozen in fear even to nod, but the look on my face was enough for her to smile with confidence, turn me around again, and escort me back into what would be my room and my world for longer than I feared. I saw the clothing on the bed, left there just as she had said it would be. The lamp on the desk had been turned on. There was a place setting with a glass, silverware, and a napkin.

On the wall opposite my bed, a large oval mirror in a dark brown frame had been hung. Why was that so important? It didn't make the room any warmer. I still thought of it as more of a dungeon.

"Change and wash up for breakfast. Dr. Kirkwell will be here soon after, and it will all begin. The more cooperative you are, the faster it will all end. But don't get your hopes up. We're not talking about days and weeks or months, are we?"

"How long, then?" I asked. *How long will I be kept here, and for what purpose?* was what I was really thinking.

"Dr. Kirkwell will know, of course, but if you're asking my opinion, I'd say years. After all, it took years to bring you to where you are."

"What do you mean? Where am I?"

She smiled, not coldly, but almost friendly because of the amused twinkle in her eyes. Why was she so happy about all this?

"Merely that you have to ask is reason enough for Dr. Kirkwell and justifies everything your grandfather decided to do," she said, and then walked out, shutting and locking the door.

Questions floated like bubbles above and around me, but all I really wondered was, who was in the grave? When would I see Simon again so I could ask what he had meant? If Mommy wasn't in the grave, was she still alive? Was everything I and Mrs. Mills had been told a horrible and dirty lie just as I hoped it was? Who else knew the truth? Did Simon, Uncle Martin, and Aunt Holly also know about all this, know I was locked in this room to be tutored and controlled by some expert in something?

I doubted they would say or do anything anyway, even if they had just found out. Who knew what Grandfather would do to them if they even thought to help me? I wanted to sit on the floor and refuse to move or do anything, but something told me that Mrs. Lawson would be pleased by my resistance. She would even enjoy being crueler to me. Why? We never really had spoken to each other much whenever my parents brought me here. Why was it so important to her to be so mean to me?

Reluctantly, I went to the bed and looked at the clothes. I could see they weren't new, and they were certainly not mine brought from Nattie's house. The dark dress looked old-fashioned, like something young girls wore in the pictures in my history book. Mommy would never have bought it. I sniffed it. It smelled like it had been recently washed. I remembered Mrs. Lawson had said there would be other things in the closet, so I looked. There were four other dresses, three blouses, and three skirts, the colors dull browns and blues. It all looked just . . . old, like clothes that had been washed and scrubbed until they looked almost threadbare. Whose clothes were they? Could they have been my mother's or even my grandmother's?

I recalled Mommy and Nattie washing their hands and splashing water on their faces following Nattie's parents' funerals. Daddy didn't do so after Mr. Gleeson's and wasn't there for Mrs. Gleeson's, but Mommy made sure I did. "You can't wash away sadness, but it gives you the feeling you left the darkness behind," she had said.

As soon as I had washed, I put on the blue dress. It buttoned in the back and had buttoned-cuff sleeves and looked a good size or so too big. It felt more like a costume. My classmates surely would laugh and ridicule me, but what choice did I have? The clothes in which I had been brought here were gone, and I certainly wanted to get rid of these funeral clothes as soon as I could. I wished I could flush it all down the toilet, along with the memory of being here.

I heard the door open and stepped out of the bathroom to see one of Grandfather's older servants bring in my breakfast tray. She avoided looking at me, put the tray on the desk, and left without saying a word. She had practically fled, not shifting her eyes from the door. What had everyone been told about me? Did everyone in the house except Emerson dislike me as much as Mrs. Lawson did?

I had been given a glass of orange juice, scrambled eggs, and toast with jam. There was also a bottle of water. I wanted to throw it all on the floor and refuse to eat, but my stomach said no, and when I began, I practically gobbled all of it. The eggs tasted just like Mommy would have made them, eggs with some cheese and some pieces of bacon. Surely Mrs. Wilson had made them. She had taught my mother so much.

Strange as it might seem, the food didn't just make me feel better; it made me feel safer, as if Mommy had reached through the locked door and thick walls to comfort me. "Everything will be all right," she often told me after Daddy had left us. "Just like it says at the end of our favorite stories: 'They lived happily ever after.'"

Would I? How could I without her?

Suddenly, now that I had eaten, I could finally cry. I didn't even try to wipe away the tears streaking down my cheeks. They felt warm and necessary. I recalled Daddy once telling Mommy that she should let me cry.

"It's the only way to get it out of her," he had said, "it" being my unhappiness over something. Mommy said that was cruel, but he said it was better than sugarcoating: "That's just another form of a lie."

"Sometimes it's kinder to lie, Morgan. Don't tell me you haven't done it," Mommy said.

Daddy stared at her.

"I haven't done it," he said coldly and firmly. I remembered she had smirked and turned me away.

I went to the bay windows and looked out, occasionally catching sight of one of Grandfather's groundskeepers. I was tempted to tap hard on the windows and shout to him. Maybe he would come running to the window and see me. He would tell everyone about me, and they would rescue me. Of course, I realized that would never happen. He'd probably be afraid to even look toward me, so I did nothing except finally wipe away my tears, take a deep breath, and retreat to sit on the bed.

I sat thinking about buzzers, darkness, old clothes, and more threats after a funeral that seemed too unreal even to be a nightmare. How could I be left so alone? If my mother was truly gone, why would my father just desert me? He had held my hand or put me on his shoulders when I was little and we all took a walk. He had spent so much of his time teaching me what he thought were important things. It was true that he sometimes looked at me suspiciously or appeared disappointed in my liking Nattie, maybe even angry about it, but did he think I was keeping secrets from him? Would I ever see him or talk to him again? Did he simply take any and all love for me and transfer it to his new daughter?

Maybe what they told me about Daddy was just another lie. It could be that he didn't know anything terrible had happened to my mother. How could I talk to him, call him?

I was so deep in thought that I didn't hear the lock turn or notice the door had been opened and closed. For a moment my heart raced with hope. Was it Daddy? Had he come for me after all? I was wishing too hard and too desperately. Reality slapped away hope. Someone was standing there and forming as if out of the shadows. Seconds passed. Whoever it was stood there studying me. It filled the air between us with static. I held my breath. It was too much like something emerging from a nightmare.

"Who are you?" I asked, or at least I thought I did. My voice wasn't much stronger than a weak whisper.

Finally, a strange woman stepped forward, glanced at my breakfast dish and empty glass, and then smiled at me.

"Good," she said. "Children with empty stomachs are like cars without gas. They go nowhere."

"Who are you?"

"I'm Dr. Kirkwell, and I'm happy to meet you."

I never imagined that Dr. Kirkwell was a woman. Mrs. Lawson didn't say. I didn't know why, but that frightened me more. She was dressed in a black pantsuit with a frilly-collared blouse. She wore thick-heeled black shoes. I saw she was carrying a large black briefcase.

Despite how my knees were clicking nervously and how I was opening and closing my hands, I continued to stare back at her silently and as defiantly as I could. I certainly didn't want to be friendly or appreciative. If I believed what Mrs. Lawson had told me, she was here to create a new me. Maybe she would get discouraged and leave me alone. Grandfather would decide to let me out, give me a proper room, and let me become a member of the family again.

For a moment Dr. Kirkwell's eyes narrowed to mere slits as if she was looking at me through a microscope. When she stepped closer, I saw that there was nothing about her that encouraged me to see her as warm and sympathetic anyway. She was tall and had graying dark brown hair cut sharply at the base of her neck. Her bangs were trimmed just as perfectly. She wore little makeup, just a brushing across her thin lips. There was a slight rose tint in her cheeks, but her nose was so sharp that I imagined she could slice her own image in half when she gazed at herself in mirrors. Narrow shoulders and a narrow waist made her look even taller, but I don't think she was taller than Nattie or Mommy.

Her eyes widened, probably because I was looking at her so hard. They were a brownish gray. Daddy would be impressed with how tidy and perfect she appeared, I thought. Her shoes looked new, with not the slightest scuff. But I didn't want to give her a single compliment, even if only in my thoughts. This was the person Mrs. Lawson had suggested would have the power to change me so dramatically that I wouldn't know myself. Right now, I wondered if she was some sort of magician who could turn a prince into a frog.

"I've seen your school records," she said. She didn't speak loudly, but her voice did seem to echo in the big bedroom. "Quite impressive. I think we can move you along in your academic work quite quickly. I'm going to continue all that but start on the tenth-grade level with your reading, your math and science. I'm sure you can handle it. Your textbooks and assignments are in this briefcase."

"I'm only in the eighth grade."

"Yes, yes," she said, waving my words off with a flick of her wrist, "but that's in a public school setting with a teacher who has to worry about twenty-five or more students. So many bright ones like yourself are lost in the haze. Actually, that almost happened to me."

She paused to look around the room.

"We're going to change a lot in here, warm it up a bit, but everything we do," she said in a sterner voice, "will contribute to our purpose. There'll be no frills. Consider this as more like a laboratory, a place in which you will learn, experiment, and improve."

She spoke as if there was never any doubt about what she said. In that way, she reminded me of Grandfather Sutherland. But as Mommy would say, "Don't be intimidated. People like that feed on signs of weakness. Even my father thought that. 'If you act like sheep, they'll act like wolves,' he would say, not realizing perhaps that he was talking about himself turning my mother and me into sheep."

"Improve what?" I asked, trying to sound stronger than I was.

"Why, you, of course," she said. "Get you balanced ethically and biologically, which will ensure that you have a normal, productive life. But let's not get too detailed and technical at the start. As the Chinese prophet said, 'A journey of a thousand miles begins with a single step.' I'd like you to think of this all as a journey we'll be taking together. Understand?"

I shook my head.

"Oh, I think you do," she said. "You're too smart for me to think otherwise, and I wouldn't advise you to play dumb. Not with me."

She walked to my desk, placed the briefcase on it, and brought the chair close to the bed so she could sit right in front of me, practically on top of me. Then she lifted the back of her pantsuit jacket so she wouldn't sit on it and sat facing me. Because she was so close, I could see the brown spots on her forehead and a small mole just above the collar of her blouse. The lines in her face were deep, especially at the corners of her eyes. Everyone over fifty looked old to me, but I recalled Nattie once saying that men were forgiven their age, but women were almost blamed for it. Whatever that meant, my mother had agreed.

She crossed her legs and sat back.

"Let's get some things straight from the start. That way we'll help each other and make all this easier and successful.

"One, I want you to say 'Yes, Dr. Kirkwell' or 'No, Dr. Kirkwell' when I ask you a question. Nodding or shaking your head isn't really an answer. It's a gesture without a commitment. When you say something, I will hear what I want in your voice. And you will, too, because you will be telling yourself yes or no.

"Besides, from now on, you and I don't pretend. You know that pretending is really being dishonest, and if there is one thing I insist we be to each other, it's honest. You understand why that's important, right?"

I stared. If I didn't talk, what could she do?

"Right?"

I bit down gently on my lower lip and folded my arms.

"You don't want me to leave to tell your grandfather you won't speak to me, do you? You'll discover I'm probably going to be your best friend. And you need a friend, now more than ever," she said.

I didn't think it was possible, but the way she said it made me even more afraid of what was being planned for me.

"Well? Will you be honest with me?"

I dipped down deep inside myself into my Daddy courage.

"Will *you* really be honest with *me*?" I countered, drawing on as much defiance as I could muster despite the way I was trembling. I thought my teeth would chatter. "And tell me the real reason why you are here?"

She smiled. She didn't look upset at all.

"You might be more like your father than your grandfather thinks."

She leaned toward me. I didn't realize how long her eyelashes were. When Mommy saw a woman or even a man who had long eyelashes, she'd laugh and say, "I'd kill for those."

"And what your grandfather thinks is very important."

"I don't know what my grandfather thinks. I don't know why he's so angry at me."

"He's not really angry at you. Actually, he feels sorry for you, and it's only his concern for you that has brought me here."

"That's not true."

"Oh, it is. Very much. You'll have to trust me."

I looked away and thought and then looked back at her.

"If you want me to trust you, tell me the truth about my mother. Did she really die? Do you know about Nattie? Mrs. Lawson won't even let me say her name."

"Of course your mother died, and we'll see about what we will and won't say about this woman you call Nattie."

"Is she alive?"

"I think we'll concentrate on you for now. There's a lot to do."

"Well, I won't."

Her eyes looked like they had turned to glass. She seemed capable of turning off a friendly look like someone could turn a faucet on and off.

"That would be foolish."

A new fear seized me. What more could be done to me?

"I don't want you to think even for a moment that I don't have sympathy for you, but we have to get beyond our emotions. Emotions," she said, tilting her head a little as would someone trying to define a word or think of the right thing to say next, "often get in the way of truth. You know what it means to be objective, to look at things as they are and not let your feelings blind you?"

Daddy had once said something similar.

"Conclude rather than believe," I said. It bothered me to think that my father would like her, but I felt sure that he would. And he'd like my answer.

Dr. Kirkwell smiled widely again.

"Precisely. If a doctor was operating on you because you had an appendix attack, his opinion of you would have nothing to do with the procedure. You know what I mean?"

"Like not caring about an airplane company when you were guiding the pilot in for a landing."

She sat back, looking amazed.

"Oh, I can see we're going to do just fine here. We'll clear things up and get you started on the right path again in no time."

"I've always been on the right path. What's supposed to be wrong with me, anyway?" I asked, feeling more self-confident.

"Let's not think of it as something wrong with you. Not yet. Just wrongly influenced. We're not sure how deep the damage goes. We'll see. I have to get to know you really well, better than you know yourself."

"Mrs. Lawson said you're going to change me until I don't know myself."

"Oh, she's not familiar with the right terminology. People like that always use hyperbole. You know what that is?"

"Exaggeration."

"Very good. I'm getting more confident. Think of yourself as having been headed in the wrong direction through no fault of your own. My job is to correct that and send you in the right direction. It's just a process of showing you the way. Nothing to fear."

"Then why am I being punished?"

"You're not being punished. Unless, of course, you become recalcitrant, disobedient. If you're cooperative, you'll do fine."

"I don't want to be here."

"No, I imagine you don't," she said, but without any sympathy. "So that's why we want to get right on it and you want to be cooperative. You've been to the dentist. You know that if you don't cooperate, you only make things more difficult for the dentist to help you."

"What kind of a doctor are you?"

"Think of me as a therapist. You know what that is, right?"

"Yes."

"I do have medical training and have written books and articles. People call on me when someone they love or care deeply about is going the wrong way or could very well do that. If you want a technical term that makes me sound more important, I'm an expert in aversion therapy."

I grimaced. What was that?

"See? You're frightened. We don't want to get too technical too soon, and anyway, let's stop talking about me."

She slapped her knees and stood.

"To start, I have to know how much about yourself you know and understand."

"About myself? Why wouldn't I know about myself?"

"Oh, there is so much we don't know about ourselves. You know what a blackboard is, of course. Well, think of yourself as a blackboard. Things have been written on you, and our job now is to get them erased and write new things. That's easy to picture, right?"

"No," I said. How could I imagine myself as a blackboard?

She stared with those penetrating eyes and nodded. Then she sat again. She had a way of looking at me that made my heart thump.

"You've had your first period, right? Or not?"

"Yes."

"Ah. How much did your mother tell you about becoming a woman? That's when you really do become one."

"I don't know what you mean. She explained what was happening and what I had to do when it did."

The look on my face caused her to nod as though she had expected it.

"You've noticed other changes in your body? Did she talk about that?"

When I didn't answer, she said, "I told you that I'm a doctor. If you went to a doctor and didn't tell her the truth about yourself, how could she help you?"

"I didn't go to a doctor."

She smiled that smile again that seemed more like she appreciated me.

"No, the doctor has been brought to you. So? Tell me what you noticed about yourself, especially this year."

Many of the girls in my class compared themselves to one another. I wouldn't participate in their discussions. I remembered how Betty Gregory would brag about how big her breasts had gotten and how she enjoyed flaunting herself in front of the boys. Mine had begun to grow but were no way near where hers were. No one else's were, but many of them looked older than I did. It embarrassed me. I was afraid they would turn to me, so I avoided them as much as I could. What had surprised me most was that Nattie saw it in me faster than Mommy.

"Are you thinking about boys?" Dr. Kirkwell asked. "Or better yet, are any thinking of you?"

"I don't think so," I said.

"You're going to be beautiful, Caroline. Just give yourself time," she said. "Well? What have you noticed about yourself?"

"I'm taller, and I weigh more."

She smiled.

"Oh, you're toying with me. I can see it in your face. You're not good at being deceptive."

She lost her smile again.

"You know I mean as a female, a young girl. Did she warn you about boys, about sex?"

I didn't answer.

"Didn't you have that famous birds-and-bees conversation with your mother?"

"No. I don't know what that means."

"No? Am I to believe that your mother has kept you an infant? With all that was happening around you?"

She thought a moment.

"On the other hand, that makes sense," she said, answering her own question. "Did your teacher in science talk about human reproduction?"

I didn't answer.

"How could your mother be so selfish?"

"My mother isn't selfish." I started to cry.

"If she didn't prepare you for adolescence properly, she was. *Mon Dieu!*" she said, a Nattie expression. "Don't tell me that we're going to have to start from the beginning. You're sexually repressed."

"No," I said. "I know what sex is. We just didn't put it all on a black-board in my house."

She smiled.

"I like your spirit."

She stood and then paced for a few moments before stopping to nod at me.

"I know exactly how we will begin, but I have some more questions for you first. I want you to answer quickly, the first thing that comes to your mind, understand? Understand? You're just going to make this harder on yourself if you pout," she said when I didn't reply.

"Yes, I understand."

"I told you I'd like you to say 'No, Dr. Kirkwell' or 'Yes, Dr. Kirk-well.'"

I looked away.

"I'll leave, and things will be even worse. I promise you that."

I took a deep breath.

"Yes, Dr. Kirkwell."

"Good. Was there a boy in your class whom you liked?"

"Yes, Dr. Kirkwell."

"Did you dream of kissing him?"

"No," I said.

"Dr. . . ."

"No, Dr. Kirkwell."

"Are you being honest? Did you tell your mother about it, and did she get upset? Well?"

"No. No, Dr. Kirkwell."

"No, I mean, did you tell her?"

"No."

"And she didn't ask if anything like that was happening?"

I started to cry, gasping with the tears. I wasn't going to tell her Nattie had asked.

"Okay, okay," she said. "We're just getting to know each other today. I don't want any hysteria. Typical," she muttered. "I'm probably here just in time."

She brought the chair back to the desk and opened the briefcase.

"These are your books. Each one, you see, has a slip of paper in it. It tells you what I want you to read before I come here again. This," she said, holding up a black-and-white notebook, "is your self book. You should start it all today."

"What's a self book?"

"You'll sit at that desk and start to write it now."

"Write what?"

"Write about yourself." She smiled, reminding me of a cat. "Come here. Now," she ordered.

I rose and went to the desk. She pulled out the chair.

"Sit."

After I did, she held up a pen and opened the notepad.

"Make it in the form of a letter. It will be easier for you that way." She handed me the pen.

"Start with this." She looked down at me. "Go on, get ready."

I did.

"'Dear Dr. Kirkwell, my name is Caroline Bryer. I'd like you to know everything about me.' Go on. Write it."

She hovered over me as I did.

"Perfect. Now, I don't want to hear about when you were born and where you lived. Just write what you think about yourself. Think about all the important things that happened to you and how you felt about them. Go back as far as you can remember."

"You mean like a diary?"

"Vaguely," she said, smirking as if *diary* was a dirty word. "This is really different because you're writing to me, not some imaginary person. And we already know, you'll only tell the truth. Nothing about you is too small or insignificant. Don't worry about that. Think about things that made you happy and things that made you sad. It doesn't have to be in any order time-wise. When you remember something, write it . . . to me. I think you understand what I want, so don't look confused. Right?"

Her words fell on me like a cold rain. I was afraid to look up at her.

"Well?"

"Yes, Dr. Kirkwell."

When I looked up at her now, she smiled.

"If this works out, I might make you the subject of a book that I can use to help other young girls and boys. Wouldn't you be proud of that?"

I don't want to be a book; I want to go home, I thought.

She patted me on the shoulder and started toward the door, stopping when she opened it and looking back at me.

"I'm going right to your grandfather to tell him we're doing fine and you're on your way."

"To where?"

"Becoming a true Sutherland," she said, and walked out.

That was the one thing, I thought, that Mommy didn't want me to become.

13

I lost track of time because one day seemed no different from any other. Just about all the time Dr. Kirkwell spent with me involved her tutoring me in the tenth-grade subject matter that I was to learn from the books she had brought me. Because I was accelerating, she said I had to work seven days a week. She gave me tests weekly, and I always got an A or A-plus. Whenever I asked her when I could go out, she'd say, "Soon. We have to be sure you're ready."

Ready for what? I wondered, but was afraid to ask. I was locked in this room. If I went out now, what was she afraid people, especially my grandparents, would see? What would they do? Was whatever it was so terrible that they wouldn't even want to look at me? When I awoke with the buzzer, I did look first at myself in the large oval mirror, searching for those mysterious changes Mrs. Lawson had predicted. Were they putting something in my food? What, if anything, already had been done to me? How angry my mother would be, I thought, and Nattie. Nattie was more like Daddy at times.

Why was Mrs. Lawson so sure I'd be a different person anyway? All

I really saw was that my hair had grown longer. My mother would have trimmed it by now. When I asked Dr. Kirkwell about it, she told me just to continue brushing it and pinning it up. The only hint she gave me about it was that I was not to be like those women who cut their hair so short and looked so much like men that people on first sight couldn't tell the difference. Nevertheless, on my own I cut my bangs. She seemed okay with that.

But what really frightened me was that I began to forget things like what day it was. I could feel myself docilely accepting my current fate. I no longer thought about pounding and pounding on the door until the echo through the dark hallway outside of it would reverberate through the house and at least get my grandmother protesting what was being done to me. If it wasn't for the buzzer every morning, I'd probably sleep until the moment Dr. Kirkwell had arrived.

Nights were harder, and I tossed and turned, sometimes into the early morning hours. The worst nightmare I had was born from the horrid way Mrs. Lawson described Mommy and Nattie's accident. Usually, I woke up from it and felt even more panic, realizing that I was locked away like some horrible criminal and that, according to Mrs. Lawson, my father had agreed to all this. Sometimes that left me in a cold sweat, battling the urge to scream and scream until my throat exploded.

Sometimes I would pause and concentrate on every sound I heard outside of my room, hoping someone was interested in what was happening to me. Maybe Daddy had changed his mind and had come back from Hawaii for me. The more time passed, however, the weaker this hope became. I tried to keep it alive by doing things he would do, like arranging everything in my bathroom perfectly. I even envisioned him counting steps from one side of the room to the other and always walking over the same path to the desk or windows. Eventually, I stopped doing that, because it was making his desertion of me even more painful.

What was more horrible than a child fighting back the memory of her father? I thought. And then I thought, wasn't that what Mommy was always doing? That realization made everything seem even darker and more dreary. Visions of our neighbors, the images of those families laughing and smiling, children holding their parents' hands and parents happily greeting each other, brought tears to my eyes. Now it seemed more like a wishful dream than a memory of us being like that. Maybe I was always dreaming; maybe we were never really the perfect family.

I cheered myself up by telling myself that the end of my confinement, more like a caging, couldn't be too far off now. In the meantime, to ward off crying inside myself, I envisioned Mommy sitting on the bed beside me, running her fingers through my hair and describing how wonderful things would be once I was out of this room.

"I promise you I'm not dead and gone," she told me in my imaginary scene. "Nattie and I are working on getting you out and home. Would I ever leave you? How silly to think it, despite what anyone has said."

I'd close my eyes and feel her lips on my cheek. How else could I fall asleep? But who could be as disappointed about the arrival of morning as I was, because with it came reality, this cold, large room and the old clothing I had been given to wear? Every time I heard the door opening, I hoped to see either my grandfather or my grandmother coming to tell me I could come out now and join the family. All would be well, and I'd even learn the truth about Mommy and Nattie.

But the only other people I saw were Grandfather's two servants who were assigned to bring me what I needed, the basics. One would carry it all in, and the other would stand in the doorway like some prison guard. Many times I was tempted to rush at her and squeeze through. But always I would think, where would I go? And surely they would have someone capture me and take me back, even Emerson, who could lose his job if he didn't.

One of the servants would say, "Here is your new linen." I'd have to have my bed stripped and ready for it. "Here are your clean towels and washcloths," she would say, and take the used ones from the hamper. Other than that, they only announced breakfast, lunch, or dinner and took away the dirty dishes and glasses. Neither asked how I was.

In fact, before I could say a word, ask a question, they would hurry out. I was sure that they wouldn't tell me anything anyway. Why waste my breath? If anything, they looked frightened that they might slip in a forbidden word. When I glimpsed past the one in the doorway into the hallway, I saw it was still kept quite dark. I never saw anyone from the family walking in and out. Once in a while I caught sight of Mrs. Lawson watching from the end of the corridor, probably to be sure I didn't try to escape.

The only way I could really mark the time was to look out my bay windows and watch the weather and the return of green leaves and grass. Perhaps, I thought, now that spring had come, they might want me to have some outdoor exercise, but Dr. Kirkwell had yet to mention it. When I saw the flow of green running again through the distant mountains and hills and the blossoming of flowers off to the right and left, the air in my room smelled more dry and dusty to me. It felt like the dark shadows in the corners were always wanting to encompass me. In nightmares, I was drowned in shadows and never to be seen again.

Once again, I would hear the unanswered questions in my mind. Why was my grandfather doing this? How much longer would it be before he welcomed me back to the family and sent me back to school? How could people who were supposed to love you tolerate your being denied even sunlight? Surely they would realize what they were doing and had done to me.

But then again, how could I have faith in a grandfather who would do this to me in the first place, or a grandmother who would let him? Should I hope he would be impressed with my schoolwork and wake up one morning thinking it was time to love me? As I looked at the world outside coming back to life, the sun nourishing, its warm kiss opening the buds of flowers, I thought again about school, our physical education classes outside, the sound of laughter, the boys teasing and some of the girls flirting, and I felt a great longing to return not only to Mommy and Nattie, but to the life I had known. I could die here from the inside out, and no one would realize it until it was too late.

All the unhappiness and frustrations I had ever felt before this imprisonment and forced learning seemed so insignificant now. I wished I could return and start again, never complaining about anything and appreciating everything. I would never be impatient; I would never sulk or be angry at anyone or anything. I'd wake up every morning with my first thought being *I'm so grateful.* I wouldn't envy or be jealous of any boy or girl in my class. The smile on my face would look unbreakable.

What, if anything, could I be grateful for here? The food, the clean linen and towels, the big bed with the oversize pillows? My own personal therapist and tutor who Mrs. Lawson said was a famous expert and to whom my grandfather was giving lots of money? I was very confused. Dr. Kirkwell hadn't stuck me with any needles or made me take any pills.

She was really no more than a regular teacher. She even had a blackboard brought in so she could write new words or do math problems with me. The library continued to fill with more books on geology and history and, of course, novels she insisted I read and write reports on, like *Pride and Prejudice* and *Jane Eyre.* She wanted me to explain what I liked about the stories and what I didn't. My English teacher at school had asked us to do that for the books we read in class, so none of it seemed especially weird. Where was all this special therapeutic treatment Mrs. Lawson had suggested?

In fact, I began to wonder, where was the woman I first met? Dr. Kirkwell seemed so different now from the woman who had introduced herself to me that first day. Her voice was softer; there were more smiles. I was beginning to think that everything else, all the things that were supposed to change me into a different person, had been forgotten. Should I be happy about that? Maybe Mrs. Lawson was just trying to frighten me when she had talked about her and all that would be done to satisfy my grandfather. This was nothing more than being tutored, though I was kept locked away.

And then after about a month, things did begin to change, especially Dr. Kirkwell's attitude toward me. I could feel it from the moment she would enter. A week ago she had brought in a vinyl record player and let me listen to the music she had chosen. She said these were classic love songs, emphasizing love between men and women. I vaguely recalled hearing some of them by singers like Nat King Cole, Andy Williams, Johnny Mathis, and Elvis Presley. Mommy liked to listen to them. When I told Dr. Kirkwell about "Sweet Caroline" and how my mother loved it and how we danced to it, she smiled and said, "For now, let's put that memory in the closet and shut the door. Think about these."

Think about these? What should I think about them? I wondered, but didn't ask. Despite that, even though I couldn't play it, even on the computer, I heard "Sweet Caroline" in my mind and danced as if Mommy was right there dancing with me. If I heard anything outside my door, I stopped immediately, my heart pounding. Somehow, I had no doubt, Dr. Kirkwell would know what I was hearing. I had the feeling that she was getting deeper and deeper inside me. How could I keep any secret from her? Maybe that was what was really happening, maybe that was how I'd be changed. I was being peeled like an onion.

She continued to review my self book every day, but up to now she didn't ask me any questions about what was in it. She simply said, "Keep going. This is fine."

Aside from Grandfather's servants who brought me my food, some different old clothes, and fresh bedding and bathroom towels and wash-cloths, no one else visited me. If I asked Dr. Kirkwell a question about my family, her response was always the same: "Let's get this underway first."

Didn't my grandmother worry about me all this time? Couldn't she at least visit?

"How long is 'underway'?" I asked, but she just smiled.

"As long as it is," she said.

I wanted to keep going, ask her why she couldn't give me a specific answer, but something told me not to. She might think any progress we'd made together in my studies was less than she had hoped. Maybe, if I could be more patient, I'd learn everything about Mommy and Nattie eventually. I was hopeful again because it seemed I was pleasing her.

Soon after she had brought me the record player and records, more began to be brought to my room: a small dining table and two chairs, a computer desk and a laptop, and the first of a half dozen paintings to be hung on the walls. Dr. Kirkwell explained that they were prints and not the actual paintings. One was a picture of Romeo and Juliet kissing the way I remembered how Mommy and Daddy used to kiss before the magic seeped out of our house. Dr. Kirkwell said she would be telling me the story of Romeo and Juliet's love. She might even read it to me or have me read it on my own and then ask questions. As if to tempt me, she left the picture on the desk beside the computer.

Another picture was of a man and a woman, both naked, the man with his lips on the woman's cheek. He had what looked like butterfly wings. She said they were called Flora and Zephyr and she would tell me their story, too. A third was a picture of a man and a woman kissing in a rowboat just beneath a walkway bridge. She called it *Forever Yours*. And the fourth was a picture of a naked man and woman, the man leaning over a boat to kiss the woman while she floated in the water on her back. She said it was called *The Siren (Green Abyss)*. The next day there were two more with a naked woman and a naked man clinging to each other and kissing.

"We'll talk about how these make you feel," she said, "so look at them hard and long every day.

"I have more for you to look at on your computer," she told me. "I will show you how to view them. We're going to use your computer for your work, but only for that. It's been formatted so you can't use it for anything else. No games, no emails, no internet. Don't waste your time trying to do that."

During these days, despite her firm orders, her voice was softer and she smiled warmly. Oddly, all that did was baffle me even more. I was still afraid to trust her even though she made a point of saying almost daily, "I hope we're becoming friends."

As time passed, Mrs. Lawson stopped by from time to time only to be sure I was taking care of my room, my bathroom. She brought me additional clothes and shoes, none of it looking brand-new. I was afraid to ask her anything. Suddenly she looked more afraid of saying anything to me anyway. I wondered if Dr. Kirkwell had forbidden it. I didn't want to feel this way, but I was having trouble resisting the thought that maybe Dr. Kirkwell was my friend now because of how well I was doing following her lessons and orders. Maybe she would really help me and protect me.

Finally, yesterday she came in, sat me on my bed, and sat in the desk chair just as she had the first day. She had her briefcase beside her. Immediately, I knew that this was going to be a very different day.

"Today we're not going to do schoolwork with your textbooks and assignments," she said. "We're just going to talk. I also have things I'll show you. So," she continued, "let's start. You've learned a great deal about human biology and animal biology. I think you have one of the best textbooks for it. We talked about nature and the laws of nature. You learned how species continue, keep themselves alive, right?"

"Yes, Dr. Kirkwell."

"What was the word we used and studied for that?"

"Reproduction."

"Exactly. And what did I tell you about sex?"

"That its purpose was reproduction."

"Why is it pleasurable?"

"You said it encourages us to want to reproduce."

She sat back, looking satisfied. Then she opened her briefcase and took out some pictures. The first was of two women kissing passionately, one standing between the legs of the other. I nearly gasped because they resembled Mommy and Nattie.

"Do you see what they're doing? They're rubbing their pelvises against each other to excite each other. It's sex, but it's homosexual sex. Did you ever witness your mother doing this with her friend? Did they make you watch? Did they tell you they were homosexuals, or did they just say they were gay?"

The questions came fast and furious as if she didn't want to give me a chance to lie. I shook my head so hard that I had pain in my neck. She studied me, her eyes searching every corner of my mind and heart.

"They never told you they were gay?"

I remembered Nattie saying something about their being the only gay couple on the street, but Mommy didn't tell it to me that way, so I shook my head again.

"'Yes or no, Dr. Kirkwell,' remember?"

She had stopped insisting on that, so I was surprised she did now.

"No, Dr. Kirkwell."

She narrowed her eyes and pressed her lips together. Seconds passed. I was getting very uncomfortable because I was so stiff, but I was afraid to move.

"What did your mother say about her relationship to Natalie Gleeson?" she asked sternly. "Well?"

I never forgot her exact words. Maybe I was shocked; maybe I was afraid.

"She said, 'You know how Daddy and I used to like to kiss and hug, hold hands, and snuggle in bed, at least in the early years of our marriage? That's something Nattie and I like to do, all of it. And the same way.'"

After a moment she smiled, satisfied that I was telling the truth.

"And how did you feel when she told it to you like that? Don't lie to me. I'll know it," she added.

"I didn't know what to say. I was . . . confused."

"So you're telling me you didn't know what she meant when she said 'all of it'?"

"Not exactly."

"But you did understand soon after?"

I was silent.

She pointed at the picture of the women in my lap.

"Well?"

I couldn't keep the tears from slipping over my lids.

"Did you love your mother less?"

"No," I said quickly. "No, Dr. Kirkwell."

"Girls often want to be like their mothers," she said. "Okay. We know what to do. Look at the picture again," she ordered. "Can these two women make a baby, create another human being, like this, doing this?"

My throat felt like it was closing.

"Can they? Well?" Her questions felt more like tacks being pressed into my head.

"No, Dr. Kirkwell."

"What if every woman alive did this and never did it with a man? What would happen to us?"

I knew what she wanted me to say, but after Mommy had told me about her and Nattie, I recalled Nattie talking to Mommy about their having a baby, maybe a little brother for me. I didn't really listen to them talking until I had heard that.

"I know some men whose sperm I'd like served in vitro," Nattie had said, and Mommy had said, "I bet you do."

They had laughed, but then both suddenly looked serious.

"I often thought about what it would be like to be a mother. Someone on the ambassador's team had the nerve to ask me if I ever felt a maternal instinct."

"Oh, Nattie," Mommy had said. She caressed her face and then kissed her. Mommy laughed and said, "I'd gladly give you the role. You're so good with Caroline. I have no fears about us having another child."

Another child? When they talked like that, they seemed to forget I was nearby. They left and went upstairs after that. Neither of them cared that I had overheard them. I thought they knew, but they certainly didn't think to explain any of it.

"Well?" Dr. Kirkwell said now. "Don't drift off to some safe place in your mind. Answer the question. What would happen to the human species?"

Dared I say it? I instinctively realized that to tell Dr. Kirkwell something different from what she was expecting would not be helpful to me. And I was afraid to tell her what I had overheard. She'd surely think I knew more of the personal things between Mommy and Nattie and wouldn't believe I hadn't ever seen them being as passionate as the women in the photograph. I had never spied on them, and they always closed their door. Were they protecting me, or was Mommy, as Dr. Kirkwell would like me to believe, ashamed?

"The human race could die out," I said.

"Exactly." She waved the picture. "Unnatural. Against nature. I know you didn't have much religious training, if any at all, so I won't talk about what it says in the Bible. Nature is enough."

She took out another picture of the two women, this time their bodies frighteningly ugly, looking like they were full of rot, kissing the same way.

"Look at both pictures. Every day. Just stare at them now for a while. Could you do what they are doing? Would you want to? Keep asking yourself the question. I just told you that children often want to be like their parents. Do you really want to be like your mother, especially in this way?"

I didn't answer. I could easily imagine how Daddy would react to someone asking me these questions. I felt the same embarrassment, even his anger. She was digging into places in myself that even I was hesitant to explore. I felt naked, without any privacy.

"Did you ever dream of this with another girl in your class? Well?"

Had I? For a few moments, I did wonder about myself, but I also knew the answer she wanted to hear right now, and right now was all that mattered in my life.

"No, Dr. Kirkwell."

She studied me with those suspicious eyes. Then she put both pictures on my lap. I could feel myself trembling, more afraid that I would knock them off me than anything else.

"Unnatural," she said again, her face full of rage. Suddenly, she smiled. "But you are a very smart girl. And from what I've read in your self book, I think we'll be able to assure your grandfather that you'll be all right. We just won't rush it. If you proved me wrong, he'd be twice as angry."

She reached into her briefcase and came up with a small recorder and earphones.

"I want you to listen to this every day before I get here. It's from one of my books and a lecture I do. I will ask you questions about it, so listen repeatedly and carefully. Look at those pictures while you listen," she said. "Start doing it now."

I took the earphones and recorder, but just as I was putting on the earphones, she grasped my wrist.

"The day will come, hopefully soon, when you will willingly tell your grandfather that you understand why he is so angry and you agree with him."

She let go.

"Listen, and while you do, look at the pictures," she said. "It's not hard. I wrote that lecture for children about your age and even a little younger. Some had a parent just like yours."

She rose.

I thought she was going to leave and there would be no more questions, but she stepped back toward me and asked, "How often do you touch yourself there?"

She nodded clearly toward my vagina. I nearly gasped. I had done that just the other day. Was I being watched, even in the dark?

Unexpectedly, she smiled.

"Don't worry about it. We'll talk about it more later today. We'll have other things to do. Just do everything I told you to do now. I know how long the lecture lasts, so I'll be back almost exactly at the end."

As she left, I began to listen to her lecture. I was afraid to look away from the pictures on my lap because I kept thinking she was watching me somehow. In the lecture she talked about sexual diseases and how other girls and boys my age would mock me and avoid me if I became what my mother had become. Eventually, I would hate myself. She rattled off statistics about homosexuals committing suicide more often. She said the likelihood was five times higher for gay men and women.

A little more than an hour later, she returned.

"Go to your desk," she said, "and complete this test."

She put it on the desk and stepped back. It was a test on her lecture. I had tried hard to listen to everything, but every once in a while, I had thought about my mother and Nattie and probably missed some things.

"Go on," she said, and I sat.

While I was taking the test, I was vaguely aware of her setting up something else behind me. When I was finished, I turned around.

"I'm sorry about this," she said, "but it has proven to be an effective technique."

She unfolded what looked like belts and suspenders, all connected and all having wires running into a single wire attached to a black box that had two buttons on it, one red and one blue.

"Come here," she ordered. Trembling, I walked toward her, and she slipped it all over me. "Go back to your computer."

I did. She leaned over and typed on the keyboard and then stepped behind me.

"You press the return key when you feel something unpleasant, something that disgusts you, and then you see another picture and another. Some will be different and you won't feel anything, and others will be the same as the first that brought you the unpleasant feeling. Let's begin," she said.

My father once told me that water was dangerous around electricity, so all I could think was that my tears would make it worse, but it was impossible to not cry.

14

I couldn't remember if I had passed out or if Dr. Kirkwell had taken the equipment off me, guided me to my bed, and tucked me in. Whatever, I slept right up until the servants brought my dinner. They did glance at me, looking hurriedly away. I don't think they even announced dinner. They were that eager to get in and out. I rose slowly but still felt dizzy. The room spun, taking my breath away, so I lay back and fell asleep again.

When I woke up I still didn't feel very hungry. I wasn't dizzy again, but I thought I should eat something. Of course, all the food was cold by now. I ate what I could and finished just before the two women returned to take the dishes and silverware and replace some towels and washcloths. I had returned to my bed just before they entered and flopped backward on it, staring up at the ceiling. Neither of them would look at me or even ask if I was all right.

"I want my grandfather," I said, sitting up before they left. They paused, looked at each other, and hurried even faster to get out. "I want my grandfather!" I shouted after them. They quickly closed and locked the door. I could hear the echo of their steps as they rushed down the dark corridor. The silence seemed even deeper. It was as if I were at the bottom of a hollow tube filled with water. Night had crept in while I was lying there. I could barely make out some lighting along the trees and the wall surrounding Sutherland.

I drifted into and out of a daze. My body seemed to have its own clock by now, and I anticipated the end-of-the-day buzzer coming, so I rose and began to undress to put on my nightgown. This one was so worn-out and sheer that I could see my belly button. It was as short as all the other clothes, the hem about six inches above my knees. If I hadn't left on my panties, anyone would see everything else. I went into the bathroom to wash and brush my teeth.

Just before I finished, I heard the door being opened. My heart began to thump in anticipation. Did they tell my grandfather? Had he come after all? Did he finally think that things had gone too far? It was possible that it was my grandfather, because Dr. Kirkwell always called out my name if I was in the bathroom when she entered. Whoever had entered was just waiting. However, when I came out, I was quite shocked.

My cousin Simon stood there staring at me. He wore a thin dark blue sweater with a white-collared shirt and a pair of black slacks. He always dressed like he was going to an important event and never looked anything like the teenage boys I remembered in my school. His hair was as trim as Daddy's would be. His left hand was clutched around his right wrist, his arms against his body. He looked like he was posing for a picture, that wry smile on his face as he took in my look of shock.

"Hello, Caroline," he said.

"How did you get in?" I asked.

He held up a key.

"Did Grandfather send you?"

"Of course not," he said.

"You came on your own? How did you get the key? Do your parents know? Is someone going to help me?"

"No one knows I'm here," he said.

"I don't understand. Then . . ."

"I was never permitted to walk down this corridor and go into this room. It was always kept locked. I've been in here before, before you were brought here. One time when I was sleeping over, I went into Mrs. Lawson's room. She has two sets of keys for everything on big rings. She never noticed this one was missing, or maybe she never told anyone. Our grandfather doesn't tolerate mistakes or accidents."

"He thinks he's the pope," I said, remembering how Mommy put it once.

Simon smirked. It was more of an arrogant grin.

"I bet your mother told you that."

"Maybe."

I paused, realizing I was standing in this practically transparent night-gown. I hurried to the bed to put on the robe folded at the foot of it.

"Self-conscious," he said. "You've become a real preadolescent."

I looked at him almost sideways. *A real preadolescent?*

He walked around the room, studying the framed painting prints, glancing at my computer and then at the books on the desk. He picked up my self book.

"Don't touch that," I said.

"Oh? What exactly is this? Wait." He held up his right forefinger and tilted his head as if he was hearing the answer. "She told you to write your feelings and thoughts, not just for now but for any of your recent memories, especially involving your mother."

"How did you know?"

He put it down, turned to me, and shrugged, just the way he did when he said something he thought was plain as day. Whether he intended it or not, it often made me feel a little foolish, always widening the gap in our ages, as if he was maturing and I was staying the same. Except for an occasional family event held at his home and seeing each other here, we hardly spent time with each other, and when we did, he seemed aloof, as if traveling on a different highway.

"Once I understood what Grandfather wanted done and found out who Dr. Kirkwell was, I looked up aversion therapy. She's considered one of the top experts in it. Grandfather is paying her a small fortune, I'm sure, definitely spending more money on you than he's ever spent on me."

"I wish he didn't spend a penny."

Simon laughed and tilted his head back as he always did, making it look like he was swallowing a pill. His laugh was always silent.

"Why did you look it up?"

"Anything even slightly medical interests me. I intend to become a doctor, however, not a therapist," he quickly added. "I've decided I'm interested in women, but more scientifically. Biologically, I find them more complex. I've been thinking about specializing in gynecology."

"What's that exactly?"

"A doctor who is specifically involved in the health of the female reproductive system. I'll probably become a gynecologic surgeon. I'm not interested in becoming an obstetrician, treating pregnant woman and delivering babies. Too simple. Glorified midwives. I assume you know what midwives are."

"I know what they are. You're not that old, Simon. How can you decide your whole life now?"

He shrugged.

"I can. So," he said, seeing the photograph of the two women kissing passionately, "what has she told you about yourself? You've been in here long enough, I imagine."

He sat on my desk chair. I looked at the door.

"If you run out of here and they find out it was because of me, I'll never be able to come here again," he said. "Grandfather will be angry at me for a while, but he'll get over it. He often brags about me. But I don't think he'll be as generous toward you. At least, not now. So? What has our Dr. Kirkwell said about you?"

"She did a terrible thing to me. If I tell you exactly what that was, will you tell Grandfather?"

"Of course not. Duh. He'd know I was in here, Caroline. Try to first think of the consequences before you say or do something. Didn't you ever hear the expression 'Fools rush in where angels fear to tread'?"

"Why do you act so old? You're only two years older than I am."

"Two years, four months, and two days," he said.

"So? That's not a lot."

"There is chronological age and mental age. I'm not egotistical when I state something that is factual. My mental age has been objectively measured. I'm way beyond the typical high school student, even college students. I simply had a good dip in the gene pool, DNA, and don't ignore it. Before you ask, that means beyond my father's and mother's genetics."

"I don't understand. The gene pool?"

"I was born with certain advantages built in, passed along from older generations on both sides of my family. What kind of science classes did you have? Or teachers? How simple do I have to make it so you'll understand?"

I was quickly losing patience with him, even though he had the key.

"I want to get out of here, Simon, but even more than that, I want to know what you meant at the cemetery."

"I imagine you do." He stood and looked around. "I think I could last here much longer than you can or will. I don't mind spending time alone. Better for the concentration."

"We're not talking about you."

He stared at me.

"Again, you're not using foresight. Where would you go if you escaped Sutherland? From what I overheard my parents say, your father practically disowned you. He's remarried with a new family."

"That's not your problem, Simon. Will you tell me what you meant at the cemetery or not?"

"I might. Let's not rush things. It could only make it more difficult for you in here."

"What does that mean?"

"You know what really makes someone an adult?"

"I'm sure you'll tell me."

"It's when you recognize what you can't change and learn to accept it, and what you can change and do it. Maybe I can help you. No. Correction. I know I can help you. This is all," he said, gesturing at the walls, the paintings, "very interesting to me."

"That's what it is? Interesting? I told you she did a terrible thing to me."

He walked toward me. I backed up to the bed and sat. He stepped closer and looked at me just the way a doctor might. I could almost feel his eyes moving over my face, my neck, and my body. I closed my robe tighter.

"I don't see any trauma."

"What?"

"You don't have any scratches or cuts, bruises on your face or neck. What did she do that was so terrible? Are you hiding something on your body?"

"She shocked me, connected me to something electric."

He smiled.

"She did that, did she? From what I read, it's actually been outlawed if it is used for this reason."

"What reason?"

"I told you. Aversion therapy. Describe what she did with more detail," he said, stepping back and folding his arms across his chest.

I had never realized how strangely different his eyes were. They were dark blue, but when I looked at him closely, I could see tints of gray.

Uncle Martin looked more like Grandfather, but Simon had more of his mother's features, the smaller nose and softer, more perfect lips. He had her high cheekbones, too. When he wasn't being arrogant, despite how he defined himself as otherwise, he was very good-looking. He seemed so much taller since I had last seen him. I hadn't really looked at him at the cemetery. I was sure he was easily close to six feet tall. He had slim shoulders, and although I knew he wasn't very athletic, he looked fit. Daddy always commented on Simon's posture, saying it was admirable that a young man held himself so well. "Most of your friends and teenagers slump," he had said.

"She put some equipment with wires over me and stood behind me with a metal box of some sort. Then she made me look at pictures."

"Of lesbians, women like your mother and her lover, right?"

For a moment, the memory of that and the shocks took my breath away. That only made him smile.

"Interesting. Residual benefits already."

"I don't know what you're talking about. It was terrible. If I didn't turn the picture quickly, the shock continued."

"And when you turned it and looked at a heterosexual woman, it stopped . . . a woman maybe kissing a man?"

"Why do you know so much about it?"

"I told you. I studied up on it. When I attack a subject, I devour it. Maybe it does work," he said, voicing a thought. "Then what happened?"

"I don't remember. I was in bed and had fallen asleep."

"Interesting."

"Stop saying that."

"Okay," he said, softening his look. "I do feel sorry for you. Grandfather can go overboard with his rage and opinions. I learned at an early age when to talk and when not to when I was in his company. My father has always been afraid of what I might say to his father. He rightly believes my grandfather would blame him.

"Despite what's happened to you regarding your father, there was much about him I liked. Unlike my father, your father is firm in his opinions. True, he's like Grandfather that way, but it's a quality I admire. Maybe because my father's always been a wimp."

He looked so ashamed and upset that for a moment, I felt sorry for him. I quickly drove that feeling out.

"What is this room? Why were you, everyone, forbidden to come here?" I asked.

"Your mother never said anything about it?"

"No."

"I always liked your mother. She was always nice to me. Frankly, I'm not surprised that she fell in love with another woman. I'm good at reading people."

"Is there anything you're not good at, Simon?"

He laughed.

"The hardest thing about being intelligent and perceptive is learning how to keep your mouth shut."

"Poor you."

He laughed again.

"I like you, too, Caroline. I actually like your innocence."

I stared at him. Maybe he really was a man in a teenage boy's body.

"Well? What about this room?"

"It was your great-aunt's room."

"Who?"

"Our great-grandfather had an affair with one of the housekeepers. Her pregnancy was kept secret. She died in childbirth right here in Sutherland. Their baby suffered from progeria, and just like your mother became an embarrassment for our grandfather, the baby was an embarrassment for our great-grandfather. They thought she would die before she was twelve, thirteen, but she lived to be sixteen."

"What is progeria?"

"A genetic disorder that causes children to age rapidly, usually start-ing within the first two years of life. From what I've learned, and it hasn't been easy to learn any of the details about her, she showed symptoms at eight months. Great-grandfather had the sister of his housekeeper care for her." He looked around as if there was still proof. "In this room. She never came out of it. Very few outsiders, besides the doctor, of course, knew she existed. Servants were terrified of even looking toward this room. He never even gave her a name. He thought there was no point; he was too heartbroken, and he thought she'd die soon. I guess the most courageous thing anyone did about her was give her a name. Her mother's sister named her Prissy. He had a picture of the housekeeper. Maybe it's still in here somewhere. She was very pretty. It's a silly little love story."

"Silly?"

"Our great-grandmother Abigail Warton, as she liked to be known, fell into a deep depression when she learned about the secret affair and the baby, which is why, like for your mother and my father, a nanny was more of a mother to Grandfather. I guess your mother thought you were too young to know any of this. Understandable. Too complicated even for some adults."

Simon moved to the closet and searched around for a few moments, then returned to the bed with a dusty box. Opening it, he pulled out a photograph of a man who looked so much like Grandfather, beaming next to a beautiful Black woman. It was the happiest I'd ever seen two people.

"This was his secret love?"

"Yes."

"I still don't understand what progeria is."

"Don't you know what aging is?" He sighed. "The child grows slowly, to below-average height and weight. They have a narrowed face, small lower jaws, thin lips, and a beaked nose."

"Oh."

"The head is usually disproportionately large for the face. There's soon hair loss, including eyelashes and eyebrows, wrinkled skin. Think of how Grandmother Judith looks, only worse and by ten or eleven. Maybe Great-grandfather wasn't wrong keeping her in here, huh?"

"No. It sounds so horrible to keep someone that young locked up; it's cruel."

"Um. Genetics determine everything, the good and the bad about someone. Understand?"

For a long moment I simply stared at the floor.

"When are you going to tell me what you meant at the cemetery?" I asked without looking at him.

"Maybe after a little quid pro quo."

"What's that?" I asked, looking up quickly.

"Latin: something for something."

"What can I give you? They took everything from me. Even my clothes. I'm probably wearing that poor girl's clothes. I have nothing from the house. What's the something?"

"You," he said, "something of you."

I sat back. He wasn't joking. What could I give him, a lock of my hair?

"I told you where my interests lie, what I want to become. I intend to be the youngest student in medical school. Although I am in high school, I've taken enough Advanced Placement classes and exams and will continue to take them so that I will graduate from high school with the equivalent of a bachelor's degree, with a major in science. I know exactly what you're going through at this age. You've had your period, correct? I saw through your nightgown before you rushed to put on this robe. You're developing breasts—rather nicely, I think."

He paused, not changing expression.

"What are you feeling? Are you excited by the idea of my having seen your breasts? Or just embarrassed?"

"Just leave me alone, Simon."

"Really? Okay," he said, shrugging. "I'll stop."

He turned away and started toward the door.

"Wait."

He spun around.

"What do you want from me?" I asked, not disguising the desperation.

"Stand up and take off your robe," he said. He smiled. "I'm not going to hurt you, Caroline." He held out his hands and turned them up and down. "No electric wires."

I didn't move.

"Once I leave here, I won't return," he said. "There's no point in my risking it. Right now, Grandfather thinks the world revolves around me because of my grades and academic achievements. Honestly, he respects me more than he respects my father. I won't have a financial worry for the rest of my life. I know I'm significantly in his will right now.

"I don't know what he intends to do about you. Maybe they'll put you in a foster home or something. Or, if you satisfy Dr. Kirkwell, you'll be part of the family again, a Sutherland. Unfortunately, he could assign Mrs. Lawson to be your guardian as she was for your mother. Not a legal guardian, just her assignment. She'll be hovering over you constantly, mostly because she'll be afraid you will do something for which Grandfather will blame her. Still, you'd be out of here. Maybe it will just be a bigger cage to you.

"I'll help you as much as I can. I obviously know my way around everyone and everything. Or maybe I won't," he said.

A few moments passed. It felt like a little knife was twisting in my heart. I could hear myself breathing.

"All right," he said. "Let it be or not," he added, and turned away again.

"Okay," I said before he reached the door. "Do you promise to tell me what you meant in the cemetery?"

"I might do better than that," he said.

"How?"

"I might show you what I meant, but we have a ways to go first."

"I don't understand. How can you show me?" I asked.

"You'll see. Maybe."

"Do you know everything, even about Nattie?"

"I know everything my parents know," he said. "And more. I listened to them talking. They think I'm buried in a book. Yes, I do know about Nattie. She worked for the American ambassador to France, right?"

"Yes," I said breathlessly. "Do you know where she is?"

"Everything in due time. Earned."

I took off my robe and let it drop to my feet. He stood there looking at me and then smiled and started toward me. I shuddered with fear, sucked in my breath, and then put out my arm like a traffic cop.

He stepped closer. I closed my eyes.

"Do you have a girlfriend?" I asked. I sensed he had stopped and opened my eyes.

"No," he said. "Most of the girls in my school are afraid of me. That's what I think, but I don't care. This might be better for you if you close your eyes. Trust me," he said.

I did.

"You are pretty. I always thought your mother was prettier than mine."

Then I felt his lips on mine, and my eyes snapped open. He pulled back.

"Kissing is like a key that opens a door," he quickly said. "Don't make a big thing of it. Was that the first time a boy kissed you on the lips?"

"Yes."

"Did you like it?"

I didn't answer.

"You liked it. We'll see about all that later," he said. "Right now, I want to see how your skin is stretching and how your mammary glands are developing." He stepped back. "Take off the nightgown. Flimsy as it is, it's in the way."

I stared ahead, avoiding looking at him.

"You've gone this far. Don't screw it up," he said.

I thought I was going to cry, and so did he.

"Don't be a baby," he warned. "This is a mature way of looking at your body. Someday you'll think back to this and be grateful. We don't have much more time. I'm taking a big risk as it is."

I had to know the answers. I had to. I took a deep breath and pulled the nightgown over my head. I held it bunched up.

"Uh-huh. Nicely developing," he said.

I couldn't speak, and I was certainly afraid to scream. I didn't think it possible, but I felt even more trapped.

"You're going to be quite a woman," he said, just as the buzzer sounded and the lights went off.

"Perfect timing. See you tomorrow."

"What? But you said—"

"I'll be back tomorrow. The same time, maybe a little earlier."

He went out before I could say another word. When I heard the lock, I started to cry. Finally.

15

When Dr. Kirkwell came in the next day, she had already been told that I hadn't eaten any of my breakfast. I was dressed in one of the old, raggedy garments but lying in bed and staring up at the ceiling, trying to relive some of the happiest moments of my childhood. For a while it felt as if I had literally transported myself back in time. Sensing Dr. Kirkwell's overbearing presence was enough to pop my memories like popping soap bubbles. I saw her look at my food and then start slowly toward me. I couldn't help cringing, my hands in tight fists.

"Aren't you feeling well?"

"No."

"What's wrong?"

"I have cramps," I said.

"Ah. Your time of the month—or, as some say, 'the curse.' I imagine you have what you need and you've taken care of yourself."

"Yes."

She stared at me a moment and then lunged forward and pulled the short hem of the dress up quickly before I could stop her. Fear brought heat to my cheeks. "I know that you were given pads to wear. You're lying, aren't you? I thought we were beyond this sort of thing."

My lips trembled, and her face softened.

"You want a day off? Is that it?"

"I haven't had a day off since I was brought here," I said, on the verge of tears. "I didn't even have a chance to cry about my mother before I was given orders and made to do things."

"Oh, I'm sure you've cried. Many times. But the only cure for grief is—"

"To keep busy. I know."

"Who told you that?"

"My mother told that to Nattie when her mother died."

"You remember every word your mother said?"

"No, but I remember that because of how quickly both Nattie's parents died, her mother almost right after her father had died. My father called it the widowhood effect."

She smiled and nodded.

"I'm not surprised that you have a good memory for anything that's affected you emotionally. You're a very sensitive young woman. There's nothing wrong with that as long as it doesn't harm you in the end.

"I think we can ease off today and just do a few important things. I told your grandfather this morning that I have high hopes for your reentry into the Sutherland family."

Reentry? I felt a surge of happiness, hope. But I had to wonder, how would things be? Would I be going from one kind of imprisonment to another?

"When?"

"Oh, very soon now, I hope. But if you start this sort of behavior, you'll prolong it. I want you to get up, eat some, if not all, of your breakfast, and then," she said, opening her briefcase and taking out a folder, "go through these pictures and the questions about each. Mark your reactions on each page. I don't want you to think long about each answer. Answer each immediately. While you do all that, I'm going to do some of my work on your computer."

She stared at me so hard that I had to look away.

"Is there something else you're not telling me? Did anything different occur here after I left you yesterday?"

I fought back the heat that tried to come into my face. Could she be testing me? Had Simon confessed or been found out?

"No," I said.

Whether she believed me or not, she took the folder to my desk. Then she turned around and gazed at me with those microscope eyes.

"If we lose trust in each other at this late stage, you'll send yourself back to day one, and you'll have no one to blame but yourself."

I held my breath. Should I risk not telling the truth? If I told her about Simon, she would tell my grandfather, and I would not get the answers to my two important questions: what he had meant in the cemetery and what he knew about Nattie.

"I know."

Whether she was or not, she seemed satisfied.

"As long as you understand," she said. "Eat and work."

She headed for my computer, and I rose. Maybe it really would be just a little longer before I'd be out of here and out of these strange old clothes. I ate some of my breakfast while I began to look at the pictures of couples and the two choices for instant reactions: APPROVE, DISAPPROVE. I knew what she was expecting from me, but I couldn't help feeling that I was hurting Mommy. It was like sticking pins in a voodoo doll whenever I checked DISAPPROVE.

Then I thought Mommy would want me to do anything to get out of here. My only hope was that I was good enough at hiding my real feelings in order to convince Dr. Kirkwell that she was succeeding with me. It was a challenge. She had those X-ray eyes.

I remembered Daddy once saying, "If you want someone to believe what you're telling them, first believe it yourself." I wasn't sure at the time if he was saying that to Mommy or me. Maybe he was really only talking about what he would tell pilots when he was in the tower. "I can't have hesitation in my voice, or especially fear."

This doesn't mean anything, I recited to myself. *It's only paper that she'll put in her briefcase. I can make her believe me if I get myself to believe that.*

When I was finished, I sat back. She was still concentrating on what she was writing on my computer. After what seemed like almost ten minutes or so, she looked at me, completed whatever she was doing, and rose. She stood beside me and looked at my responses. I was confident they were the answers she wanted, even though I wasn't sure how I really felt.

"Why did you check DISAPPROVE on these?" she said, flipping to the pictures of naked women kissing and fondling each other.

"They can't make babies. It's unnatural," I said. A new thought occurred to me. "People might pretend it doesn't matter and say they respect them, but they don't."

Those were her exact words in her lecture. I tried not to sound like I was parroting her. I put all my emphasis on "don't."

Her eyes were burning into me.

"We'll see how much of that you truly believe and accept," she said, and returned the folder to her briefcase.

I thought that was it, that I was finished for the day, but she took a box of stationery out of her briefcase and brought it to me. She opened the box and took out sheets of letter paper.

"I want you to pretend you are your mother and you're writing a letter of apology to your father. She will apologize for what she has done to him and what she has done to you. I want you to get very detailed when you come to what she has done to you, how she has confused you and how hard she has made it for you to grow up normally. If the letter is honest and true and I tell your father that you wrote it, he might want to see you again. Do you want to see him again?"

"Yes."

"Well, then put everything you've learned from me into your letter. If you lie, I'll know, and I'll rip it up. If it's good and true, I'll show it to your grandfather first, and then we'll mail it overnight to your father in Hawaii, with my detailed explanation, of course. He'll see it's in your handwriting. You could be quite happy again. When you're done, just put it in the envelope, but don't seal it."

She took out an envelope. It was addressed to Morgan Bryer in Maui, Hawaii. *Daddy*, I thought. I did miss him, but to see him again, I would have to betray Mommy and hurt her like I never had.

"Eat your lunch and your dinner, but first bathe and change your clothes after you write the letter. I don't think you did that last night. Am I right?"

"Yes."

If she knew that, how much did she really know?

"Start thinking about what your mother will tell your father," she said. She returned to her briefcase, closed it, and looked at me. "I will return to pick up the letter before your dinner is served. Hopefully, tomorrow will be a very good day for you."

I watched her walk out. When I looked at the blank stationery, I felt sicker than I had this morning. I decided to bathe and change into another one of the old dresses first. Before I stepped out of the bathroom, I heard Grandfather's servants take my breakfast dishes and leave my lunch. *I had better eat it*, I thought, *or they'll tell Dr. Kirkwell.* As I ate, I stared at the stationery. How would I even begin? But I knew that if I didn't do it, I might be in here for months more, maybe years!

"Help me, Mommy," I whispered.

We'll do make-believe, I heard her say, just as she always had when I was little and something had saddened us both. I imagined her adding, *Don't worry about me.*

I picked up the pen. For a moment it felt more like a knife, but I drove that image away, swallowed hard, and began.

Dear Morgan, I wrote. I could hear Mommy call out his name. She used to make it sound longer: "Mooorgan." Sometimes he would just look at her as if she was speaking a foreign language. Or he would imitate her and say, "What, Linseeee?" In the early days, they would laugh at each other, but toward the end, neither liked the way the other pronounced his or her name. There was just a "What is it?"

I took another deep breath and continued, picking and choosing words and ideas from the articles I was made to read and Dr. Kirkwell's lectures.

> I am so sorry about how I hurt and disappointed you. I should have paid more attention to your feelings. I ignored your suspicions and pretended they didn't matter. You don't think of what I did as adultery so much as an attack on your manhood. I understand. I especially understand the pain that would bring to a man as proud of himself as you are and should be. I was simply selfish.
>
> I certainly should have considered how everything would hurt our family, especially Caroline. She had to face her fellow students in school, many of whom were whispering behind her back. Some parents even forbade their children to have anything to do with her. How could she have real friends? How could she grow up enjoying her youth, her school? She suffered because of that, because of me. I don't want her blaming you even in the smallest way.
>
> Now my father is suspicious of her and thinks she might turn out like me. She's not me; she's her own person. I'm sure she is both confused and angry, and that's my fault. Please don't blame

her for my actions even though she didn't cry to you or complain about me. It wasn't that she loved you less. She is torn between us now, and I'm sorry about that. I never meant to drive her away from you.

Caroline needs your love and attention more than ever, Morgan. She needs you in that tower, watching her take off and watching her land. I know she respected your wisdom and guidance. She often quoted you and was always concerned about your feelings.

I am also sorry for the hurt I caused my own family, all the Sutherlands. People are surely whispering behind my brother's and sister-in-law's backs. Even though they wouldn't dare say anything to my father or mother, both of them feel it. I've deeply disappointed them.

I've embarrassed the people I should have protected. Everything is my fault. I don't ask your forgiveness. I just want you to think of our Caroline. It's all right for you to forget me and have a new and better life. Caroline will be happy to be a part of that.

Linsey

I put the pen down, not realizing until I did that I had been crying the whole time I had thought of the words and had written them. Deep in my heart, I knew this was a betrayal of my mother. I could feel the flood of tears and regret falling inside me.

"Mommy," I whispered, "forgive me. I know you'd tell me it's all right. You understand, but it hurts; it really hurts."

I placed the letter in the envelope as Dr. Kirkwell had ordered, and then I went to the bay window and stared at the world outside.

"Mommy surely would forgive me. Mommy surely would forgive me."

Was it a prayer or a chant? I couldn't stop saying it. What frightened me the most at the moment was the possibility that Dr. Kirkwell had succeeded. She had convinced me enough for me to believe that what I had just written wasn't completely wrong because a family had been destroyed, and that made me feel even more guilty. I hated even the smallest possibility that Grandfather was right to be as angry as he was and to do what he had done to me. The most frightening thought was that Dr. Kirkwell was correct with her prediction: someday I would thank my grandfather; someday I would forgive him.

It would truly be like burying Mommy again.

Which made it even more important than ever to know what exactly Simon had meant at the cemetery. *Damn him*, I thought, but then I feared that he would not return, that maybe he had already left Sutherland, satisfied with what he had gotten from me. Or perhaps, as I also feared, Dr. Kirkwell knew about his visit and had told our grandfather.

When Dr. Kirkwell returned, I was sitting up in bed, reading *Romeo and Juliet*, mostly to take my mind off the path of fears.

"That's very good," she said after she had entered and saw me. "I was wondering when or if you would choose to read it yourself. What do you think so far?"

"Love can be stronger than family."

She held her half smile. She wasn't sure she liked my answer.

"Yes, I can see why you might think that, but it's much better to have both, isn't it?"

I nodded and then quickly said, "Yes, Dr. Kirkwell."

She walked over to the desk, took the letter out of the envelope, and read it. Then she folded it and put it back in the envelope, but didn't seal it.

"You did well," she said. "Your grandfather and I will decide if we'll send it. We will discuss your continued education once you leave this room. I will return after you have had your breakfast in the morning."

"Will I get something else to wear? Maybe my own clothes once I'm out of here?"

"Why do you want those? Your mother bought you some of those with someone else's opinion. From what I've been told, some of it was quite ridiculous for a girl your age."

"I just want something different to wear. These dresses itch."

I certainly wouldn't mention what Simon had told me about whose clothes these were. She would then know for sure he had been here, and everything would be ruined.

"We'll see," she said with that suspicious tone in her voice. "One thing at a time. Enjoy reading the play. Perhaps someday you'll see a performance."

I watched her leave with the letter I had hated to write. I did finish reading the play after dinner and cried about what happened to Romeo and Juliet. Then I reread some of the beautiful lines they had spoken to each other. I tried not to think of tomorrow. Would I be free, or would I be told not yet? Maybe because of *Romeo and Juliet*, I envisioned myself dying in here.

If I committed suicide, would it even matter? The room would be locked up again, and no one would be permitted to come in or even talk about it. I was tired of crying, and I was tired of looking at all these paintings. The only thing that brought any relief was the bay window. Even in the overcast darkness, it was something of an escape to look out and imagine the world I knew beyond the gates. I know I fell into a daze, because I never heard the door being unlocked and opened. Finally, I sensed he was standing behind me.

"Are you going to give me the answers you promised?" I asked without turning around. "Is that why you're here?"

Then I did spin on him, pointedly.

He smiled.

"How come you don't wear a bra?" he asked. "You need one now."

"They took all my things and never brought me any. I guess they never let Prissy wear one."

He laughed.

"No, I don't think that was important. Last night, did you dream about what we did? My kiss?" he asked, sounding more like Dr. Kirkwell. He narrowed his eyes similarly.

I could sense he was hoping I had somehow liked what he had done. Maybe he needed to feel that. Perhaps he wasn't as perfect as he thought he was. But I wasn't ready to give him any satisfaction.

"No, I didn't dream about it. I had trouble falling asleep, if you want to know."

"Sex can do that to you, make you restless. A part of you has been awakened for the first time. I was thinking of writing a paper about it, 'The Emerging Woman.' What do you think of that? I won't mention your name, but you'll certainly be a reference."

"Stop changing the subject, Simon. I let you do what you wanted. I think it was sick, but I let you do it because you promised the answers. Why did you say what you said in the cemetery? What do you know about Nattie?"

"I might have to spend some time with you afterward," he said, sounding more like someone giving a warning.

"After what?"

"After we return."

"From where?"

"Once we go out that door, you have to be as quiet as a shadow. I'm taking a very big risk for you," he said, instead of giving me a specific answer.

Why was it that something I had wanted for so long now seemed frightening? Then I told myself that Simon was exaggerating the danger. He wanted to be so important.

"Why is it such a big risk?"

"I won't say another word. What you'll see and learn will say it all for now. You'll have more questions, for sure. I'll see about answering them later," he said, and smiled. "Quid pro quo."

Another cloaked threat, but I would risk it.

"When we walk out, stay a little behind me and hover close to the wall. The kitchen staff has gone for the day, and no one is doing any cleaning now. Grandmother's nurse is with her upstairs, and Grandfather has gone to his room. They've always slept in separate bedrooms, you know. Grandmother Judith always complained about his late comings and goings, and Grandfather complained about her keeping him up with her jabbering about social news and such. At least, that's how my father explained it to my mother."

"Are your parents here now?"

"No. I'm in one of the five guest rooms upstairs."

"Don't you have to be in school?"

"I'm on my own schedule. I go in when I have questions or have to take an AP exam."

"Don't you have any fun? Go to parties?"

"There's time for all that later," he said sharply. Then he relaxed and added, "My mother nags me about that all the time."

"So that's why you have no girlfriends and why girls are afraid of you."

"We're not talking about me right now. Do you want your answers or don't you?" he snapped. He looked ready to run out.

"Of course I do."

"Then keep quiet."

He unlocked the door and opened it slightly to peer out.

"Close the door softly behind you. Remember, stay a little behind me so if someone appears, he or she will see me and not you, and I can handle it. Quiet as a shadow," he reminded me, and went out.

An astronaut stepping out of the space station might not feel any different from how I felt when I walked out behind Simon and closed the door. He glanced back at me, and we started down the dark corridor. It was so quiet that I could hear my heavy breathing. At the end of the corridor, Simon gestured for me to stop while he looked around the corner. I held my breath until he beckoned for me to continue. Days had run into days so that I couldn't remember when I had been this far from the room.

When I stepped around the corner, the vastness of the entryway and the sight of the large teardrop chandelier gave me pause. I was always impressed with how big Sutherland was, but having lived in such a confined space for so long made really big rooms look even more immense and intimidating. Simon stood so still that he resembled a rabbit anticipating having to flee. He was holding his breath, too.

The silence coming from all sides sounded deep and foreboding. There wasn't a footstep or a voice. It was as if everyone had deserted Sutherland and Simon and I were the only ones left.

When he was satisfied it was safe, he beckoned to me to follow as he crossed toward Grandfather's office. Never had the large, embossed dark oak door looked more forbidding. He turned toward me when he reached it, his eyes shifting to the stairway. I held my breath again and didn't move. Was someone coming? He gestured more emphatically, and I hurried toward him. He opened the door slowly, and then we both entered and he closed the door softly behind us.

Why were we coming here? What did this have to do with Mommy? Of all the rooms in this estate, this was surely the most forbidden.

A single green glass desk lamp was on and casting a glow over Grandfather's very large marble-topped cherrywood desk with his well-worn black leather chair. On the right was a long metal desk covered with neatly stacked papers. I hadn't been in his office for some time, and really only when I was very young, but I remembered being impressed by the nearly wall-width painting of Sutherland that hung behind his desk. Even though the house was smaller when the picture was painted, it loomed over the property like a castle fit for a king. Its walls glistened under the captured sun.

Half the wall on the right was a set of paneled windows that looked toward the pool and the golf course. To our right was a grandfather clock that I remember being told was actually our great-grandfather's. It either never worked or Grandfather didn't care to have it working. Its hands were frozen at twelve o'clock. I wondered if whenever Grandfather looked at it he thought he had the power to stop time.

I thought the floor was different. I vaguely recalled polished wood, but this floor was a light gray tile done in very large blocks. To the right of Grandfather's desk was the old ruby-red leather sofa I recalled having lain on while Grandfather and Daddy talked almost in a foreign language about investments and interest dividends. Mommy wasn't there at the time. She was with Grandmother Judith in the den off the kitchen.

I remembered all the plaques and awards Great-grandfather Sutherland and Grandfather Sutherland had won or been given. There seemed to be at least five or six more on the walls and shelves. There was a picture of our great-grandmother and great-grandfather dressed in very fancy clothes at some event on the grounds. I recalled thinking that neither looked terribly happy. When I had told Daddy, he'd said people back then didn't think smiling in pictures was dignified. Mommy had blown air through her lips, looked at me, and said, "You're probably right, Caroline. They weren't terribly happy. Being dignified was usually a way to cover it up."

Simon stopped, so I held my breath. After a moment he nodded at the bookcase on the left.

"Your mother is behind that," he said, nodding.

"What? What do you mean, behind?"

"The only reason I know about the door is I was sleeping on the sofa one day. I don't think I was more than four, but I have a great memory. Grandfather didn't even notice me. He pushed a button on the wall here," he said, stepping toward it, "and the bookcase slid to the left. Then he unlocked the door and went in. He was in there for a while. When he came out, I was afraid to show him I had seen him, so I kept my eyes closed and pretended I was asleep. I was pretty smart even then.

"Later, I told my mother, who told my father. He warned me never ever to mention it. He was so frightened about it that I never forgot his warning. You're the first person I've told, actually."

"What's in there? What did your father tell you?"

"Something about Grandfather's different assets, paperwork, a safe. That was all my father ever told my mother and me, but I never let forbidden rooms and secrets keep me from exploring Sutherland. Someday it could all be mine, you know."

I just stared at the wall. Was my mother really there, kept perhaps as I had been?

"Ta-daaaa," he sang, smiled, and pushed a button I really would never have seen. The bookcase slid open, just as he had described, and there was the door.

"Is it locked?"

"Yes, but . . ." He walked to Grandfather's desk, opened a drawer, and showed me a key. "He keeps it in a gold cigarette case. I discovered it a while back. Not an especially brilliant place to hide a key. I found it almost immediately," he bragged. "If you want to become a doctor, you had better be a good detective."

He went to the door and inserted the key. Then he turned the handle and opened it slightly. He stepped back and gestured with a theatrical bow.

"Madam, your mother," he said.

Truly terrified, I stepped toward the door. He kept his smile. I paused.

"Quid quo pro," he said, and opened the door wider.

It was a small room with metal shelves, two file cabinets, and a safe at the right corner.

"I don't understand," I said.

"Just go in, Caroline, and look to your left."

I stared at him, my mind reeling with the possibilities. He read one in my eyes.

"I'm not going to lock you in there. Why would I want to do that? My grandfather would not only be furious, he would disown me."

I took a breath and stepped in. On my left were wider shelves, and on one was a pewter urn. He stepped up beside me.

"Your mother's ashes are in there," he said, nodding at the urn. "That's why I told you at the cemetery, at the grave, that she wasn't down there."

"But . . ." I couldn't take my eyes off the urn. "Why? Why are they here?"

"Grandmother Judith wanted her buried in the family cemetery, but Grandfather didn't. She insisted, so he manufactured the funeral for her. My father told my mother he thinks Grandfather had a bag of cement or something like it put into the coffin. Then he had this done. Grandfather always manages to win one way or another, doesn't he?" he said.

We heard a door slam.

"We'd better get back to your room."

He looked from me to the urn and then said, "You could touch it, but do it quickly."

"That's not my mother," I insisted.

"Yeah, well, I don't think he'd put just anyone in here."

He stepped back. I considered touching the urn but walked out quickly instead. He closed and locked the door. We could hear voices coming from the front entrance. He hurriedly returned the door key to the cigarette case in Grandfather's desk drawer and then went to the office door, opening it very slightly. He held his hand up so I wouldn't move.

"Emerson. He just went in and out," he whispered, opening the office door wider. "C'mon."

When we were both out, he closed the office door gently.

"Stay quiet," he said, and led the way to the dark corridor and back to the door of my dreadful room.

I was in such a state of disbelief that I couldn't feel anything, even fear. He unlocked the door. For a moment I considered turning and running. Maybe Emerson didn't know what Grandfather had done. Maybe he would be just as upset and help me. I had to find Nattie to tell her. She would so angry, maybe even angrier than I was. I had to get out of here.

"You'll only get us both into trouble," Simon said, holding the door open. "And you won't be able to find anyone to help you. Get in. I'll tell you the rest of what you want to know. But you have to get back inside. Now."

I glanced back and then walked into the dreadful room. Never did I feel as trapped as I did at this moment. As soon as Simon closed the door behind us, I spun on him.

"Where's Nattie?"

"You have to calm down. You have to relax. It's a lot of stunning information, I know. I'm trying to feed it all to you slowly, carefully. I'm pretty smart about this sort of thing. There's such a thing as emotional overload, you know."

"Just tell me about Nattie."

He stood there, silent, that wry smile on his face.

"You don't really know, do you?" I said.

"Oh, I know. I know it all. My parents are oblivious. They have these secret, whispered conversations while I'm supposedly absorbed in a book. It's been that way most of my life. My mother gets my father to tell her everything. One of these days, when I don't care anymore, you could thank her."

He patted the bed.

"You want to know about your precious Nattie, don't you?"

He reached out for my hand.

"C'mon. Quid pro quo."

"Get out of here!" I shouted at him. "Get out!"

"You're making a big mistake. You'll never get out of here."

"I don't care. Get out, or I'll scream and scream."

"I was just trying to—"

"I know what you were trying to do."

He stared at me a moment and then smiled.

"You should have been more willing, more excited. Maybe you are like your mother. Dr. Kirkwell just might have second thoughts about you when she knows."

It was like someone had thrown a pail of ice water over me.

"You'll tell her?" I said.

"I might. Or I might just say it wasn't an opportune time."

For a moment I couldn't raise enough breath to speak. The best I could do was a loud whisper.

"She knows you were here?"

He shrugged.

"I'm kind of like her intern."

"I'll tell Grandfather everything. I'll tell him what you showed me."

He shook his head.

"Thought you'd realize it by now, Caroline. Nothing happens at Sutherland that Grandfather doesn't want to happen. I learned that faster than I learned anything, maybe." He smiled. "If he lives long enough and I'm old enough, he might just bypass my father and leave it all to me. I think I'm more of a Sutherland than my father is, anyway."

"That you are," I said. It was better than shouting profanity after profanity at him.

"Whatever."

He started toward the door and then paused and turned around.

"To show you my feelings aren't hurt . . . your Nattie is in very long-term, maybe forever, therapy. She's paralyzed from the waist down and can't talk . . . makes crazy sounds, as I understand it. Someone from the American ambassador to France is taking care of all her needs. The point is, she can't help you. She can't help herself. In my opinion, which you should seriously consider, you're better off pleasing Grandfather, who might get your father to reconsider taking you back. If not, you'll always have a place here. Not this room, of course. It's your choice. Don't make the wrong one.

"Maybe I'll see you soon . . . at dinner," he said, and left, locking the door behind him.

EPILOGUE

I knew where my mother was. In my mind a pewter urn glowed in the darkness. I could hear her voice, and I could see her face.

This was a house full of lies and secrets. What good was the truth in such a place?

I did learn from Simon. Here you kept yourself under lock and key to survive.

In the morning, when the door was opened, I could only hope that I looked sufficiently helpless and grateful.

Mrs. Lawson entered and immediately set down new clothes for me to wear: a plain blue skirt and a white blouse, new but quite unattractive shoes, socks, and underthings, including even a bra. She told me she would brush my hair.

"After you're dressed, you will have breakfast in the dining room with Dr. Kirkwell and your grandfather. Simon," she added before I could even think to ask, "has left for a school exam, and your grandmother is not feeling well enough to come down."

I said nothing. I did exactly what she wanted and waited for her to look me over and approve.

"Frankly," she said when she opened the door again, "I never thought you'd come out of here."

"Neither did I," I said, which made her hoist her eyebrows.

I walked down the dark corridor and waited for her to show me into the dining room. Grandfather, in a three-piece gray suit, sat at the head of the table. The knot in his black tie couldn't have been any tighter or any more perfect, just like Daddy's ties. Dr. Kirkwell sat to his right. He nodded at the seat to his left. I hurried to it.

"I've been hearing good things about you," he said as soon as I sat. "You have a long way to go, of course, but Dr. Kirkwell believes you have had a good beginning."

I looked at her to show her my gratitude. She smiled.

She's not as hard to fool as she thinks, I thought.

"Here is how things will be for a while," he continued. "You're being moved to what was your mother's room. Mrs. Lawson will take you shopping. She will buy your necessities and choose your new clothes, just as she did once for your mother."

"More than once," Mrs. Lawson said. Grandfather looked at her sternly, and she pulled herself up, pursing her lips.

"For the remainder of this school year, Dr. Kirkwell will continue to tutor you. If your father agrees, you will visit him in Hawaii during the summer. If he wants to keep you there, we'll make the necessary arrangements. If not, you'll return here and we will arrange for you to attend a private school I've financed. In the meantime, you can walk the grounds of Sutherland but not leave it."

He paused and pressed the tips of his fingers against each other as he looked at me.

"What you have of your mother in you we will overcome. I will expect obedience, a sense of responsibility, and always economy and efficiency.

That is the way to maturity. Childhood at Sutherland is considerably shorter."

He looked at Mrs. Lawson.

"Please, see to our breakfast now, Mrs. Lawson."

She left immediately.

I reached for my napkin and placed it on my lap. The closest Grand-father came to a smile occurred. He nodded and looked at Dr. Kirkwell.

"You can employ my personal study as your classroom."

"How generous," she said. "And how comfortable a classroom it will be. That's right next to your office, is it not?"

"Exactly."

They looked at me because I was smiling so warmly.

Neither understood.

I'd be close to Mommy.

We'd set each other free.

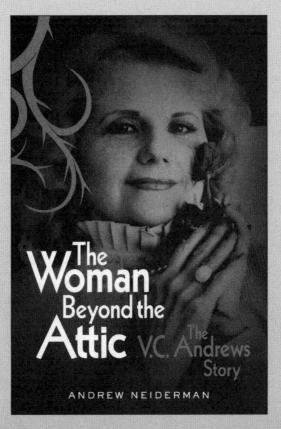
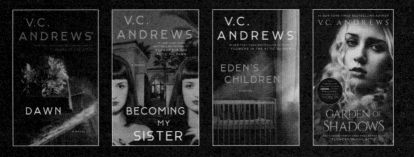